PENGUIN BOOKS

TRAILERS

Kate Le Vann was born in Doncaster. She has written for *Vogue*, *Sky Magazine* and various football magazines. *Trailers* is her first novel.

TRAILERS

KATE LE VANN

PENGUIN BOOKS

PENGUIN BOOKS

Published by the Penguin Group
Penguin Books Ltd, 27 Wrights Lane, London W8 5TZ, England
Penguin Putnam Inc., 375 Hudson Street, New York, New York 10014, USA
Penguin Books Australia Ltd, Ringwood, Victoria, Australia
Penguin Books Canada Ltd, 10 Alcorn Avenue, Toronto, Ontario, Canada M4V 3B2
Penguin Books (NZ) Ltd, Private Bag 102902, NSMC, Auckland, New Zealand

Penguin Books Ltd, Registered Offices: Harmondsworth, Middlesex, England

First published by Viking 1999
Published in Penguin Books 2000
1 3 5 7 9 10 8 6 4 2

Printed in England by Clays Ltd, St Ives plc

London
Wednesday

I'm more afraid of being old than most people I know. Maybe I just think about it more because, at twenty-six, I've already done so much of it. Not because trauma makes you mature before your time. No, I've been getting used to the real stuff, the day-to-day facts of being old. Slowness. Pain. That breathless envy when people my age swing carelessly past me and I know they're out of my league, that I'm not viable, not do-able any more. They run across the road without looking, while I wait with the blue rinses for the green man. We've the same concerns, the old women and me, including whether we'll make it all the way over before the man goes red. We group together when the cars rev their engines: there's safety in numbers.

I never used to feel like this. There's been some sort of turning-point because in the past the ageing effect happened in reverse. As recently as six or seven years ago, when my mother pushed me around town after an operation I felt young, younger, almost as if I were a baby again. She'd make sure I had a carton of juice with a straw. I'd be selfish and grumpy and say when I wasn't happy. I was allowed to stare at people in the street, the same people who were morally barred from staring first, but did, all the same. That stage, the defiant infancy, is over. It could be because I moved away from home; that's what most people would think. When I was seventeen my mother's friends used to tell her she worried too much about me: that all her attention was making me dependent, stopping me from growing up. That's a laugh. Unloved people are always looking for a home, even if it's not the right one. Loved people think everywhere's home.

What's changed things is that, before, I thought my life was all in front of me. Then I realized I was already in it.

It shouldn't be this hard. And yet, I see people who are worse than me, walking; I'm not sure if I admire them or just want to tell them to give up. The harder it becomes, the more overrated it seems. We're conditioned to think that nothing else matters, by the old films and corny soap operas that use walking for climax; the strings and tears as people rise up and leave their chairs behind – as if it's synonymous with pride. But when it hurts so much and looks so bad, I don't think we should be under so much pressure to keep it up. Still, we're all out here, trying. It's strange how many of us there are, and you don't notice until you're among them. Like the very first time I went out in a wheelchair, I saw so many others, and crutches and sticks, that it felt like a convention. My mother and I laughed a little about it, because we could. We thought of it as a gimmick: temporary. And so it was, because I may never *have* to use one. It's just that now it's . . . it's not an option, it's a possibility, not even that – it's just that sometimes I'm standing in the street and I can see where I want to be and it looks so far away, and I think it would be easier if I could only sit down. That's all.

Anyway, I suppose the fact that I'm okay, and reasonably boredom-free now, should have positive implications. Why should things get worse? Obviously, I'll get uglier still, and slower, but if I can deal with this concept, at this level, surely I always will. Actually I don't have too bad a time of it. I manage. Every now and then I apply for jobs that I don't get, but the rejection is always something of a relief. I joined an agency, even, but then I unjoined when I realized I was turning down everything they offered me, because it involved catching the tube or standing a lot. The jobs I did take, what was hard wasn't the work, it was the rest of it. Like when the receptionist thinks she'll do the new girl a favour and ask her to lunch and the new girl has to wheedle out of it because Prêt à Manger's fifty yards away. Only I never told them why. Idiot. Frankly, I'd rather not even try, now. My life is like being on holiday alone. I read magazines, and buy interesting food, and go shopping. There are always new magazines, and different food things and shops. And television. Television is only boring when you don't have to watch it. The more you see, the better it is: like anything, the detail only pops out when you look at it closely.

And then there's my best friend, Alice, and my parents. They all visit, quite often, and I phone them every day. So, I speak. I don't ever go very long without speaking. And a few words with any of them is better than an evening with Sara. I can do without the effort of talking to Sara. She believes, because I've been telling her this whenever she calls, that I'm too depressed and too broke to go out. I'm both, but I'd still go out. If Alice lived anywhere near I'd go out with her, I'm sure I would. It's still important to me to be involved, to go to the places I read about. But Sara's not interested in going anywhere new and exciting. She wants to go to a smoky pub and discuss politics, and my brain can't spare the neurone damage that I'd waste getting pissed to make Sara's conversation tolerable, and my skin can't spare the free-radical damage I'd suffer from sitting in a pub inhaling her cigarette smoke. My skin is fabulous, and if they ever find a cure, I don't mean cure I mean system or something, for dealing with my disability, I want my skin to be as good as it can be. I want to look young, to offset the time I've wasted. If I get another chance, I don't want to have thrown my skin and brain away on Sara and a pub and conversations about the headlines in the *Guardian*. It's only when you lose things that you realize nothing lasts and everyone's falling to pieces a little every day. This is why I make such efforts to conserve. I'm keeping a tight check on the things I have left, the genetic advantages – great ankles, smooth skin, ambiguous smile. One day I may have use for them.

I believe, because I've always been hopelessly optimistic, that I will get another chance, that they will come up with something. They invent new things all the time. Maybe this is what keeps me from getting too depressed about it: I won't really accept that it's over. Still, I worry about hope. When you come down from it, is the feeling even worse? Is it the safety net or the tightrope? But it's like regret. You can't help doing it.

I don't always wear make-up when I go out these days. Lots of sunscreen, obviously, to protect my skin. To maintain myself for anything that may come later. But right now, what's the point? This is London. We're all tourists. And I got tired of being looked at by strangers on buses, and flirted with in cafés, only to watch them look down, and away, when I stood up and moved. It hurts, being disappointing. So it's jogging bottoms and big sweatshirts and, hey, I'll even let my hair get greasy now. It's better not to be looked at at all. Although sometimes I smother myself with Estée Lauder, the full works, like I used to, even if I'm just going to the newsagent on the corner. I still like putting on make-up. I'm not immune to its magic. It's just that I'm not subjugated by it any more. I'm free to be plain. Although sometimes I feel so ugly that I think I'm attracting even more attention, and that people are staring because I look so bad. Which is ridiculous, because it's not my face that's the problem, and at least one in five people looks worse *with* make-up than I do without it. But it crosses my mind. I know it's paranoia, but it's not all paranoia. I used to be looked at, sometimes, when things were good, and I still am and although I assume the reasons have changed, it's confusing. I'm always suspicious: I have so much potential for being hurt now. What I want to feel is invisible, and I don't, not yet. It's the part of old age I haven't encountered.

Manchester

1992

I

Heather was making bread again. Some people just bake: Heather brought to it the flamboyance of a Catholic ritual. She spent the day clearing more surfaces than she could possibly need and nagging at all of us for being so untidy, and unloading ingredients from rustling KwikSave bags, lining them up in order of size and usefulness. The air was heavy with steam because the hot tap was constantly running, cleaning spoons and dishes and trays that Heather might choose to involve in her baking process. I liked to sit in the kitchen and watch her, because it felt a little like being at home, even the nagging, and she liked to be watched, because she was so very good at this.

'I wish I could cook,' I said.

'Grace, you're a terrific cook,' she said, generously, 'you're always eating something fabulous.'

'Yes, usually something my friend St Michael prepared for me,' I said, which was pitifully not funny, but she smiled as if it were, because it was her joke, which she had set up. I was happy to play the stooge. Plenty of girls who've grown up only knowing feminism have a secret fear of being naturally accomplished at anything domestic – exhibiting that kind of delicate incompetence made me feel liberated and modern. Heather, on the other hand, liked to be seen as grown-up and capable. Both acts strained reality, but in some important way the exchange made each of us feel more female. So we were both happy.

Heather sneezed and a cloud of flour blew into the air. She reached for a tissue and wiggled her nose until it rattled.

'So, who were you snogging last night?' she asked me, with tears in her eyes.

'Which one?' I said.

'There was more than one?' she squeaked.

'Actually, there were three,' I said, trying to sound rueful rather than horribly pleased with myself, 'but they were all hideous.'

'Three?' (The voice went even higher.) 'You're such a terrible slut. No wonder Finlay was mad.'

'I don't care if he was mad,' I said. 'I fail to see what it has to do with him.'

'Oh, come on, Grace, the poor guy's in love.'

'Of course he's not,' I said impatiently, loving it. Finlay did have a terrible crush on me, and I did everything I could to encourage it, short of sleeping with the sap. I was as fond of his seedy attentions as he was happy to indulge himself in persisting with them. It was a two-way street. He had a perpetual excuse for not getting a girlfriend, and I had constant reaffirmation of how desirable I was, and we got to act out all our favourite film roles in creating the little contretemps. This was particularly satisfying for us both, both film buffs, and more excited by fiction than by the mundanities of real life – I should say real student life, which is something else. It was the sort of relationship I was most comfortable with, the sort I attracted. Even as early as school, the couple of boys who sent me valentines and pestered me at parties were the boys who, in retrospect, exhibited homosexual ambitions. At school I was superficially snotty, bookish and not much of a dater; the reputation must have made me look like a safe bet. The complicit stalemates we engineered protected them from the kind of accusations that sensitive boys tend to attract in the rougher comprehensives, and I wasn't all that pretty: I was grateful to be able to turn down anyone. Finlay wasn't gay, and didn't, I imagine, set out to be strung along, but he clearly derived enough compensation from the rejection to keep on asking for it. The idea of a romance was the thing; the fact that it was unrequited made it all the more fictional, therefore idealized. It had so many more possibilities than an affair.

'So who was the guy with the red T-shirt? I saw you with him before Daniel and I left.'

'Did you stay at Daniel's last night?' It was my turn to squeak. She had announced it casually, but the build-up to the consummation of her flirtation with Daniel had been a tortuous, meticulously planned affair, and I personally felt a sense of triumph at this revelation, having followed it every step of the way, nurturing and assuring and leaving off trying to seduce him myself. Heather looked demure. 'Did you sleep with him?' I said, sternly. My other role in the house was the prudish, disapproving, old-fashioned girl who never had sex. It was one of my most popular turns. Heather nodded. I switched back to squealy girlfriend. 'And were you wearing the date underwear?'

'D'you know, I wasn't,' she said, with brisk annoyance. 'I just wasn't expecting it. He told me he wouldn't be going to the party. And then when he showed up I was like, oh, no, grey pants and the boingy bra . . .' And so we talked, although we didn't go into details about his performance, the way girls are meant to when they talk about men without men. I wanted to hear the dialogue, as I was desperate for a little vicarious aural sex, and I knew that Heather would embellish it and furnish her inarticulate boyfriend with an enviable script. And the boy in the red T-shirt, and his fellow losers who I managed to do the rounds with were forgotten in the excitement. Snogging people at parties was something I did a lot. I enjoyed it all: the feeling pretty and wanted, the making Finlay seethe and strop, the contribution I could make to the morning-after house gossip. When we went out in the evening, we would always leave together, in a group – we were known by our close friends as the Orwell Street Seven – but on any given night, about half of us would pull, and never more than two of us came home together, so our evenings were mostly unknown to each other. We all had to catch up the next day.

Mandy came into the kitchen looking odd and guilty.

'I heard you two laughing,' she said. She was wearing her dressing-gown, although it was nearly two.

'And what sort of time is this to get up, madam?' Heather asked her.

'I didn't hear you come in last night,' Mandy countered.

'That's because I didn't. I, er, spent the night at a friend's,' Heather said, barely able to contain her excitement.

'Did you . . .?'

'Yes!'

There was some more high-pitched squealing, a bit of a hug, and I got to hear the best details again, along with the worst details, during which time I sort of switched off.

'When I last saw you you looked like you were going to get off with Dave the geologist,' Heather said, and Mandy grabbed her by the shoulder and pulled her down to the table.

'He's upstairs now,' she whispered.

'Oh, my God!' In unison.

'You brought Dave the geologist back?' I whispered. 'I didn't know you were . . .'

'We're not. It was a mistake.'

'Does he know that?'

Mandy shrugged.

'Did you sleep with him?' This was Heather.

'Not really.' We both raised our eyebrows. 'I gave him a blow-job.'

We were so close that we didn't notice Richard had slipped in and was standing by the door listening.

'Why are we all whispering?' he boomed.

'Shhh!'

'Dave the geologist is upstairs,' Heather told him. I thought I saw a twinge of jealousy in his eye, and the way his mouth tightened. It was my opinion that Richard had the hots for Mandy. They'd had a thing the year before when we were all in halls together, but it had come to nothing and it was all very friendly on both sides now. But still, sometimes he looked at her the way I look at Sachertorte, and when he talked about her it was with an unusual respect for her opinions. Out of all proportion to their validity.

'I suppose I'll have to get rid of him now,' she whispered, with a kind of theatrical, eye-rolling ennui. An awful lot of men were incredibly fond of Mandy, and she dealt with it gracelessly. She was the kind of girl who has always been attractive and popular and takes it for granted, although her affected disdain showed that it made her happy enough. She was the only girl I knew who liked every bit of her body, and was pleased to tell us all. Some of the things she 'complained' about to me were insufferably conceited, although she tried her best to express it as dissatisfaction. Her breasts, she would say, were far too high. ('Practically in my armpits,' she'd say, and I'd have to resist saying, 'But that's just when you're lying down, isn't it, dear?') Her eyelashes were too long. ('I actually have to trim my own eyelashes or else they look really false.') And pressed by absolutely no one, she was always prepared to own up to possessing the perfect bottom. ('The lads back home always said I had the best arse, and they made such a fuss when I wore my wetsuit. I don't know what they could possibly find sexy about an all-in-one rubber catsuit that clings to every bulge of my body.') But although she was very pert and pretty, and reasonably bright, she still slept with the most unsuitable, unworthy men, which was something I could never understand. Perhaps somewhere deep down she was really insecure. I doubted it. She said she liked sex. I found that even harder to believe.

That was how we lived. People came home with people, or stayed out all night with people, and in the middle of it all, I hoovered up the gossip but never stayed out and never brought anyone back. It wasn't that the girls I lived with were unusually promiscuous, except Mandy, perhaps, and no, not even Mandy. It was just what everyone did. It's what everyone does now. It's normal. It's modern.

'So I hear you made a fool of yourself last night,' Richard said to me, and I took a deep breath in preparation for the telling-off I'd have to give him for listening to Finlay, and then I looked up and saw that he was grinning and his eyes were twinkling.

'I did, actually,' I admitted, over a huge sigh. 'I don't know why I do it. I just don't feel like I've achieved anything in an evening unless I neck with someone dreadful.'

'So you could always give Finlay another go.'

'I usually do. You're always telling me I lead him on.'

'You're right, I do. I'm just kidding. You tart.' Some days I fancied Richard, and this was one of them. He was splendidly good-looking in a tall, beefcaky way, which didn't usually attract me to men, but he was nice with it, and had a clue. Most male students didn't. 'So who was it last night?'

'Oh, I don't know. One of them was called Titus. Really. I saw his driving licence and everything. I think I fell asleep with my tongue in his mouth.'

'Nice.'

'I was tired. And one of them was in my tutor group, so at least I don't have to see him again.'

'You're so hard.'

'As nails. And the other one I mistook for the bloke on my course who I used to fancy and when I realized . . .'

'There were three? Finlay said you snogged two men.'

'There were three. He must have missed one. Good grief, I can score more than twice a night, you know.'

'You really are a teenager, Grace.'

'Where is Finlay this morning?' asked Heather. 'Did he pull last night?'

Richard and I exchanged looks. Finlay had spent the evening sulking and accusing me of being pathetic before I tired of it and found solace in the soporific arms of Titus, at which point he had to go somewhere else to sulk. He'd gone home with Richard, and I heard them discussing me in Richard's room when I got in that night.

'She just doesn't want to go out with you, mate,' Richard was saying.

'I know that. I just don't see why she has to virtually fellate ten men in public every time we go to a party,' Finlay slurred. Although it's always a treat to listen to people talking about you, I shut my door and went to sleep.

'So?' Heather was waiting for an answer.

'No, he didn't pull. He's in his room listening to A-ha,' Richard said. 'I spoke to –' He stopped, because at that moment Dave the geologist came in looking sheepish and we all froze in embarrassment.

'This is Dave,' Mandy said, with a smile so manufactured it looked painful. I don't know if Dave caught the expression behind her eyes.

'Hello, Dave!'

'Hello,' he said. 'Mmmmm. Is that freshly baked bread I can smell?' His voice clanked with the uniform irony that passes for wit wherever there are students.

'I just put it in the oven,' Heather said, looking worried. She didn't want some Tom, Harry or Dick eating her labour of love.

Dave seemed to realize that he'd sounded as if he wanted some and made an effort to show that he didn't. 'No, I think it's really clever, making your own bread. Erm, I wondered if you wanted to go for breakfast today. Well, lunch now. Erm, brunch,' he said to Mandy. He tossed more pointless words after his hopeless pitch while looking searchingly at her, to get some idea of how she felt about last night. It gave them an air of intimacy that made me feel like an eavesdropper.

'Oh, babe, I can't. I promised to go shopping with Grace this morning.'

Bitch. Morally, I have no problems with anyone lying, but I had to sit there and not say, 'Oh, I don't mind,' so I looked like a total mad cow who couldn't go shopping alone and guarded my girlfriends like a jealous spinster. I blushed and looked at my fingers.

'It's already the afternoon,' he said.

'God, is it? Jesus, Grace, I'm sorry. I'd better get a move on. Is there hot water?' Mandy started to scoot about the kitchen madly, and ignored Dave the geologist until he began to look uncomfortable.

'Well, I have to go round to Ranjit's to pick up my bass . . .' he offered, and Mandy looked sweet again.

'Okay, honey,' she said, looking up at him. He bent his head to kiss her and she looked shy and pleased like the housewife in *Bewitched*.

'I'll give you a ring tonight?' he said, still looking for encouragement, permission. He had that smitten look that all of her men got.

'Okay,' she said, in a baby voice.

'Bye, then.' He stood and looked embarrassed for a few moments, until it became clear she wasn't going to see him out. 'Bye, everybody.'

'Bye, Dave,' Heather and I said.

'See you, mate. Nice meeting you,' added Richard.

We were silent until we heard the door slam.

'Oh. My. God. What have I done?' Mandy said. She sat down and rocked her chair back, balancing it with her toes on the table. Her dressing-gown was very short and I envied her smooth long thighs and careless confidence.

'He seemed really nice,' I said.

'Oh, he is,' said Mandy quickly. She wouldn't admit to being fancied by anyone who wasn't a bit of a catch himself. 'He's really nice, really brainy, really funny. He's just so clingy.'

'Well, that was a good way to make him unclingy,' Richard quipped, but his disapproval hovered like a martyr's halo and Mandy threw him a dark look.

'Are you going to see him again?' Heather asked her.

'I'm going to bloody have to. He doesn't take no for an answer.'

'He will if you say it enough,' I said.

'You don't know him. Anyway I don't want to talk about it.' So we changed the subject, but she got to sit in the middle of us and look dramatically worried for some time. Richard tried to lighten the mood.

'But anyway, what about you, Heather? I heard you coming in this morning. Can I assume that you finally did the deed last night? And if so, what are you doing back here already?' Heather smiled like a cat.

'Well . . .' she began.

And then we heard about last night again. I'd had enough. I went into the living room, where Finlay was sitting, watching *The Word* on video. Obviously he had skulked downstairs while we weren't looking. But I could hardly go out again, just because he was there. We ignored each other for a good ten minutes, and then he started smirking. When there was a silence, one or the other of us would soon surf it with a smirk. It signified indifference, how aloof and civilized we were compared to each other. He coaxed the smirk into an amused sniff. I ignored it. More time passed and then I smirked. We spent ages doing this sort of thing.

'You seemed to be, er, enjoying yourself last night,' he finally said. The smirking was over. Let the games begin.

'Oh, you know.' He seemed to think about saying something else and didn't. We watched *The Word* in silence.

'It's quite embarrassing, you know,' he said at last, but continued to stare at the television. 'Snogging ugly men just because you can. It's quite desperate-looking.' I couldn't think of anything smart enough to say, so I maintained a prim silence. That was always more infuriating for him anyway, and it saved me from looking stupid. I was never the mistress of the witty riposte that people often took me for, but I had struck lucky once or twice, enough to establish the reputation, and I had cultivated a supercilious look that suggested there might be a subtler, second meaning to my sentences. It really is easy to fool people into thinking you're clever. Stupid people, anyway. Finlay was still waiting for me to rise to the challenge. For breakfast, he liked nothing more than one of the little exchanges that began with him being mad at me, and the nicest thing I could have done was play along. He said horrible things more to provoke than to wound, and I wasn't exactly easily offended anyway, at least, not when it related to my behaviour; naturally, if he'd said I had very big hips it would have lived with me for a lifetime. But I wasn't yet ready to be picked on – a string of liaisons with unknowns, despite the cheap kudos it brought, often left me drained and defensive. Much as I enjoyed the chase, and even the snogging, it was as if I surrendered some of my privacy with each conquest, and it took me a while to recharge. His insult faded, I let it go.

'I gather Heather finally, er, made the beast with her ginger boyfriend,' he said, giving up. His voice, as always, was heavy with implied inverted commas.

'I've heard the story three times now,' I said. 'If I hear it again, even if I'm telling it, I will actually die of boredom. You'll have to get it from someone else. Heather's making bread in the kitchen. She can tell you herself. Make her skip the part about them taking acid. It's too pretentious for words.'

'They took acid? They did it on acid?'

And I ended up telling the story anyway.

I saw him first. No, not quite true, I *heard* about him even before we met. His reputation preceded, and there's something quite thrilling about a personality so pushy that it creates a bit of a stir before it arrives. So that was interesting. If he'd been a girl I would have hated him by then, because he was known for his intelligence, and my weakness was competitiveness, specializing in intellect. It's a character flaw that goes back a long way, although it's impossible to tell whether it stems from nature or nurture.

You decide. My father's father was a European Jew, whose parents took him off to America before things got really hairy. As an adult, he spent enough years in Britain to impregnate my grandmother three times, then lived the rest of his life with a different woman in Canada, where he practised as a psychiatrist. In the sixties, his hospital non-consensually sterilized dozens of teenagers who, in the view of the hospital, were educationally or mentally sub-normal, and therefore deemed unfit to reproduce. In the nineties, the same teenagers, now adults, were suing the local authority and the hospital for the violation of their human rights and the loss of their chance to have children. I saw a documentary about it. The claimants were all normal people of at least average intelligence. My grandfather wasn't mentioned by name in the programme, but the hospital was, and my father, who called to tell me to watch, said that his father had been the chief psychiatrist there at that time. Dad's voice was a collision of twisty pride and amusement and appalled shock when we discussed it.

'So your Jewish grandfather became a Nazi doctor,' he said. 'This is obviously where I get my fixation with intelligence.'

My father, though all too apparently desperate to establish a genetic connection with the parent who had abandoned him, did indeed take an unusual interest in these matters. When I was a small girl, at the age when most fathers told their daughters how pretty they were, mine only praised my IQ. When I was a little older and didn't have boyfriends he told me that I just hadn't met an intellectual equal at school, but promised I'd come across a few at college. He was complacent. In the seventies, the in thing was to develop children's minds with educational toys and constructive regimes, but my brother and I were free to indulge in as much crap television and as many comics as we liked, in spite of the trend, not instead of it. Any toys I did have which could be considered at all tutorial were those I'd requested myself, and there weren't many. An abacus, the fruit of a tantrum in Hamley's, and a talking robot who told jokes and asked multiple-choice questions about the *Guinness Book of Records*. Before I was twenty the only books I read were Enid Blyton and Mills and Boon, although, to be fair, the attic at home is fusty with more estimable choices that he suggested and I rejected – mainly because he suggested them. The combination of chippy ignorance and rebuttable arrogance ensured an echo, a similar preoccupation with my brain, which, given the retarded development of prettiness in my early teens, I came to think of as my only relevant endowment.

Whether I should blame the ravings of my ancestors or the pushiness of my closer relatives, I did – do – have a thing about this. And despite my father's efforts, I wasn't confident of his evaluation of me. Another modern notion is that parents should heap praise on their children, so they grow up feeling secure. But it doesn't really succeed, just as pretty girls whose fathers made a fuss of their looks are the girls who worry too much about looking pretty. It's as if being defined in one way, having the importance of that quality impressed upon you, makes you depend on it, fear its loss, or doubt its strength. For a long time, I'd grind my teeth with envy when someone I didn't know was described as being 'really clever', automatically on the offensive in case we might come to be engaged in a battle of wits, and my best attribute be outclassed. Now an aspiring heterosexual, if the conditions arose I still had pangs of competitiveness with both sexes, but also considered clever men as potential boyfriends. Which is why I wanted Finlay before he even knew I existed. Realistically, given my unrealistic expectations, he could only disappoint.

For a long time, he didn't. He looked the part, with an artistically wasted physique, and mad, recusant hair, like Einstein after an application of Grecian 2000. He wore clunky black glasses that were just awful enough to be knowing, and had good bones. And when we first spoke, although I was out to impress, he wasn't, and he did. He spoke deeply about shallow things, an attitude that has become stale, but was hip and pertinent at the time. I wasn't aware of my attractions by then – ironically, he would go on to play a large part in establishing my confidence in that area – but from the beginning, he made me feel like a valid object of desire, and I behaved accordingly. In place of my usual stream of self-consciousness, I found myself relaxing into important silences, monosyllables and wry understatement. In spite of this, he didn't appear to be pursuing me at all, which rendered him safe enough to play with. It was benign and friendly, but we spoke the same language and I left clues. Then, after about three encounters, all get-to-know group outings of the household we would imminently become, there was a change. It was a bit like one of those Magic Eye posters that were beginning to appear at every student fair those days: when the picture was revealed, it was a little startling, but seemed always to have been there. So it was with us.

This, I think, is the conversation that swung it. It wasn't the content that mattered, but the timing: we were simply ready to move on. We were at the Sanam restaurant, drinking wine, eating naan and discussing television.

'That was the best episode,' I was saying, 'I really fell in love with him, then, because he was so dominant, for once, and he's normally so shy and sweet but this time . . .'

'So you like to be dominated?' Richard said. Such an annoying, typical male-student question. It's impossible to know which side to come down on. Say nothing and you're repressed, say anything and you give them a nice little scenario to explore recreationally. There's nothing in it for you. Another favourite: do you masturbate?

'I said he was dominant, not dominating. There's a difference.'

'So do you?' Richard said, smiling with his teeth showing.

'Intellectually.'

'Really?' Finlay said. 'Why's that, then?'

'I don't want to have to explain,' I said.

'Why don't you try?' Finlay said.

'That *is* the explanation. I never want to have to turn round and tell the person I'm with what I mean. He should know. I don't want to teach someone how to behave, or wait around for him to catch up. I don't want to be the funny one, you know –

the smart one, the one who knows where to go all the time. I want to take, not give. Otherwise, what's the point of the relationship?' I crunched cucumber and shrugged.

'Well, what's in it for him, if he's the one explaining things to you?' said Richard.

I laughed darkly. 'I don't know. I suppose I'd have to come up with something to make it worth his while. I'm just saying that the situation couldn't work if he was stupider.'

A challenge, then, and Finlay picked it up. It was a flirtation that appealed to his vanity.

The period of mutual partiality was the most fun. It was flavoured with something of the spice of incest, as we knew we'd be moving into a house together, but were still virtually strangers, holding back, holding back. I would have continued to enjoy things if they had stayed the same, but nothing ever does. The odds were tilting in our favour and I got scared. I began looking for problems. I remember exactly when it cooled: I was lolling on the lawn of my halls of residence with some girlfriends, watching the boys play frisbee. Finlay's blouson leather jacket, despite the shrill summer heat, was placed in a careful fold on the outskirts of the game. He was shouting things and running. I looked at him and realized that the moment had passed, the momentum slowed. There was no reason; just another change.

'Do I *really* fancy him?' I said, to a girl whose brutal propensity to judge had always stirred my admiration.

'I can't imagine why you would,' she said, and turned over to tan her back.

'No, I don't,' I said, and that was that.

I hated the library. I frequently saw people I'd snogged there, and had to duck behind bookshelves to avoid being seen by them. And there was never any space to sit, and you weren't supposed to eat and I was too wimpy to flagrantly break the rules and too hungry all the time to go without food. So I'd sit there furtively eating from noisy packets, slowly rolling Maltesers out of the bag one by one and wishing I was somewhere else: this channelled my concentration until it was time to go. And I didn't talk to most of the people on my course, but we were on smiling terms, so I had to spend a lot of time smiling, or making three-word comments about something course-related to everyone I bumped into. Because of all this I rarely went there, but I'd promised to give Sara and Mabel, the other two girls in the house, a lift in, and while I was there I decided to do some photocopying. Mabel and Sara both did sociology with other bits, so they took some lectures together and had areas of discussion in common. Sadly, they were rather assiduous about it all, and I got away from them as soon as I could. There's nothing worse than people who like what they're studying. They want to talk about it, and convince you that it's the most interesting thing in the world and make you jealous and hint that they must be terribly bright to be doing something so wonderful. It was more than I could stand.

But today I was in for a treat. Jim McFadyean, the tutor I spent most of my spare time lusting over, was standing in the queue for the photocopiers, holding a big pile of books. Unfortunately I was looking very bad that day. I had only one coat of mascara on, gummily and hurriedly applied, my cheap weekend foundation, and I hadn't set my hair in rollers, just tonged it in a fairly random bend after drying it. It was a low-maintenance day. I sucked on my lips to darken them and joined him in the queue. He looked extremely pleased to see me. He flirted terribly in tutorials, and I believed we had some sort of rapport, that he spotted in me a lazy, cynical maturity that the other girls lacked. His were the only classes I ever went to, and I didn't do any work for them, but I would always introduce some debatable lowbrow topic, and the hour would be wasted considering it, while the other students looked on and tried to interrupt with their carefully planned homework. He wore threadbare jumpers with holes in the elbows, his chin was suedy with a manly growth of stubble and his blue eyes were very dark and penetrating.

'I don't expect to see you here, Grace,' he said, in his low Scottish brogue. 'You never give the impression of actually reading books before tutorials.'

I laughed a little too enthusiastically. 'I'm not staying,' I said. 'I'm going to the pictures later.'

'Oh!' He looked excited. He loved films: it was one of the things we talked about. Actually it was the only thing we talked about, but that was just because we had no mutual friends, not because he was boring. 'Have you seen *Cape Fear* at the Cornerhouse?'

'No, I'm going to something trashy with a girlfriend. Her choice.' This was a really atrocious lie, because I was going alone and it was a film I was dying to see and there I was, disowning it to impress my groovy teacher. As well as pretending I had a friend I didn't have. 'I really want to see *Cape Fear*, though.' I held my breath and waited for him to ask me.

'Yeah, it's a great movie,' he said.

Curses. 'Oh! You've seen it, then?' I gulped back the disappointment. 'Is it as good as the orig –'

'Excuse me, there's a machine free.' We both turned round to see the impatient, imminently sweaty face of a fat girl, dressed as female students love to, all batik print and exploitative Indian cotton with tiny mirrors and gold thread. I let an audible tut escape before I could help it.

'Do you want to take it?' I swooned inside, thinking he meant the fat girl, thinking he wanted just to stand and talk with me longer, but he meant me. 'I know how much you hate spending time here.' A reprise of his successful opening gag. I simpered and said I couldn't possibly push ahead of him, and he took it without arguing back and forth a bit more – I was hoping to be gradually persuaded – and the machine I eventually had to go to was nowhere near his, and before I knew it he had finished and was waving to me as he backed away up the escalator, piles of warm paper tucked in his arm. He was dreamy.

I caught up with Mabel and Sara in the sociology department. We had arranged to meet for a coffee break but I wasn't in the mood to drink watery crap and hear about sociology.

'I'm just nipping into town,' I said. 'There are some law books I need from Dillon's.' I always felt the need to lie when I went to the pictures. I preferred to go alone, because I hated that moment when the movie ended and the audience filed out and the loud voices of men who thought they knew what they were talking about rose above the muted, pretentious over-analysis coming from me and my friends, and everyone tried to talk and listen to other people at the same time. And even more than that, I hated that thing people do when you see a comedy with them, when there's a joke in the film and they turn around to look at you in the dark, to see if you're laughing as well. Chiefly, I liked to go to the pictures alone because sometimes I just needed to get away from it all. Away from the stress of always smiling and being nicer than I felt. So, with a happy, selfish afternoon ahead of me, I thought I'd better just nip over and tell the girls they'd better not expect a lift home.

'Oh, are you really?' Sara said. 'I need some stuff from town.'

'Well, are you all done here?' I asked. 'I don't want to rush you. Why don't you make me a list and I'll get it for you?'

'I don't have any cash. I'm going to have to write cheques. It'd be easier if I just went in.'

'Well, okay then.' I picked up all my stuff and started to head off, but Sara wasn't following.

'Oh, God, listen,' she said, in that voice I hated, 'I'm so incredibly nearly done here. I'll be thirty seconds. Honestly.'

'That's fine,' I lied. 'I'm not in a hurry.'

Hell can't be much worse than a series of car journeys with Sara. She was rude about my collection of tapes, and made me feel I should justify them to her. Every time she sat in my car, she used to pick them one by one from the passenger door, where I stuffed them, and read out the titles, sarcastically.

'Barry Manilow, *Hidden Treasures*?' she'd say, and snort. 'You have the weirdest taste.' Oh, just fuck off out of my car, I'd think. She had strange ideas about conversation, too. She thought it had to be important and intelligent, and that arguing was something positive and mentally stimulating, rather than tiresome and annoying. Except her theories were all too apparently regurgitated from her course, things she had spent nights working on or had heard her lecturers say. Because I was conceited I could never resist bluffing, and although the issues she wallowed in wrestling bored the hell out of me I was dragged into defending positions I didn't know about, didn't care about, and didn't want to hear about when I was supposed to be at the pictures watching *Other People's Money*. Sara was the most earnest person I knew. She cared about everything, she read newspapers from the beginning, not just the arts pages, and she had obviously been brought up by sincere, self-important people who thought that a fine mind was an indispensable attribute for a young woman to possess. Our parents would have hated each other. A generation on, we were half-way to reconciliation.

Worst of all, she used to joke that I couldn't drive. Anyone who has driven around Manchester for the first time knows that the one-way system isn't all that easy to negotiate. And if you're looking for parking spaces, rather than paying the five pounds an hour or whatever it is at the central car-parks, it's possible to take a wrong turn and then have to take a long route back to where you started, going along the same streets more than once. The process is baldly harder with someone next to you giggling, and saying how amusing it is that you're hopelessly lost. She'd tell the story when we got home, too. Tales of how Grace sometimes takes the wrong turn-off. I've never been the sort of person who can laugh at herself and don't believe anyone really is. We like to be teased about the things we're proud of, and then pretend to have a self-deprecating sense of humour. I didn't mind when, for instance, people made jokes about how vain I was because, really, I thought being vain was quite cool. Or when they chose to interpret my indiscriminate snogging as a sign of promiscuity, because sometimes I'd have loved to have the confidence to be a bit of a goer. Or even when they reminded me of my prissiness, because in a world where the old vices are the new chic, being prissy could be contrarily hip. But I happened to be a great driver, and I was doing Sara a favour anyway and just the sight of her having a jolly old time at my expense was more than I could bear. Ordinary people only attain this pitch of annoyingness deliberately. If she wasn't so vacuously proud of her own personal goodness, I might have supposed that was her plan.

I parked outside Marks and Spencer and binge-fed the meter. She watched and sympathized.

'Do you want to meet in about an hour?' I asked her.

'Well, where are you going?' she said. I racked my brains to think of somewhere she wouldn't want to go.

'Well, Dillon's, as I told you, but if they don't have my book I'll have to go to the legal bookshop on John Dalton Street. In fact, I may as well go straight there, because I know they will have it and Dillon's probably won't.' It was about four-thirty now, and getting colder already. I intended to get a cup of coffee somewhere, since I had missed my film, and maybe look for a new bra. Then buy something tasty from Marks and Spencer and suffer the censure when I got home. (Marks's food was considered wildly extravagant: I was routinely made to feel like Marie Antoinette when I brought home groceries: Let them eat focaccia!) 'Where are you going?'

'Boots,' she said. I realized she wanted to shop with someone, and felt a bit bad about trying to get rid of her, and a little obliged to go with her. She never went shopping with other girls, the way the rest of us usually did, because thrift was her neurosis: she never bought from a normal supermarket what she could get from the Aldi, or a discount shop, and she resented paying money to have people bring her a cup of tea. Mabel and I took her with us when we went to get a piece of cake once, and she was all for it until she saw the prices.

'Bloody hell!' she had virtually choked. 'Two pounds for a piece of cake!'

'It's really good cake,' Mabel had said.

'Yes, it looks nice, but bloody hell, Mabel, two pounds for a piece of bloody cake. I'm not paying that.' She had sat and watched us eat the cake, which felt as dry as sawdust, crumbling under the pressure of its audience. We had offered her some of our cake but Sara would never expect other people to pay for her. Because even her meanness was admirable. It was part of a contradictory character trait that could have been customized to exasperate: on a personal, everyday level she was aggressively generous, constantly endeavouring to promote general use of her purchases, her possessions and her time. She would offer, lend and foist things with relentless selflessness, buy bottles of wine and insist you shared them. She only objected to giving needlessly to the fat cats who ran our capitalist society. Which is all very good and everything, and meant I felt like frozen, concentrated evil for condemning her. I hated feeling like that. But virtue creates as many enemies as iniquity. My impatience with her was by no means unique. Others noticed and said things. Inevitably, she spent a lot of time alone, hunting for bargains, I imagine, but I could sense she didn't enjoy solitude as much as I did.

'I'll come with you to Boots,' I said, generously. 'I need some contact-lens stuff.'

2

I was never much of a judge of character. My first impressions more often than not turned out to be quite sound, but I couldn't stay faithful to them. I'd phone Alice to rave about someone I had started to get to know, and she would remind me that I'd hated them the week before, and I'd say yes, I just didn't know her very well then and actually she's lovely. Then I'd spend more time with them and little things would irritate me, and then I'd realize that they were wholly despicable and phoney and I'd been right to hate them. I went through much of this indecision before settling on liking Mabel. She was the kind of girl everyone instantly warms to. She was incredibly pretty, half Chinese with high cheekbones and warm olive skin, and she smiled all the time. She lived next door to me in halls in the first year and I liked her as soon as I spoke to her, and then as time passed and we hung out with different sets of people I decided she didn't like me, and was bored stupid by everything I said, and she was probably quite shallow really, and her smiles weren't real. I didn't think these things in any kind of active, external way, but I had those general feelings towards her. And then we somehow just started talking more, and I found out she was every bit as nice as she looked and she didn't hate me and she wasn't shallow. Especially compared to me. But you know what paranoia is, it can ruin perfectly good relationships.

When we all started living together, I often felt rather embarrassed if I happened to be alone with anyone. I was good in a group, mouthy and opinionated, but it was kind of showy and didn't work well to an audience of one. With Mabel, I never felt as strained or uncomfortable. She was less intense than the others, and she liked to watch trash television as much as I did, and not even to analyse it. She was also very sensible, a quality I admired in others because I liked it in myself, and the defining trait of most students was an inability to see sense, a compulsion to treat everything as a drama. They were always having tantrums and crises over the most mundane things. They'd fall out because one of them might make a flip comment, and the other would happen to be in a bad mood and take it the wrong way, and days of bitterness and resentment would ensue. I couldn't stand such wanton theatrics. Neither could Mabel, and I never tired of liking her because of this. She was braver than me, too, and in the middle of one of Mandy's wobblers, she wasn't afraid to say: 'Oh, calm *down*, for Christ's sake, you're being hysterical. If you're so desperate for a pint of milk I'll *buy* you one.' Like a coward, I resorted to sly, silent disapproval until the danger period was over.

Mabel was also the only person in the house not to give me grief over my thing with Finlay, although she was friends with us both, and Finlay liked her more than he liked anyone. Her link with both of us prevented the situation from ever being as serious as the others tried to pretend it was, and I was grateful for that. The rest of the girls, who enjoyed gossip and the coup of a male friend who confided in them, let him get unnecessarily heavy about it all, more than he actually felt, which made things more of a chore than they needed to be.

Mabel's Achilles' heel was her boyfriend, a dental student in Oxford, who was generally perfect and lethally charming, but a no-good blackguard. He would tell her about his infidelities and beg for forgiveness, and she always gave it. I often saw her sitting on the stairs, the curtain of dark shiny hair in front of her face as she whispered into the phone, giving in gradually. It was the only area of her life where her normally sound judgement seemed to desert her, but it wasn't something I felt I could comment on. I was the type of girl who waits until a friend has dumped a boyfriend until I start getting nasty about him. Not much use, but people hear what they want to hear anyway, so why force them to edit? Round about that time they were going through a period of trial separation, to see if they were really sure about each other. This was blatantly his idea, but she spoke as if it were her own. They were still together, she said, but they had been cooling things until they saw each other again. Whatever that meant – I mean, what would the alternative be? Dirty phone calls? Steamy letters? It sounded more like a licence for him to do what he liked and accuse her of breaking the bargain if she complained.

'We're going on holiday together!' she said one day, when she got off the phone with him. 'To Blackpool!'

'Oh, Blackpool! I've always wanted to go there.' This wasn't sarcastic. I dreamed of having an old-fashioned relationship with an old-fashioned boy who took me to the pier and won soft toys for me at the funfair. I wanted to drink murky tea in greasy spoons to shelter from the rain, and keep the napkin because he'd written 'I love you' on it, to stroll along beaches and wear his jumpers and kiss in the drizzle as the tide rolled in. 'When are you going?'

'The tenth. For a week. I can miss the lectures, and I'll call in sick for my tutorials from Blackpool.' It baffled me that people called in sick for tutorials. If you didn't turn up nothing happened. It wasn't school.

'I'm so jealous,' I said, truthfully, and I was also thinking selfish thoughts, because I hated the house without Mabel standing up for all that was reasonable and normal. 'It'll be so unbelievably romantic.'

'Blackpool? How, er, incredibly romantic!' Finlay said sarcastically, when he heard.

'Oh, shut up. You can be such a wanker sometimes,' Mabel said.

'But what about our party?' said Richard. Of course. We were supposed to be arranging a party for that week. I was always secretly impressed by the amount of people everyone knew when we did that sort of thing. I hardly knew anyone who wouldn't have been invited by someone else, and I couldn't have rounded up enough new people for a dinner party. I certainly didn't contribute much to the claustrophobic affairs we ended up having.

'Shit! Can't we postpone it?' Mabel said. The boys, who decided these things, hummed and haaed.

'We could have it before you go,' Richard said.

'We haven't got time to arrange it,' Finlay said.

'We have. We have,' said Mabel, jumping about a bit. 'We told everyone we were going to, and we didn't set a date, so everyone knows what's coming up. If we have it the Thursday before, rather than the Saturday night, it's a difference of two days and nobody has lectures on a Friday, so everyone can stay out all night.'

'I have lectures on a Friday,' Mandy said, sullenly. She was a chemist, and her schedule was notoriously exhausting and eventful.

'Couldn't you skip them for a day?' I asked. I may have been affectedly lazy, but I really couldn't see why everyone was so dedicated to their lectures. It's a comedy basic, isn't it? Students don't go to lectures. Except the ones I knew.

'Oh, fuck it, why not?' she said. Sometimes she surprised me.

We told Heather when she got home, and since she had a preposterously popular image to maintain she made a bit of a song and dance about having to uninvite 'about fifty people', at which point Richard went nuts and said we couldn't all invite so many people anyway, and Mabel said she only had to tell them to come two days earlier. They were teetering dangerously on the threshold of taking it all too seriously, and Mabel had surrendered her bargaining power by imposing the change in the first place. It was up to me to point out that there was no great disruption to our plans and we could even get a little more excited because the deadline was closer, and these things are always better with a slightly frantic aspect to them.

I did no work at all for the next couple of weeks. I spent time trying to rustle up at least one friend to bring (Sunita, my best friend from my course, never did things out of working hours, because it was that kind of friendship, and I knew she wouldn't really show up, and Michelle, my shamelessly stereotypical Essex Girl friend – although she was from Kent, not Essex, not that I could tell the difference; all the south is the same to me – also from my course, only ever went out to drink gin with strange men, and wouldn't dream of doing something as hopelessly bourgeois as a student house party) and scouring the shops for something to wear, and trying to come up with some kind of fashionable, artistic way of decorating the place for the party. I loved walking round the city centre. For someone who had never really made a point of knowing much of my home town, the scope for belonging here was a greater temptation; I took to the streets whenever I felt I ought to be in the library. I had spent most of the year before university in a wheelchair, and the operation I had just before I came was one of the more successful ones. My legs felt new and restless, and I had an overwhelming sense of freedom, compounded by leaving the places I'd grown up with, and being able to drive. I was trippy with the possibility of motion. It surprised me that the other students were so insular and inert, perpetually squashed in the union and the well-known student haunts. I spent my days walking through the cobbled area around St Anne's Place or hunting for weird things in the gorgeous Corn Exchange, or buying pineapples from the market stalls and looking at diamond engagement rings in Mappin and Webb, hoping that people who walked past might think that I was about to get married. That I had a boyfriend.

There was a little antiques shop that no one else seemed to know about, that sold furniture and home accessories from the 1950s. It was part gallery, part shop, so I could walk around without feeling compelled to buy something, although the things they sold were pressure enough. A week before the party I found a dusty little book about mixing cocktails, full of line illustrations of black-lipped women wearing New Look Dior, and canapé recipes and deliciously quaint fifties-style instructions on being a good hostess. I bought that, and an ice-bucket shaped like Elvis, and some delicate glass swizzle sticks. Not that I was expecting our party to be a lounge-style soirée, but I longed for a bit of sophistication then, and I just wanted them, just to pretend to myself that my life was even slightly going the way I meant it to. I also found a gorgeous pair of shoes that I could hardly walk in, spike-heeled mules with marabou feather trim, in Shoe Be Do's sale, and I bought those as well. I was a little over-enamoured with the charms of kitsch, then, it's fair to say, but again, at the time, it was fashionable. Actually, it was just about to be fashionable. The others would never have appreciated this. Most students, though obsessed with their images, have no real connection with fashion. They know it only as something they despise, something they disapprove of. It is a waste of money, a capricious mistress who keeps on taking, and they regard it with disdain. The sixties will never go away for students, because it was the time when students ruled the world. So they keep on buying their joss sticks, their second-hand Kerouac books, their tie-dyed T-shirts, their ethnic crap. They consider themselves morally superior to the whimsy of designers. Not that buying a bunch of fifties tat was particularly forward-looking or innovative, but at least I was always ready to change along with the rest of the world; it was the *right* retro. The students I knew just wanted everything to freeze. Including their lives. Further education keeps the wolf of responsibility from the door for as long as you like.

In the days before the party, I wasn't eating, because I wanted to lose enough weight to wear a shirt that was really too small for me, and I always dieted before parties anyway. Mabel was dieting, although she didn't need to, because she was planning on sleeping with her boyfriend for most of their holiday in Blackpool, and she didn't want him to get a shock when he saw her bottom. Sara was running three miles every morning, not because she wanted to lose weight, but because she thought it was important to be healthy. I've always been wary of people who want to live longer. It's as if they're introducing an element of competition into something I can't be bothered with, but I feel insecure about not trying. I'd prefer it if we all agreed to do nothing and died at the same time. Heather wasn't eating because she was in love and there were more important things than food, you know, Grace. And Mandy was eating wall-to-wall bacon sandwiches and French toast and explaining to anyone who dared mention that they were skipping lunch that she never skipped a meal and she could eat anything she liked without putting on weight because she was born with an abnormally high metabolism and was really lucky that way. I know dieters are boring, but they're not in the same league as thin people. No matter what they tell you, effortlessly thin women are absurdly smug about their condition. I had a friend back home, about my height, thinner than the Duchess of Windsor's corpse, who was always moaning that she was too skinny. But if you pointed out another emaciated freak when you were with her she got competitive and wanted to apply a ratings system. 'Is she thinner than me?' she'd say, frantically craning her pipe-cleaner neck for a better view. 'I bet she's not.' Then she'd want me to count up the calories she'd consumed in any given day to prove she ate normally, because she knew I knew the calorific content of everything. They're easily as obsessed with their size as overweight people. And despite what they say, they're truly contemptuous of fat people, saying they have chips on their shoulders (and their plates, ha ha – thin girl's joke) and are jealous and out of control. They pretend to be so victimy and self-critical and they're pure venom. Hang out with one if you don't believe me.

We went on a house outing to the supermarket to buy things

for our party. I drove, because I was the only person with a car there, although others had them at home, which meant Sara had ample opportunity to make jokes on the way. The tape collection was dragged out again, along with a few priceless anecdotes about my taking the wrong road and ending up in Chester. (Not entirely fictional: we drove past a signpost for Chester.) The Sainsbury I went to was another of my favourite places. The rest of the house shopped in Banto, one of those German supermarkets where they pile it high and sell it eventually, but I had wheels, and I could drive myself all the way to Salford and wallow in the aisles and aisles of choice. Best of all, it was the haunt of Manchester's top celebrities, and I had bumped into Terry Christian from *The Word* there, and Take That, on the cusp of their fame, relaxing in the café with milky tea and sticky buns. They seemed a little surprised that I'd want an autograph. The rest of the house, whether or not they were impressed by the names I dropped, were somewhat enthused by the potential glamour of the place.

But that day, there were no showbiz sightings. We went straight to the alcohol section and bought a few wineboxes, then argued about whether we should provide food or not. House outings like that were about the best fun we ever had. Away from the house, we became friends again, the way we were before we moved in together and got in each other's hair. Finlay would put on funny voices and tell jokes and in spite of myself I found them irritatingly amusing and had to laugh. And Richard would act like a kid with the trolley and push Finlay and they'd scoot around scaring old ladies and the girls would pretend to be cross and embarrassed. It was so nice when we were like that. Of course, Sara had to pretend she was a Russian defector from 1980 and she'd walk around saying things like: 'I've never seen a supermarket this big. What are all these things? What, you can actually buy ready-prepared vegetables? What a complete waste of money. That's like paying someone to chop up a carrot.' But the supermarket was my turf, and the atmosphere was so light and relaxing that I found it easier not to be impatient with her. All that space allowed me to regard her from a distance, as a curiosity.

When we split up to do our individual shops, Finlay bought as if he was five and his mother had allowed him to do the shopping that day, ice lollies and marshmallow sweets and enormous bags of frozen chicken that he'd never in fact ever cook. Heather bought lots of ethnically adventurous food, like couscous and lentils and matzo meal. Mandy bought red meat and butter. Mabel bought fish-fingers, Marmite and oven chips: traditional British fare. Sara bought very raw vegetables like turnips and carrots. That was all she ever cooked. Richard bought sensible ingredients for a variety of well-balanced meals, and nursery-style puddings, all ready-made. Many male ex-boarders have a notably unmasculine love of pudding, because it stood in for their mothers from an early age. It was quite fascinating to watch them. Oh, and I bought whatever was fashionable that year: bagels, blinis, lychees, Poptarts. We picked different queues and raced each other through the checkouts. It was one of those moments where life seems to imitate art, and you can almost hear an American teen-movie soundtrack accompanying you, although really there's just the muzak piped over the supermarket speakers.

We made detailed plans for the party. Sara put together tapes, and we worked out which rooms we were going to focus on and which would be kept locked. We made a bowl of punch, because we decided it would be an ironically bad-taste thing to do, as well as a cheapish way of providing alcoholic drinks for dozens of people with little more than cider, lemonade and past-its-prime fruit cut into lumps. We could always add more lemonade and chopped banana when it ran out because people would be too sloshed to notice. Heather, Mabel and I made one of those hedgehogs with cocktail sticks and bits of cheese. It had been decided that we weren't going to buy food for the guests but the three of us wanted to do this so much that we split the cost. We wanted our closest friends, who would arrive first, to see it and think we were too, too witty. All of us felt very lively, the boys in particular. The usual sarcasm and careful cleverness had given way to a rare, uncomplicated enthusiasm. Mandy even let up on moaning about how Dave the geologist was literally obsessed and never stopped calling. We should have had parties more often.

It was all going so well that it was inevitable that something should go a little awry before we started. In fact it was Heather, who gave in to a bout of hysteria while we were getting ready. She was so excited about Daniel coming round and seeing her as the perfect hostess of the perfect party that something inside her just cracked. Mandy came to tell me. I had rollers in and only fundamental make-up and I wasn't too pleased about the boys seeing me in the chrysalis stage of development but I was nothing if not a true friend. Sara came out of Heather's room looking grave, as if it were a hospital and we were visitors.

'I don't know what she wants,' she said. 'I have to get ready now, anyway.' And she went.

'She's flipped,' Mandy said. 'I've never seen her like this before.' We went in and Heather was sitting at her dressing-table, crying and breathing in huge, rasping gulps. 'What's wrong, babe?' Mandy asked her tenderly. She could be a very sweet friend. Perhaps this was the side she showed her boyfriends.

'Nothing's right, nothing's any good,' Heather shrieked. 'I look horrible. I'm fat. Nothing's right.'

'What is it, Heather? You can't be worried about the way you look. Nobody dresses better than you. You look stunning.' I said this, and it happened to be true. Normally I'd be too jealous to be so generous, but I could see she was really distraught.

Outside her door we heard Mabel whispering and Finlay shouting. 'What's wrong, Heather?' he called. He was already drunk.

'Go away,' Mandy shouted. Mabel came in and shut the door behind her, making the most of a single, harassed tut.

'He's practically legless already,' she said. 'Are you okay, Heather? Is it Daniel?'

'No, it's not Daniel, it's me,' she sobbed. 'I've got nothing to wear. Everything's wrong. I look like shit.' We took turns to assure Heather that she looked great, and she hiccuped and spluttered denial all the time.

'Has anyone got a paper bag?' I asked. 'She's hyperventilating.' Mandy, naturally, had a McDonald's bag, which smelled of McChicken Sandwich, and Heather was a vegetarian, if you didn't count pepperoni on pizzas, and she didn't. It couldn't be helped. She sucked on the bag until her colour dropped and she looked a bit more normal.

'Jesus, my head,' she said at last. 'And my lips are buzzing.'

'It's the bag,' I said. 'Now, are you feeling any better?'

She nodded. 'But I still don't have anything to wear,' she began again, and Mabel slipped her arm around her.

'Come on, now,' she said. 'Daniel'll be here soon. He doesn't care what you wear as long as he can see you naked before tomorrow.' And that did it. Heather giggled, and she was fine suddenly. We left her with Mandy.

'What a palaver,' I said, when we were outside her door.

'Ah, bless her,' Mabel said. 'Sometimes it's not easy looking as perfect as she does. The pressure, you know.' Sara popped her head out of her bedroom door.

'Is she better?' she asked. It was strange, the way she had disappeared, because Heather's loopy turn had been quite good fun, really, if you thought about it, and it was an authentic female bonding moment. But, then, Sara never seemed to fit in all that well with female bonding moments. She was strange, with a studied lack of vanity that I found exhausting, and couldn't connect with. She was too efficient and sincere to endure the sort of attention-seeking Heather had just treated us to, but she went too far in the other direction, possessing a sort of masculine detachment from the display. It wasn't as if she wanted not to take part, more that she couldn't. We all feel like the outsider at times, I'm sure, but you could see when Sara felt that way, and it was embarrassing to look, to be able to read someone so easily.

'She's fine. It was just a panic at-*yeek*!' Mabel squealed as Richard ran up the stairs behind her, picked her up and twirled her round. It was my turn to feel out of place. I'd never been good at the relaxed, tactile playfulness that goes on between boys and girls. I learned the finer points of sexual etiquette on my back – from matinée pictures: this is what comes from not being the outdoorsy type in the important teen years. While my best friends ran around with rough boys, I atrophied at home, studying the silver-cold actresses in the black and whites, thinking that was how it was done. In practice, their sort of appeal wasn't easy to emulate. Physically, I always looked untidy and flustered – more early Sally Field than early Betty Bacall – so to counter this I worked too hard at being detached and wry, and never felt I could let my guard down and just be with men. I was jealous of the way Mabel and the boys behaved so naturally together, apparently without thinking about it. Finlay joined us on the landing, Sara slipped back into her room.

'Has Heather, er, abandoned her tree, then?' he said. Already his eyes were glazing over, but he was still fairly sensible and still well up to poking fun at Heather's fit. The four of us often stood together like this and whispered rude things about the rest of the house. We were the saner core of our artificial family, but Mabel was the essential part of it; we fragmented when she wasn't around.

'No, she's not out of her tree, she's just stressed,' I said, but with enough of a sneaky, selfish glint to show how silly I thought she was being.

'She's having problems getting dressed,' Mabel said, with a similar, but kinder glint, although we both sounded as if we were ticking off the boys for their insensitivity.

'It's a pity she can't just throw any old thing on, the way you do, Mabel,' Finlay said, and Mabel swiped him on the shoulder.

'You sod,' she said. 'You really know how to make me feel like shit.'

'Oh, come on, Mabel, you know you always look gorgeous,' Richard said, with soft sincerity and a glimpse of flirt. She blushed prettily. 'But, Grace, were you planning on being quite as . . . white as that tonight?' he asked me, and I remembered with horror that I still hadn't put most of my make-up on, and I was standing in public with naked eyes. I hated to leave Mabel and the boys when we were all getting on so well, but it had to be done. I shut myself in my room and fixed my face.

We were, as it happened, a good-looking bunch of kids. Nothing wildly head-turning or supermodelly, but a consistence of youthful symmetry and the kind of attractiveness that comes with intelligence. When we were trying we were more than presentable, particularly as a group, rather than individually. Between the five of us, the girls represented all tastes, like Charlie's Angels. From Sara's long, athletic twigginess, through Mandy's flawless dimensions, to my abundantly slutty curves, which rebelled against the more pristine image I hoped to project, there was something for everyone, even perverts. We gathered in Heather's room for a bit of ego gluttony.

'You all look amazing,' Heather said, as everyone walked in.

'You look pretty amazing yourself,' Sara said.

'And I have the new underwear on,' she whispered. Much falsetto giggling.

'Time for a spliff?' Mandy said.

Everyone got excited, because the thrill of doing something illegal, something nobody's parents would ever have approved of, was taking its time to wear thin. I liked the shared sucking part of it much more than the actual drug, which was another facet of my love-hate relationship with other people's saliva. Like, I could neck with complete strangers, but on the street, I found the stuff really, really offensive, and I couldn't look at chewed chewing-gum without feeling nauseous. But the moistened end of the last half-inch of a joint I found, for whatever reason, comforting. Mandy rolled it on a textbook and forced everyone to admire the gently tapering lines. The herby smell was soothing and Heather could pull the most incredibly sensual, quasi-orgasmic faces when she inhaled, which were always a treat to watch. The camaraderie and the midnight-feast daring were the drug's strengths. Without these, it was little more than a roughly put-together fag. We listened to the Red Hot Chili Peppers on a tinny stereo and tried very hard to feel stoned.

Thursday

I wouldn't be in this dilemma if I'd screened that call, the way I screen all my calls. It's Alice's fault. She rang off to get her doorbell and the phone went twenty seconds later and I answered and, of course, it wasn't Alice, it was Heather. The truth is, I was excited to hear from her. Her voice was soft and pretty, unsettling, because in my memories she's always hysterical. How long has it been now, since we talked? What year did we graduate? Not that I spoke to her in the third year. A couple of chance meetings at parties or in the union, that was all. Anyway, I answered and I said I'd go. If I'd screened the call, I could have thought it over and I wouldn't have had to go, and now I do.

I'm a glib liar when I'm put on the spot like that, but my excuses are full of holes, which is why I'm no stranger to reunions. Every December I begin dreading the annual Christmas Eve get-together down the local by the river in my home town, when school-friends still show up to find out who is engaged and who is losing the fight. The sole, consistently notable exception is the school villain – my original best friend – a predatory sort who spread malice like marmalade and made no attempt to conceal her scandalous, swaggering confidence. The rest of us wait, salivating with anticipation, for the year when she finally crawls in, poor and wretched and, if there is justice on this earth, fat. For those who make it yearly, the changes are steady, and seldom dramatic. I am always worse. That's a constant. But it's easier there. There are fewer expectations.

In my home town I was always ill. A sickly child. No doubt I'd have died of consumption if I'd been born into another century. Measles, shingles, mumps, rubella, foot and bloody mouth – the full check-list of disease; and then Perthé's, the one that I still live with. Everyone feels sorriest for little kids in wheelchairs but, actually, it's not such a big deal. I spent a couple of years (age eight to nine) with my legs in braces, set widely apart like the men who sit on tubes and take up three seats with their knees. When you're a kid, everything's fine, everything just is. You feel a little sorry for yourself because you can't ride on the roller-coaster, but to be truly honest, I was secretly rather glad about that: it looked frightening. And you'd expect the other kids to be cruel, but they're not. They've a strong sense of morality, taught by the Saturday-morning cartoons. They're capable of genuine viciousness, of course, but that's part of play, and random. I remember the day my mother took me back to school in the shiny red chair, and left me. I think, looking back, that the headmistress must have had a serious word with all the pupils in a morning assembly, they were so reverent and well behaved, though it might just have been a wave of embarrassment, unease, pity, fear. There was silence, staring, and then gradually the noise crept back and everything was normal. Within weeks, they were using the wheelchair like a cartie, pushing each other around, while I ran after them, laughing, jerking from foot to foot with my legs rigid, like a plastic soldier.

Nobody expected any further problems until at least my forties, but when I was sixteen it began again. I tried to conceal the fact for as long as I could, but the pain soon showed. I was doing things differently, standing in a twist or leaning on walls for support. Things happened fast: I stopped going out, saw doctors and cried at whatever they said, then went through semi-experimental operations designed to delay the need for hip replacements. In hospital, fastened to a bed for months on end, I refused all visitors except Alice. She wasn't officially my best friend, then, but she was always my favourite friend. And I must have needed someone. She came almost every day after school. Almost always, she brought flowers, saying the man on the stall liked her so much he gave them to her for next to nothing. She saw my parents lurch into a kind of concerned insanity, brought chocolates and anxiety when my weight fell to five stone, understood when I threw fits about nothing and didn't believe me when I made light of things that mattered. Because I lived for months at a time in that bed, in the tiny room just off the geriatric ward, she saw all of me. No one outside my family ever came as near.

Separated through the college years, nothing has diminished, but things between Alice and me have changed. The older I get, and the more this looks like the way things are going, rather than a detour, the more I've recalled my competitiveness. It isn't angry or destructive, but based on a need to present my life as being valid and equal to hers. So I gambled the reassurance of her sympathy for a shot at winning her respect. I've outgrown the desire for pity, even Alice's pity, which is not to be sneezed at. To be pitied is to have a bad life, and there's no pity in the world that'll make up for that.

Now the Orwell Street people, back from wherever: they went all over the place – I *think*. Actually I just didn't bother to find out, or pay attention when anybody told me – the only one I kept in touch with was Sara, which was a mistake, because she lives here, and she makes the effort. I've just realized, it's a year since I last saw Sara. It was February, because it was just after my birthday. Have I been screening calls that long? I've been trying to imagine what they're all doing: no doubt their relentless capacity for ambition has been amply rewarded. God, though, how do I make this life sound good? I should have been a solicitor. I could have been a solicitor. I almost was a solicitor. Would that do? But why would anyone want to be a solicitor? I couldn't stand it: all those books, all that law. This is the excuse I give. The truth? After skipping another year for another op I thought everyone doing the practice course would be younger than me and I'd fit in even less than I did at college. I know how stupid that sounds now, but when you're young and you're wasting time it feels like you'll never make it back. Particularly when you used to be precocious.

I've made better decisions – let's face it, even perming my hair in the eighties was probably a better decision. At least I'd have had money now, at least I wouldn't have to be so afraid. So pitiable. I certainly don't want *their* pity. I never had it before. Although I was never exactly overflowing with promise, I always had an airy indolence, which represented a certain glamour, with the further charm of being a yardstick for the rest of them. The years erode cool. The pose has lost its allure.

So, achievements. Well . . . what I can come up with is excuses, and they're good excuses, honest and valid and considerable. But excuses never made anyone happy, or jealous, for that matter. And I know I don't want to go into all that with them. When we lived together, I mentioned to the girls that I had problems with my walking, but only once, really, when I wanted a good cry and needed something to blame. And I just talked about scars, not pain; disfigurement is something girls can relate to because they're convinced they're hideous anyway. Pain sounds too much like whining. I never told the boys or talked about it in front of them. Too vain. Too desperate to be desired. I explained away the disabled badge on my car as a perk, the spoils of a medical family, which, to an extent, it was then. Besides, I was okayish. I don't think I let any of it show, most of the time. Once in a while, people on my course would walk out of a lecture with me, and say, I thought you were limping, then, and I'd just laugh and mumble an excuse, usually a lie, and change the subject. I have no idea whether Finlay knew. I assumed he didn't. And I assume that because I assume that he wouldn't have wanted me if he'd thought I was anything other than perfect.

If only I'd known then how good things were. At college, I walked almost normally, and I was energetic and, compared to now, probably fairly gorgeous. But I wasn't a hit. The good-looking rich boys didn't know I existed; or if they did, they must have pulled muscles trying to pretend that they'd forgotten who

I was when I met them for the third, fourth, eleventh time. Instead, there was a lot of snogging but very few phone calls. There was Finlay, and Greg, and heavens, in the third year, the toothsome Mark the Tart, who was handsome and funny and good, but he did put it about a bit, which scared the heck out of me. If I had my life over again, though, the first thing I'd do is Mark the Tart. But I digress.

What's odd is that now, even now, *especially* now, I'm never a long way from a proposition. It's mainly to do with me living in the part of London that thinks it's a holiday resort. We've got a Butlin's, a hundred and four tacky bistros and a constant stream of suitcases along the pavement. Most of the men on the streets in the day-time are foreigners, and men abroad are bolder than men at home. So they approach, introduce themselves, ask me where I'm from and if I'd like to have a drink. And even if they're awful, you'd think this could still make me happy, but it doesn't. I think too much. Yesterday an Italian hairdresser came out of his shop while I was waiting at the bus stop outside. He started chatting, flattering and asked for my number. I didn't give it to him, but I smiled prettily and he kissed me on the cheek. When I got home I called Alice to laugh about it and boast a little, but this was a pretence: I wanted to slip in the serious question.

'Do you think these men, the ones who ask me out, do you think they think I'm going to be easier, you know, more desperate because I don't walk so –'

'That's such a load of rubbish. I'm going to pretend you didn't say that.'

'Well, I did say it.' Silence.

'So is that what *you* do now?' Alice said, after a while. 'The men you fancy are those who are unattractive enough to be grateful?'

'No, of course n–'

'But men do? That's what you're saying?'

'I don't know. Who knows what men do? There has to be a reason.'

'There is. Have you looked in the mirror?'

'Oh, come on.'

'Oh, come on yourself.'

Textbook best-friend script. She does it very well. Still, it was awkward and awful trying to bring up the whole subject with Alice. Alice is something of a fair-weather friend – she blocks it out when I'm doing badly – and despite what people say, they're the best kind of friend. I'm the other kind, I've always got time to hear about someone's problems. But I want to know the bad news for my own protection, my own peace of mind. To compare and contrast: it helps. Sadness upsets Alice, and it's not my job to upset her, even if it's her job to be upset. We're supposed to protect each other. I don't think I'll bring it up again.

1992

3

The thing about a student party is you always forget how late they really start. Through a combination of their wanting to appear too cool to come early, and actually being too cool to come early, and waiting until the pubs shut, you can have a complete dearth of guests until nearly midnight. But the party-people can't go out because they've said come at ten and someone just might come that early. As we sat there, wilting and drinking the wineboxes, I began to worry that nobody would come at all and we'd be exposed as friendless bad-party-givers.

'Daniel said he'd be here before eleven,' Heather said.

'Have you packed for Blackpool?' I asked Mabel, not wishing to start on the Daniel thing.

'Almost. I'm going to put this dress in as well, and I still have to get my make-up together. Look, don't eat the hedgehog, Finlay.'

'How many pairs of knickers are you taking?' Mandy asked.

'Well, I'm going for two a day because we'll be going out for dinner, and an extra pair, just because you never know when you'll need another pair of knickers.'

'Yes, you should always take an extra pair,' Heather said.

'Yes, but I usually wear them in bed and I'm not taking any to sleep . . .'

'Put the telly on, Dick,' Finlay said, with the strained loftiness that little brothers adopt when they're surrounded by too many of their sisters' friends.

'We can't be watching the TV when people come,' Sara said. 'They'll think that's what we do.' The rest of us started giggling.

It could have been the three or four joints we'd got through, but I'd like to think it was collective amusement at Sara's irrational fear of being associated with watching television. Specifically, she had it in for all things American, and couldn't be persuaded that any programme they produced might be more sophisticated than even the worst ITV sit-coms. Like a lot of British people she had read too many articles about US manipulation of sentiment, and didn't want to appear gullible enough to have her feelings messed about with in the name of something so mainstream. We watched television anyway and almost forgot about the party until the doorbell went. There were about half a dozen girls there, our sworn sisters from halls in the first year, with whom I was already losing touch, due to the usual paranoia and an inexcusable lack of effort. It was still good to see them again, and they took a tour of the house, although they'd seen it before when we first moved, because we all felt fairly grown-up about renting houses and wouldn't have missed an opportunity to do grown-up things with them. We sloshed cheap wine into chipped glasses and spilled lager and dished dirt like the old friends we were, and I wouldn't have minded if no one else had come at all. But they did. People I knew, people I didn't know, people I didn't want to know. They turned up and spread out and filled in as more came. Sara's tapes were playing at nosebleed volume and soon enough we were shouting and laughing and feeling damn popular again.

The best areas of a party are the stairs and the kitchen. My personal preference is for the kitchen, and that's where I headed. I looked fairly terrific, and although I'd decided I wasn't going to snog anyone, I wanted to mingle and sass and strike a pose while I still looked this good. I wasn't going to snog anyone because I never brought people back to my place, and in your own party, there's very little choice in the matter, unless you pretend you don't live there. This rule was the result of a disastrous encounter I had in the first-ever term of college, when I went to a ball and a blond boy who looked uncannily like a pig spent the evening following me around and saying, 'I'll be right back. Don't go anywhere!' whenever he went to urinate, which was often enough to cause me some concern. This was back in the early days, when I still didn't suspect I possessed sex-appeal. My behaviour was still very much inhibited by my school image: I was unsteady in a situation where refusal was not expected by both parties at the outset, and too flattered by his interest to dismiss it out of hand. After doggedly hanging on my every word, this porcine character informed me he lived too far away to get home, and could he sleep on my floor as I lived close? I scraped home on my gold stilettos, too drunk to muster enough attitude to turn him away. He slept on my bed, with me, although I kept my dress on. No, there was no unpleasantness, no date rape, no sex, no unwanted attention asserted. But I woke up the next day feeling wretched and unclean. I couldn't look at him, couldn't speak to him. I felt my space had been invaded. I believe this was the very moment at which my hygiene obsession kicked in, or at the very least, the first time it kicked out. I washed those sheets five times before I allowed them back on my bed, and when I did, I spent half the night reliving the sordid, soiled feeling. I didn't use them again. This story only goes to show how weird I really was, but it sums me up pretty well as well. I overreact to intimacy with strange people to an unnecessary degree.

There were no chairs left in the kitchen, but a chiselled Asian boy asked me to sit on his knee. It's always uncomfortable doing this, because you have to put virtually all your weight through one big toe, to pretend you weigh a fraction of your actual weight. Somebody suggested a drinking game, and everyone else called him a fucking student and wouldn't. So instead we started the usual philosophical crap that students are so fond of. They like to leave clues about themselves which have nothing to do with their opinions and everything to do with sex. They'll throw in half a double entendre and look smug about it. A lot of young men take a long time to learn that the things they find most attractive about girls, specifically, being up for it, don't produce the same erotic response when they replicate the effect for us. It was no wonder I hardly ever fancied anyone. But the boy I was sitting on seemed a touch more astute than most, and had a perfect nose, and I was drunk enough to have benefited from a personal testosterone surge, and we diverted ourselves by flirting disgracefully and making private, whispered jokes about anyone who struck us as ridiculous, for the sole purpose of unsettling them.

'Grace, can I have a word? It's really important,' Finlay said. He had been in the room, glaring silently, but I hadn't really paid him much attention. I knew he just wanted to start up the whole me-and-him business again, and I wasn't in the mood.

'Yeah, in a minute.'

He looked pissed off. 'Look, it really is, er, quite important. I wouldn't ask you otherwise,' he said, with sulky piety.

It had started to occur to me, in my alcohol-deluded state of self-confidence, that I might be encouraging the boy underneath me, and now seemed as good a time as any to break it up, just in case. So I went.

'Can we go in your room?' Finlay said. A reasonable request, as it was one of the locked, out-of-party-bounds rooms. The relative quiet, when we closed the door, was unexpected, given the wafer-like nature of the walls, and my ears were whistling like a long, steady note on a harmonica.

'What's wrong?' I said, when we were sitting on the edge of my bed. There was no chair, it was a tiny room.

'You know what's wrong.'

'I don't know what's wrong. I thought you had something important to say. So say it, for Christ's sake. There's a party going on.'

'You know what's wrong.' I stayed silent. He inhaled and exhaled in a manner I thought a little hammy. 'I just don't see why every time you meet a bloke you –'

'Oh, change the bloody record, Finlay. You're not still pretending you fancy me?' Always, I had to make him say it. If we had to take a vote on who was more pathetic, I'd have had to cheat not to win.

'Of course I do. I can't just stop fancying you because you decide it's not *cool* any more, or it doesn't fit in with your plans.'

'Look, we've had a couple of snogs, nothing more; they can't have been that memorable.' Oh, I had no shame at all.

He chuckled softly to himself as if I just didn't understand something blindingly obvious. I enjoyed the softness of his voice. 'Actually, er, they were.'

Our faces were dangerously close, and he had positioned his hand so it almost – but not quite – touched my thigh. I found our situation unspeakably arousing.

'We live together,' I said. 'It would be a disaster.' I watched my bosom heaving and hoped he was too. He moved closer, until I could feel his breath on my neck, and lifted his hand to my hair. I carried on talking while he twirled a lock close to my cheek, shivered once as his hand touched my skin. Then he leaned in further and kissed the side of my throat, dipping his hand deeper into my hair.

'Please don't do that,' I said, the way Ingrid Bergman might have, if her scriptwriters had skipped college. His other hand was around my waist now, gently, gently fitting into the curve and resting on my hip, and he was whispering to me, his lips brushing my face. My whole body was experiencing waves of guilty pleasure. He may have been as irritating as hell but he really knew how to kiss. He had mastered the one basic prerequisite: he adored me. A little bit of unqualified longing, and I'm putty.

It would have been so easy to stay there and let it happen, but I never lost sight of my practical side. I knew from experience what the consequences of another rerun would be, and this time I summoned the willpower to stand up. I straightened my clothes for effect, for something to do that looked conclusive.

'Look, you know I always fancy you when I'm drunk. Alcohol makes me easy. I can't help it. I don't really fancy you. Leave me alone, for Christ's sake.'

He stood up, too, and leaned against the door. 'You're not going.' We both knew this was a question – *almost* a whine, even – but he added the slightest inclination of statement, just to sound a little tough, a little sexy. Our faces reflected the kind of fierce seriousness that's one degree from laughing, and I gave in first, but gently.

'Come on, get out the way. Before I hurt you,' I said. He smiled too, perhaps because I was revisiting one of our running gags, the one where I mocked his masculinity. I used to take the lids off jars or the corks out of bottles when he'd struggled with them. (Endurance of pain is the secret there, not strength, incidentally.) I pushed him to the side, not quite easily. He took hold of my wrist. I have absurdly slender wrists, and I never tire of people noticing. His hand dwarfed it.

'You know, you come on to some twat you don't know just because you think it's . . . funny or something, and I'm supposed to just –'

'I *am* going now,' I said, 'and I'm not leaving you here. Come on, you're not staying in my room to go through my knickers.'

'But that was why I wanted to come in here in the first place. I intend to try them on as soon as you've gone.' Beneath the lightness of our words we were both losing patience. He was on comedy auto-pilot, playing for time, competing with my nonchalance to cover his resentment. His eyes had hardened. 'I just wish you weren't, you know, such a bitch to me.'

'Fine, I'm a bitch,' I said, all weary condescension. 'So stop talking to me, stop . . . pissing me off.'

I could tell it was time to stop. In the sober bleach of day this sort of thing was amiable; at night, alcohol would make him aggressive, which I didn't like. I came across all ballsy and don't-give-a-shit, but the implicit violence of men was something I couldn't predict, so never felt completely in control of. My father never lost his temper or raised his voice, and I couldn't gauge men who did, or guess how far it went. I was tired of this anyway, tonight: it was a waste of a good outfit and I wanted to get back to the people who only ever saw me looking plump and frumpy.

He sat down on my bed again, raked his hair with both hands. 'I just don't see why we can't have, you know, a civil conversation any more. A normal conversation. That's all I want.'

'We talk,' I said, used to this complaint. He didn't mind that I let him think he had a chance, he didn't mind the tease of almost-contact that happened increasingly rarely now, when I got drunk. What he objected to, he claimed, was the withdrawal of the drollish rapport we used to have. But this was semi-mythical anyway, and the fact was that even where it was true it was his fault, not mine, that it was gone. The success of our relationship had been based in sparring and insults, a mostly conscious, mostly mediocre attempt to re-create the flirty fighting that occurs in all good fiction. But he just didn't joke so much with me any more, and when I did he took it all personally, jumped at the chance to take offence, to tell me how unpleasant or immature I was – 'immature' being the nastiest insult one student can give to another.

'I don't know what you want me to do,' I said. 'Tell me, and I'll do it. Tell me how to be, and I'll be like that. If I annoy you so much, you'll just have to learn to ignore me.' I liked saying that because it tormented him. Me being reasonable, pliant. Him being unreasonable, demanding. While it brought an unarguable finality to all discussion, it dangled tantalizing acquiescence. I was still standing by the door, he was still sitting.

'Don't make me drag you off there,' I offered, but it was too late for that. He sat still, to show me I couldn't force him to do anything, then finally got up. Clearly, *all his decision.* I locked the door behind us and went downstairs. I assumed he was following, but when I turned round he'd disappeared.

It had been presumed by the rest of the house that my designs on Finlay were honourable, but hesitant. The misapprehension, if indeed it was one, had grown from our brief, infrequent, but nonetheless several kisses. I think the general feeling was that I wouldn't have contributed to these if there'd been no sincere affection behind them, which may even be true. The first came about when we'd been living together for a couple of months. By then his famed cleverness had been exposed, through the emergence of recognizable patterns and important gaps and limitations, as nothing to be afraid of. He had a tendency to be a little grubby. And I didn't like his fingers, which were spindly and moved too much. I researched and catalogued his faults until I was securely over him. With the danger of an emotional attachment on my side having been averted, I felt it was safe to continue. There are plenty of psychological shortcomings, I believe, that are even more pathetic and futile, and I don't give myself too hard a time when I think about mine. It was harmless.

The first authentic collision came about at the summit of a process of gossip and consultation that was so immature it made me blush to think about it. I seem to remember getting drunk and telling a male friend I had a bit of a thing about Finlay, just to put him off. Tim, the friend, was one of those effeminate heterosexuals, the kind who are celebrated cissies at school and only bond with girls. All their subsequent relationships with the opposite sex are close and chatty and apparently platonic. Occasionally, they use this position to angle for sympathy sex – *very* occasionally, it works. They're my favourite type of boy, because they never make you feel obligated: they lead you to believe that your company – just that – is the whole objective of their charm. They like you. Normal boys wear ulterior motives like slogan T-shirts; there's a constant feeling you should be impressing them or putting out, which can lead to insecurity or guilt. Perhaps, later in life, the cissies insinuate themselves into the best relationships, with the brightest, prettiest women. I hope so, because they deserve to. Tim, an exemplary cissy, must have achieved this parallel sort of intimacy with almost every woman in the university, and was as close to the other Orwell Street girls as to me. He discussed my revelation freely with them when I wasn't there and later claimed I hadn't declared the subject to be restricted. The girls challenged me in private and I confessed that there had been an interest, but it was now a shadow of its former self. They refused to believe it could be over when they hadn't even noticed it happening. Only Mabel had seen the signs.

'I knew you did,' she said, and casually changed the subject, but the others wanted to flog it.

'I'm sure he fancies you,' Sara said.

'Have you thought that before?' I said.

'No, but I didn't know you liked him. If you like him, I'm sure he'd be up for it.'

'Well, "up for it" isn't enough. Anyway, I've gone off the idea.'

'I'm going to find out if he does,' Heather said. She looked bouncy with pleasure at her new toy: an excuse for a deep chat with Finlay.

'Oh, don't,' I said, weakly. But, you know, the idea was suddenly looking interesting again, and we had been drinking. For the next few days, the house was talking about the two of us, which was, of course, enjoyable, in a classroom note-passing way. But by the end of it, everyone knew everything about everyone, and it was no longer possible to ignore it. There was a party looming, and there were assumptions and it all drove me mad. I athletically avoided him all night. The cocktail of reported attraction and unavailability meant there could be only one result: a bona fide crush on his part, stirred up out of practically nothing. Boys are so malleable. Another social event came about, and when I found myself alone on a couch with him, I drew attention to the formality and falseness of our situation. I suggested that, now the inevitable looked inevitable, the expectation of it was more than I could bear and it could only be an anticlimax. I talked and stalled and rationalized. At the time, he was trying to create a façade of spontaneity, and my admission trampled all over it, putting the affair on an unromantic and controlled platform. Which was just where I liked it. I let him proceed.

How cool. In retrospect, I *was* as cool as all that, because that's what happened. We thrashed and rehashed the situation so many times that it became external and theoretical. But at the time I was just as nervous and stupid and embarrassed as he was keen and earnest, and none of it was as deliberate or controlled as I convinced myself it had been. On the contrary, sometimes he made me shake with longing, sometimes I shrank with doubt and couldn't understand him at all. There were days when he intimidated me with opaque silences and I thought he'd discovered how ordinary I really was and I'd lost him. And the opposite: he'd deliver great intelligent monologues that I sat at the edges of, in dumb admiration, wondering if I'd misread everything from the start. But some people say that real memories are just as imaginary as false ones, because none of the past exists. If we get to choose our own recollections, I don't see why I can't be the hip one in mine.

Back in the kitchen, Heather was talking to a thin, handsome, older man. Early thirties, maybe. I was so envious that it must have shown on my face, but I remembered that Heather was in love, although the all-singing, all-dancing Daniel was nowhere to be seen.

'Where did you go?' she asked.

'I've been with Finlay. The usual.'

'Did you succumb? Christ, you did. You succame.'

'No, the usual refusal, followed by the usual post-mortem. He's just pissed.'

'Ahhh, the poor boy. He just can't get over you,' she said. 'There's a guy in our house who's crazy about her,' she explained to the stranger, with a coy little smile that I found disarmingly sexy, so he must have. 'This is Grace, the most sophisticated member of the house.' That would do, I supposed.

'Hello,' I said. 'I'm not sophisticated, really.'

'I'm Adam,' he said. 'I'm not sophisticated, either.' But the tilt of his smile told me a different story. He had an old-fashioned

Robert Mitchumy appeal that used to be described as rugged, but his face was open and intelligent. Just my type.

'No, I think you are,' I said, narrowing my eyes to scrutinize his. 'I can usually tell these things too.'

'Then you must be sophisticated,' he said. Not exactly David Mamet, but I was drunk and he was a complete stranger.

'Adam's our neighbour,' Heather explained. 'He's a teacher.'

'A teacher? But you're so . . . *normal.* We never had teachers like you at my school,' I said, realizing too late that I sounded like Jimmy Tarbuck interviewing a Miss World contestant. I was practically leering. Fortunately, he was laughing at me, but kindly.

'I'm pretty sure my kids don't think of me as "normal",' Adam said, glancing at Heather. 'All kids hate their teachers, anyway.'

'I bet yours don't. Do you have the whole building?' I said. He looked blank. 'Next door.'

'First and second floors. Someone else has the ground. He's a bloody weird man, and he probably sleeps with corpses and collects stuffed birds, but I don't see a lot of him and the mortgage is cheap, and the area's nice, so I'm happy.'

'Then you're the one who plays non-stop Piaf, and has about a million messages on his answerphone a day. I hear it bleep, not the messages,' I said quickly, in case he thought I had a glass to the wall. 'So how did you – why are you here?' I was rushing things and doing badly. Faced with his irrebuttable maturity, my own was looking like a poor impersonation. I had to slow down and let him show me if he might be interested at all.

'Well, Heather came into the pub for ciggies and got talking to Justin – my boyfriend – and asked if we'd like to come along, and I could but he couldn't.'

'Your b– you're both living next door, or . . .?' It was a good recovery, but we all saw it happening. My cack-handed seduction plot dissolved like Aspro-Clear.

'No, just me. But listen, I'm sorry about the Piaf,' Adam said. 'I can turn it down if it's bothering you.'

'I wish you'd turn it up,' I said. 'It's lovely, honestly.'

'I teach French,' he explained, 'and I find French music really helps me think in French. Films just don't do that.'

'Who's the woman you play who sings "I Wish I Were In Love Again"? Is it Judy Garland? Not that you'd have to listen to Judy Garland. Oh, God I'll shut up now before I say something that *isn't* really offensive.'

Adam cocked one groomed eyebrow into a perfect arch. 'Can you hear my music all the time?'

'Only when I'm putting on make-up in my bedroom. No more than three, four hours a day.' I wrinkled my nose, fetchingly. A straight man would have found it impossible to resist. Adam laughed, a deep, maple-syrupy laugh. I was already half in love with him. Shame, that.

Richard and Sara were nowhere to be seen. And Finlay. Heather, I had left in the kitchen, along with Mandy and Mabel who were talking to our old girlfriends from halls. There were some scary-looking big boys taking out little polythene bags in the living room. There was a bunch of travellers with a pretty little dog on a piece of string. Did we know them? As I walked past the line of girls on the stairs, I realized I didn't recognize a single one of them, and they looked back at me in the cool, defensive way that girls at parties look at each other until they bond over the queue for the loos, or a search for something to eat. I suddenly had the feeling that I was at somebody else's party, surrounded by strangers. I wanted to tell people that we had left the living room unattended and anyone could just walk off with the television and it was hired. Nobody else ever seemed to worry about this sort of thing, while I always found time to behave like a parent. I stood in the hall between the rooms for a long time, talking to nobody, feeling the cool, scratchy wallpaper on my back. I wanted to be somewhere else, somewhere with cleaner, older people and a piano. When I closed my eyes the room was spinning horribly, and I went with it, feeling my head being whirled around. People started leaving: some drunk boys tried to assemble sentences on their way out of the front door and gave up. One of them kissed me wetly on the cheek as he said goodnight. I'd never seen him before, not even at the party. It was all winding down now. There was a sleepy feel to the rave music, the beats were fusing together into white noise. The scary big boys were drifting into their own blue haze, the girls on the stairs were sitting down, Mabel was yawning and looking at her watch while a tall boy who wasn't good enough tried to impress her with borrowed humour. I wanted to have a bath and go to bed.

Richard appeared and squeezed my shoulder. There was a slowness, a heaviness to his touch that made his exhaustion palpable.

'Are you tired, lovey?' I asked him.

'It's only four o'clock. Are you calling me a pansy?' he bellowed, comically, as Adam walked by.

'I'm going to head off next door now,' Adam said to me. 'If you ever want to pop in for a coffee . . .'

'I'd love to,' I said. 'Now I know who you are.' Adam smiled and went.

'Woh ho ho,' Richard said. He nudged me suggestively. 'Who was that, then?'

'That was Adam, our neighbour. He's a pansy.'

Sara came downstairs and walked past without talking to either of us. She looked mad about something, but that was hardly unusual.

'What's wrong with her?' I asked him. He shrugged. There were just a few people kicking around now, and they were gathering together in the living room.

'Where's Finlay?' Mabel said.

'He's upstairs, sleeping with Donna,' Sara said, flatly. A few people looked at me and, not knowing how to react, I put on a disaffected smile. I had no idea who Donna was, but I didn't want to seem interested enough to ask. But then I didn't want to look too bothered not to talk about it. It was something of a challenge, how to broadcast a complete absence of concern.

'Who's Donna?' Mabel asked. Bless her.

'Donna is Natasha's friend,' Heather said.

'Blonde Natasha, who used to go out with Steve?' I said, picking the exactly right note of interest in the conversation, by focusing on a secondary character.

'No, the other Natasha, from Newcastle. Donna's the tiny redhead who used to be an anorexic.'

'Oh, is she the girl who rollerskates everywhere, and used to have half a slice of bread with brown sauce and ketchup at dinner last year?' Mabel said. I didn't have a clue who they were talking about.

'That's her.'

'And he's sleeping with her? Now?' said Heather. 'Are you sure?' She glanced at me again, to see what my reaction would be. I made sure there wasn't one. Really, everyone behaved as if we were some sort of item, as if I was as keen as he was and would be jealous if he found someone else to bother. And I was jealous when he found someone else to bother, but not because I wanted him. It was more that by fancying someone else he would have gone beyond giving up, and actually discovered something defective or unattractive about me. I just didn't like the idea of him changing his mind. It felt like criticism.

There was a boy in the corner of the room who kept looking at me. I kind of knew him as one of Finlay's friends, Trev, or something. Later, we were all talking about some commercial pop record that I was defending and everyone else was being unnecessarily negative about, when the boy in the corner said, 'No, it's a good record,' and then smiled at me as if he'd just made some kind of Sir Lancelot-style joust for my honour. He sounded fairly stupid, and I felt that his support did my argument no end of damage, and I didn't even want to be sided with, so I ignored him. 'I've got one of their albums,' he said to me. 'I can bring it round for you.'

'Actually, I'm terrible about borrowing stuff,' I said quickly. 'I have about thirty books that belong to other people and I tend to scratch CDs when I touch them and just generally stand on things and break them, so, thanks, but I don't think that would be a good idea. Thanks, though.' I had a nasty feeling that this boy was beginning to show too much of an interest in me, and I didn't want him to. There was something a little odd about him. Finlay had a lot of weird friends, and I didn't talk to most of them. I didn't want to be drawn into some kind of album-sharing understanding with this one. But as the party withered even more, he remained, clinging fast like ivy. Mabel said she had to go to bed, and I leaped up with her, saying I did too. I didn't get to see this Donna girl before she left, or Finlay again that night. I lay awake in bed, listening to the door slamming, and Heather going nuts over the mess, then going nuts over the fact that Daniel hadn't come. I heard Richard and Finlay whispering about Finlay's conquest, although I couldn't make out much of it, and then they were whispering about something else, and Finlay shouted, 'Fucking hell!' and Richard said 'Shhhh!' really loudly. I grinned in the dark. It was all so trivial but they took it so seriously, were always so excitable. We're forever being told that life isn't a rehearsal, but college sure as hell is. It's a place for middle-class kids to feel what it's like to live away from home, and they spend their time there imagining what it must be to have real relationships and real problems, while they pick up their beer money for doing nothing. I did all this just as much as the next person, but I never, even for a moment, felt like anything was actually happening. I always knew I was still a kid. Shopping, cooking, arguing, watching television like a family – it had an unreality about it, like a radio play. As with the best comedy, it depended on everyone playing it absolutely straight, but I often wished they didn't also have to upset themselves so much.

In the morning, I woke with a hangover at about seven, less than three hours after I'd finally slept. I showered, dried my hair and put on a light, naked face make-up. I got downstairs at nineish and Heather was already up, collecting beer cans in a bin bag.

'Look at the place,' she said. My shoes were sticking to the carpet; I had to peel them off when I stood still for a while. The smell of fags and beer was rancid and assertive. The living room was a tip, but it was a fairly standard party aftermath. I got a bag and started helping her, except I was lazier than she was and kept trying to encourage her to sit down, take a break, talk over last night. I would have been happy to leave it all alone for a day, spend some time away from here, clear my head, have somebody cook breakfast for me, and then come back to tackle it all much, much later, when I felt personally clean enough to handle it. The filth of the party was trapped in my head and lungs. But Heather was well brought up and responsible and I couldn't just sit there while she did all the work, regardless of the fact that everyone else had stayed in bed and I should have. So I looked as useful as I could, even though every time I bent down to pick something up I would cheerfully have vomited if only I'd been able to, and don't imagine I hadn't tried. I took deep breaths as I made my way through calcifying evidence of other people's mouths. Stale saliva stood out in matt smears on shiny surfaces. I went to get a large bucket of soapy water. As long as I was touching water and soap, I could just about cope.

Sara was the next to join us, only she hadn't just woken, she'd been for a run round the park. I bustled from one room to the next looking virtuous, and I realized that she was saying something of grave importance to Heather. A little put out that they had started without me, I sat down with my bucket and asked what was going on. Sara looked at her feet.

'Sara and Richard . . .' Heather said, meaningfully.

'What, you . . .?' I said, and Sara nodded, looking very serious indeed. 'What did you do?' I had to ask, because I didn't know how much to infer. 'What, you fell out, you shagged, what?'

'Yes, they shagged, Grace,' Heather said, with some impatience, as though I was extremely young or extremely stupid, and then carried on from the middle of the conversation that I hadn't been having. I'm afraid I'd already stopped listening. I did that a lot. I wasn't actually interested in gossip and was far too self-contained to pay much attention to the drama of other people's lives. I preferred it served to me by the television, where the lines were a bit more structured, people repeated themselves less, and they didn't expect me to react properly – I faked emotions badly. Later, of course, when I couldn't contribute to the circle of advice-giving, couldn't withdraw my own comfort from the feeling of belonging that's created by the intimacy of secrets, then I regretted not paying attention when I should have. But when it was just a story about other people, I didn't really want to know. Me and the bucket just carried on as normal. So they had sex, so what?

Mabel left early that morning, to meet her boyfriend at the train station for their Blackpool holiday. She apologized for about twenty minutes for not helping to tidy the place. I was sorrier that she was leaving, because the house without her was going to be more of a struggle, which I hated. The cleaning up at least gave me something to do. Not much had changed, considering Finlay had scored in a big way and two members of the house had learned something very new about each other. Really, to see them all, you wouldn't have thought we'd even had a party. We all began again where we'd left off. Finlay discussed his conquest, of course, with an abundance of candid detail and an absence of minimal decency that made me feel very glad I'd never allowed him nearer me. Sara and Richard just pretended nothing had happened. Heather called Daniel in a strop, and was soothed by whatever he had to say. The only excitement to have come out of the whole tacky affair was that Richard found a bag of coloured pills under one of the armchairs.

'Whose are they?' Heather said.

'There were some scary people there, with bags of something. I saw them,' I volunteered, exaggerating my greenness like the kids who grass at school. 'What are you going to do with them?'

'We'll sell them,' Mandy announced. She, rather impressively, had a warm relationship with a very minor drug dealer, a friendly, harmless lad who sold her cannabis resin and sometimes took her to the pub. Predictably, he was stupid with unrequited passion for her. She and the boys started discussing market prices, and identifying the pills and talking knowledgeably about them. Inwardly, I couldn't deny that this was exciting, but I made it clear that I didn't want anything to do with it.

'So, we sell them to Tony,' the drug dealer pal, 'and swap them for money and a quarter of blow,' Mandy said. Her languid tone was just a touch too smooth to pass for true awelessness.

'What if they come back?' Heather said.

'What are they going to say?' Richard laughed. 'May we have our drugs back, please?'

'What if they're really bad ones, full of shit?' Sara said.

'Tony can usually tell. He'll just try one. His head got fucked up long ago.' Mandy chortled.

So they got to make these plans and talk about them for hours on end and feel very pleased with themselves, not to mention very mature and law-breaking and with it. Taking drugs was one thing, but bargaining with them and indirectly selling them on the open market was a whole new world of daring. They were in the big league now. This was really living. This was hanging out, taking risks, living life on the edge. These were the tales we'd have for our grandchildren, the memories that'd stay with us.

And they pulled it off. Tony the drug dealer came round, referred to the tablets with cool-sounding names, like Roobarb and Custard, and Dennis the Menace, and did a deal with them that gave them a few quid each and a generous supply of whatever they made joints with. The brown stuff, I think. Mandy, Richard and Finlay split it between them, the rest of us observing in admiration or foretelling doom-ridden consequences (Sara). I wasn't there when the exchange took place, but I heard about it in vivid detail later. I played the kid sister, taking exaggerated, hasty breaths at appropriate moments to please them. The other revelations raked up by the party were eclipsed. You just couldn't buy entertainment like this.

Finlay and I seemed much more relaxed together than normal. The shag had worked wonders for him, restored his confidence and revitalized his sense of humour. Which wasn't to say that I wasn't a little miffed at being so not so unforgettable after all, but, you know, anything for an easy life. The only thing I couldn't stand was the undisguised admiration all the girls had for his scrawny, carroty little bint. Whom I still hadn't seen.

'She's unbelievably feminine,' Sara used to say a lot. I took this extremely personally. What was it, if not a comparison with me? The fact was that, although physically I was about as voluptuously lumpy as a slimmish girl can be, and small-chinned and long-haired and generally female-looking as the next girl, I had always felt butch. But, then, it's not down to the shape you are but what you do with it. Audrey Hepburn's figure was ostensibly androgynous, but every move she made set off her gamine delicacy better than any amount of lip-gloss and bra padding. I blamed my mother for a while – and why not? – as she'd dressed me quite sportily compared to the other girls, who were allowed to wear boob tubes and ra-ra skirts when they were twelve, and we used to hold beauty contests among ourselves in the lunch-breaks, and I would stand there awkwardly in spectacles and jersey, unisex clothes, and always come absolutely last. But it wasn't my wardrobe and four-eyes that held me back; just attitude. I got older and learned the moves, but behind the scenes nothing changed: my lack of interest in gossip, my reluctance to commit to relationships, the sense that I was faking something when we got drunk and sang songs from *Grease.* It just wasn't convincing: there was an *effeminacy* about my girlishness that looked like hard work – big breasts, concrete hair, frequent public application of pressed powder on a complexion that didn't need it: there's a fine line between made-up and dragged up. I didn't want to be found out as a fraud; part of me never stopped believing that could happen. That was why the 'Oh, Donna's soooo feminine' talk hit so hard. Not only had the one chump I could count on to be absorbed in me moved on, but he had done so for reasons of my inadequate bloody femininity.

4

'You're what?' I couldn't believe what I was hearing. Neither, it seemed, could anyone else. If I could have dropped something so that it shattered, I might have felt I'd reacted appropriately and treated this news with the sensational response it deserved. As it was, I just made her repeat it.

'I'm getting married. I'm engaged. I'm going to be Mrs Jonathan Ong,' said Mabel. There were ten solid minutes of squealing and leaping about on furniture and hugging. We forgot about how much we disapproved of the ratbag boyfriend, we forgot the hours Mabel spent on the phone, struggling to keep her voice normal when she wanted to cry. We behaved like girls.

'You can try on wedding dresses!' I said. 'You can make wedding lists for John Lewis and Heal's. You can buy *Brides* magazine! But I can't believe you're really getting married! Oh, my God, you're going to be the first one of us to get married. You're going to be the first one to get pregn– to have kids.' I had to correct myself, since Mandy and Sara had both had abortions long before they came to college.

'Actually, there's not much point trying on wedding dresses,' Mabel said, twisting her face in embarrassment. 'The thing is, we're getting married now. I'm going to live with him in Oxford. Now.'

Silence.

'But you can't,' Sara said. 'You can't leave university to get married. What will you do?'

'I'll get a job there,' Mabel said. 'I've got A levels. A degree doesn't matter anyway, these days.'

'Then why does he have to have his?'

'Because he really loves what he's doing. And there's a point to dentistry. There's a job at the end of it. What am I going to do with sociology?'

'I thought you liked sociology,' Sara said quietly. The crowd was turning against Mabel, showing signs of discontent, and she was starting to look upset.

'I do like sociology. But it's not a proper degree, is it? I mean, it is for you but I'm . . . I'm wasting my time here, wasting my life. I really love you guys, you know I do, but I really, really love Jonathan. And I need to be with him. I'm not getting any younger. I want to be with him when I'm young. I want him to see me when I'm at my best. I need to be where he is. Don't you see that?'

'What the hell are you talking about?' Heather said. 'You're twenty. You've got a year and a half to go. You're talking like a madwoman. Why can't you wait?'

'I thought you guys'd be happy for me,' Mabel said.

'We are happy for you, Mabel, it's just, well, have you thought it through? What if you break up with him? What if something happens? Are you sure you want to leave here now, when you're so close to finishing?'

'We've been together for four years,' Mabel said. 'That's longer than most marriages. And I'm two years from finishing, and I'm tired of it all. Look, you all know how unhappy I've been this year.' We all blushed. I don't think any of us had noticed that Mabel had been unhappy this year. She never said she was, she never had tantrums like Mandy or panicked like Heather. She never lashed out at people the way Sara did, or sat moodily alone like me. She was always easy and jokey and normal. Except when she was on the phone to Jonathan. 'Do you really think I shouldn't?' she finally said.

'Of course you shouldn't,' Heather shouted. 'Are you crazy?'

'I don't know,' I said, with a stout seriousness that lent more weight to my opinion than it merited. 'Perhaps you shouldn't rush into it. But if you're sure. If you know what you want, we can't pretend we know any better.'

'I think you'd be mad to give up now,' Sara said. 'And we're going to miss you, Mabel.' She laughed, and looked sad.

Mabel burst into tears. 'Jesus, what am I doing?' she wailed. 'I don't know what to do.'

'Oh, honey,' Heather said. 'We just don't want you to make a mistake.'

'I'm so in love with him. And I'm so unhappy here.' Her voice cracked and a lump leaped into my throat. I had always been emotionally suggestible. 'I'm behind in sociology. I never do any work, I never hand in any essays. My tutors are getting at me. I've got no money. My bank's taking away my Switch card. Nothing I'm doing here means anything. I never enjoy myself when we go out. And the rest of you are shagging and fucking and screwing everything that moves and every night I come home alone and sleep alone and I just can't stand it any more. And the only man I've ever loved is hundreds of miles away, fucking other women, and I just want him so much I can't stand it.' She broke off to sob. I resisted mentioning my own celibacy. I was hardly a good example of an enviable romantic life.

'If he's fucking other women, why the hell do you want to marry him?' Heather said.

'Because if I marry him he won't fuck other fucking women, he'll fuck me. He's only fucking other women because I'm not fucking there.' And then she laughed. We had all started screaming at each other and it was as if she had just noticed. For a moment, she was normal, although tears rolled down her cheeks. 'I'm going to phone my mother,' she said.

When she had gone, we sat and stared at each other, pulling faces and looking like everything was obvious, really, and just waiting until she was far enough away not to hear us talking about her. Heather looked impatient enough to explode with undelivered judgement.

'She's gone bloody mad,' she said, when the coast was clear.

'She says he's sleeping around. What does she think she's doing? I mean, for Christ's sake, this is the *nineties.* Who the fuck gets married now? At twenty! Listen, you guys, we've got to talk her out of it.'

'I didn't know she was so unhappy,' I said. 'I talk to her, and I didn't know she was unhappy.'

'We all talk to her, Grace,' Heather said. She wouldn't let me get away with that suggestion that Mabel might confide in someone other than her.

'I know that,' I said. 'I just mean, I should have known.'

'She hasn't been depressed,' Heather snapped. 'She's just decided that now because she wants a reason to go off and marry that bastard. I mean, what was he doing asking her, anyway? What a bastard.'

I sniggered. 'Yes, how despicable. The swine. I don't know, men these days. He doesn't get her pregnant, and then he asks her to marry him.'

'This is so serious,' Sara said, an implicit scolding as clear as day. 'We have to make her think about it. But if we're not careful, she'll just go crazy like she did then. Maybe she'll change her mind if we leave it a couple of days.'

'What if this is really what she wants, though?' I said. 'I'd love to get married.'

'No, you wouldn't,' Heather said. 'You just say you would for effect. I hope you don't say this to Mabel.' She said it quite nastily. I didn't want to argue.

Mabel came back in. 'Jesus, that was hard,' she said. 'She went mad, of course.'

'Is she going to let you?' I asked.

'Of course she's not. But there's nothing she can do about it. Look, I know you all think this is mad, and I've just had my mother crying and I know how mad it sounds. But I've thought about this a lot. Jon and I have talked about it before. And I'm just not happy here, I know I'm doing the wrong thing keeping on with it, and I don't see the point of wasting any more time. I need to do something. This is it.' There was a long silence that throbbed with our negative vibes. 'So be happy for me, hey?'

'We are, Mabel, it's just . . .' Heather gave up, but she pursed her lips and her disapproving look was as good as any lecture.

The Saturday after Mabel's shock announcement, most of the house went out together to a fashionable nightclub in town. Mabel wasn't going, she said she had some stuff to work out and she wasn't in the mood. I stayed at home too because it would have involved dancing. I bought a bottle of red wine from the shop down the road and we put on *West Side Story* and drank together.

'What the hell happened in Blackpool?' I said, casually. I would never have lectured her on my own. 'It must have been one hell of a week.'

'It was a hell of a week. It was hell.' Mabel dipped her finger in her glass of wine and sucked it. Then she took a big gulp and rolled back the corners of her mouth in a grimace. 'Now that's rough,' she said.

'It was supposed to be fairly good,' I said. 'Anyway, it gets better after the first glass. Have more.'

'Blackpool was the most racist place I've ever been,' Mabel said. She traced the edge of her glass absently, as if she didn't want to pay attention to this part of her story. 'I've never . . . at school nobody ever . . . well . . . When we went out, on the pier, round the arcades, there were kids shouting, "Fucking Chinks," at us. I've never known that before. But I could stand it, you know. Jon couldn't. He was so mad, and so protective, and he just couldn't do enough for me. I said, "It's fine, don't let it bother you," but he was just so serious and so macho, I really couldn't get enough of him, being so strong and protective. Then one night at dinner he said, "I can't stand not being there for you. I can't take the fact that you could be treated like this all the time up here and I'm not here . . ."'

'Not all of the north is racist,' I said, lightly but defensively. 'I didn't know Blackpool was like that.'

'Neither did I. Well, you know what Jon's like about the north. I mean, no offence, but he does think you're a load of cap-wearing, ferret-eating factory workers . . .'

'No offence taken. But we put ferrets down our trousers, we don't eat them.'

' . . . and this just sealed it for him. He said he didn't want to keep coming up here, and he wanted to see more of me and it was tearing him apart that we couldn't be together. And then he said, "Are you happy here?" And I started crying then, because he was being so nice, and I said, no, life was shit, and he said, "Let me take you away from it all. Let's get married." Then I laughed and he kissed me and just looked at me for a really long time, and he looked so strange and then he said, "Look at me. No, *look* at me. You *know* me, you know when I'm being serious. Come down. Live with me. No, fuck, marry me. I want us to get married." And I knew he was serious. Am I doing something stupid?'

'He has slept around,' I said.

'It's just fucking,' Mabel said. 'When you actually have sex, you'll realize it's not so big a deal.'

I smiled, softened. 'I know it's not,' I said. 'That's why I never do it. Look, do you want to know what I really think?' Mabel nodded, and she suddenly looked scared. 'To be perfectly honest . . . I think I'd give the world to have been proposed to like that. I think I'd love to be in love like you. And I think I'd give up tomorrow if I could find someone who wanted to take me away from all this. But don't tell Heather. She'd kill me.'

'Thanks,' she said. She had started crying again. On the television, Natalie Wood was singing 'I Have A Love.' We laughed at the coincidence. 'I'd already decided, anyway, but it helps to have even one person not telling me how stupid I am.'

'But what are you going to do about your mum?'

'She got married at sixteen. To a Chinese man. And she was a Catholic. She knows all about scandal. She'll get used to it. And Dad'll be relieved he doesn't have to pay for some big thing.'

'You're really doing this?'

'I really am.'

'But where? Oxford? Can we come down? Dress up anyway. You have to wear white. Oh, let's make a bit of a big deal about it. You know you want to.'

Mabel poured the last dribble of wine into her glass. 'Is the shop still open?' she said. I nodded. 'Then get another one of these, and a copy of *Brides*. Let's get slaughtered.'

The other girls had not approved of the fact that I hadn't managed to talk Mabel out of marrying her dentist. They frowned on my purchase of *méthode champenoise* sparkling white wine at the corner shop instead of a second bottle of red. This, they felt, was tacit approval, maybe even active encouragement, and they responded as if to betrayal; for several days my name was mud. The boys stayed out of the whole tricky business. They could tell it wasn't their place, although they liked to listen to the rest of us discussing it. It was such a bombshell that it was all we could discuss. Mandy, who had been away for a few days with the chemistry society when Mabel broke the news, was at first shocked, then negative, then she seemed to settle on agreeing with whoever was speaking about it, provided that person wasn't me. Mabel planned to go down to Oxford at the end of term. Jonathan had a flat there, because he was already implausibly wealthy, by our standards, but he had to give the bloke who rented a room enough notice to find a new place. They'd be fine, Mabel said. She could get a job straight away and they could be together. Despite it being a small register-office do, I had suggested to Mabel that she could still wear a white dress. We went round town looking for something short and sexy and white, and it was every bit as much fun as putting on something sticky-out and starchy from Pronuptia. Almost, anyway. As it became a project, the others couldn't help being a little sucked in. Despite their official hard line there was something in all of us that sensed this was the ultimate rebellion, the only genuine way of beating the system. We were all clones, our neat little student lives set out for us at the age of twelve, if not earlier, and what Mabel was doing was really brave and . . . cool. It was hip to get married now. It had a working-class nihilism that appealed to all of us on some level, and to me, totally.

It was our first real wedding. This was a landmark, like an eighteenth birthday or a funeral or a first kiss. That made it compelling and important, even if someone's life was going to be ruined in the process. I thought we were all feeling much the same way now, that even though Sara and Heather disapproved on a rational, daily level, they were caught up by the pace of it. For me, it was like watching my own life-plan in fast forward, and carried all the significance of something that personal. I began to picture Alice and me in every permutation of the scenario. These daydreams always had to end, and it was then that I felt most envious of Mabel, with her clean-cut ideas of love, and her certainty about Jonathan, the feeling that she had found someone who wasn't disappointing on the most mundane, trivial level. Alice had finished with all her boyfriends for the most shallow reasons imaginable. She had been put off by one careless shrug at the wrong moment, or pseudo-archaic vocabulary, or his parents. The last boyfriend had been rejected on the basis of a single instance when he walked into a newsagent and requested a box of Pontefract cakes. ('It was the way he said it, Grace. He was smug to the point of indecency. It was like watching him masturbate in public.') And I was no better. I hadn't committed to people because I knew I couldn't have endured the way they laughed enthusiastically at the wrong pictures, or made religions of their CD collections, or wore more than one piece of denim clothing at a time. But Mabel had found a man who, although he may have screwed around like someone trying to repopulate a small planet, at least didn't make her want to hang her head in shame when they bought confectionery, or at any other time, which was almost more important.

In the real world, the strange friend of Finlay's who had tried to lend me a CD at the party turned up on our doorstep one day. I said that Finlay wasn't there, and he said he'd come to see me. He knew I had a car and he had some heavy electrical stuff to take into town and would I mind giving him a lift? I minded very much, but he'd asked me outright, and I didn't really see the harm in dropping him off somewhere. I still wasn't sure what his name was, so I didn't use it. I had to pick him up at his house, which was just round the corner, to save him carrying the heavy stuff over. He was a part-time DJ, and the heavy stuff turned out to be turntables and speakers and lights he had borrowed from an electrical hire shop. It nearly filled my little car. We set off, talking shyly at first. He was illegally dull.

'So what kind of clubs are you into, then?' he asked me.

'Well, I'm not really a club person. I like bars a lot. Smoky bars with jazzy music and cocktails and nothing happening too quickly. Places where you can hear yourself speak.'

'Oh, yeah, that's nice. I'm a bit of a raver, but, yeah, I like bars too. Do you know the Ten Bar? Stop, that's the place.' I braked and parked fabulously. He noticed. This was at least an improvement on Sara, if I was going to be imposed on. He unloaded the things, struck up a loud, tactile conversation with the bloke in the shop and got back in.

'The thing is,' I said, 'I have to go to a legal bookshop now . . .' (Ah, my old friend, the legal-bookshop excuse) '. . . so I can't take you all the way back to Vicky Park.'

'That's okay,' he said, 'just pull in over there and I'll get a bus back.' We stopped in the quiet street, and he unfastened his seat-belt, but he didn't get out. Instead he leaned over, no, he climbed over the car seat and pressed his mouth fully on top of mine, tongue and everything. I pushed him away. It was ten in the morning and I was, fairly literally, gobsmacked.

'What the fuck do you think you're doing?' I spluttered. 'Get out of my fucking car.'

It was his turn to look horrified. 'God, I'm sorry,' he said. 'I just thought, with the lift and everything . . .'

By now, I was actually more embarrassed than affronted. You know, stranger things have happened, and I didn't feel really threatened by him by then, just dazed. 'It's okay,' I said. 'Forget it. You made a mistake. No harm done.' Get out of my fucking car, I was thinking. He got out and waved cheerfully as he walked away. Well, that was odd, I thought, but I thought no more about it. Hey, these things can happen. They didn't, as a rule, but I could see the possibility of reason behind it.

I didn't mention it when I got in because, quite honestly, I was really fairly ashamed of the experience. I was ashamed of having put myself in a risky position with a man I didn't know, even if he was a friend of a friend. I was ashamed because I prided myself on always being rational and sensible and safety-minded. For a second, when he'd leaned over, I was aware of his strength, and my weakness, and I hadn't liked it. Even though nothing had happened and it was fine now, I didn't want to talk about it. I wanted it to go away. I'd learned my lesson: don't give lifts to strangers. But later, when I was making a celeriac and barley soup, Heather came in and told me Finlay was furious.

'He's what? What about?'

'He says you snogged his best friend.' My mind was honestly blank.

'I did? Who, Richard? Finlay thinks I snogged Richard?'

'Not Richard.' She started laughing. 'All right, not his best friend, although that's what he's saying. He says you snogged Greg.'

'I don't know anyone called . . . Wait – you don't mean that Trev person?'

'Trev? Do you mean Greg?'

'Is Greg the big tall bloke who stayed at our party until everyone went home?'

'Yes, that's Greg. Is that your Trev?' I nodded. 'Did you snog him?' I told her the story. 'What, he just kissed you? What happened before that?'

'Nothing,' I said. 'It was strange. I just forgot about it. But it wasn't my idea and it was over in a matter of seconds. How the hell does Finlay know? I can't believe Trev would have told him. What did he say?'

Perhaps Finlay had been listening at the door. It would have explained his perfect timing. He strode in, and stood dominantly at the table, and although none of his limbs were literally akimbo, his posture implied that they were. I suppressed the urge to mock.

'D'you know, Grace? I credited you with a little more than this, snogging my best friend,' he said. He was a picture of wounded good form.

'How did this start?' I was incredulous. 'He's not your best friend. I didn't snog him. And you have a girlfriend now.'

'I don't have a girlfriend,' he said. 'There's nothing between me and Donna.'

This felt like bad soap opera. 'So what?'

'So how could you snog my best friend? It just shows a complete lack of, you know, respect for me. Oh, don't pretend you didn't. He told me himself. He says you had talcum powder on your face.'

'Trev said I snogged him?'

'His name is Greg. And I know you did because you *do* put talcum powder on your face.'

'Okay, stop, stop, stop. Let's start talking sense right now. First, and I'd like to clear this one up for good, that's not talcum powder, it happens to be Guerlain translucent silk base. Two, I've never heard of this Trev, this *Greg* character until he shows up at the party and then asks me to give him a lift this morning, which I very kindly agreed to do because I thought he was a friend of everybody's. Three, he made a pass, I rejected it, the story ends there. Four, whether you go out with Donna or not doesn't alter the fact that whatever I do has nothing to do with you and I don't appreciate you coming in here getting shirty about something completely made up which happens to have nothing to do with you. Does that satisfy you?'

He calmed down. He seemed to consider these facts. 'He made a pass at you?'

'Obviously. What, you think I've started taking men out in the morning to seduce them?'

'Well, I wouldn't put it past you,' he mumbled.

I chose to take offence. 'Right, that's it. Get out of my sight. I don't want to hear from you again.'

'I'm sorry,' he said, and looked it. 'It's just that Greg came up to me, looking really smug, and told me you'd snogged him in your car. What was I to think?'

'You were to think maybe you shouldn't have friends who pounce on girls at ten in the morning. I still want you to get out. I wasn't even going to bring this up, but as you mentioned it, I have to say I was pretty unhappy about the whole thing.' That really seemed to please him. He apologized again and went. Over on the hob, my soup was boiling over.

The next day Greg turned up to see Finlay. Clearly, they hadn't fallen out over the incident. Whereas, of course, it had been fine to give me grief about it, but I let that go. I didn't know how to behave, didn't want to look like the mad, frigid anachronism I was secretly afraid of being. I wasn't sure what the correct behaviour of a normal girl who was assaulted in her car by a virtual stranger was these days. I just kept a low profile and didn't look at him but didn't obviously ignore him, and got out of the way as soon as I reasonably could. But before then, we all had to listen to Greg's absurd stories about the people he knew and the connections he had. He told Finlay he was going on tour with the Stone Roses, as an assistant roadie, and he knew the manager of Man United like a friend. It all sounded like so much bullshit. I really hated this Greg, who could violate my generous lift-giving and then come over and act as if nothing had happened. I supposed he just wanted to show that everything was like it was before. I had to do some work, anyway, because I had a tutorial with Jim McFadyean, and I thought I might show how clever I really could be when I put my mind to it. I was in my room, watching *Coronation Street* with a textbook open in front of me when there was a knock on my door. I told whoever it was to come in, thinking it'd be Mabel. But it was that bastard Greg.

'I came to say how sorry I am,' he said.

'It's okay. It's fine. I've forgotten it already.'

'I just thought that when you gave me a lift . . .'

What did you think? I wanted to say. That because I gave you a lift I had the hots for you and fancied a quick bit of the other with a stranger in the middle of the morning? Are you mad or something? I said none of this because I just wanted him out of there. And then he came and sat down on my bed. I stood up. 'Do you think you could go now, Greg?' I said. 'I've got a lot of work to get through.' He was touching my duvet and swinging his legs.

'I really didn't want to upset you. That's the last thing I'd have wanted.' His voice was reasonable; I didn't look at his face. I was fumbling around for something to say. He lay back, first supporting himself with his elbow, then all the way. His head. My pillow. His head. I tried to stay calm but I could feel my blood pressure panicking.

'Well, look, I'm pretty busy, so I'm going to have to get rid of you now. You're going to have to –'

'Don't be cross.'

'I'm not cross, I'm busy. So, I'll see you . . . whenever.'

Greg stood up and rubbed his chin. I let go of the breath I'd been holding. He nodded, smiling sheepishly, and made a move towards the door. And then the bastard swivelled and lunged at me again, aiming his mouth for my neck, like a human mosquito. I knew that there was something I should have been doing to stop this; maybe I should have slapped him, but I'd never hit anyone and I wasn't sure how it was done, or when it was appropriate. I was as unsure about violence as I was about sex. 'Get the fuck out, Greg,' I shouted.

Richard opened my door and came in. 'What's going on?' he

said, heroically. I felt mad enough to murder someone, and cross with myself for looking like I needed rescuing. 'Come on, mate, I think you'd better go,' he said.

'I just wanted to talk to Grace,' Greg said.

'Look, she goes out with Finlay,' Richard said, quickly. At the time it seemed like a good lie, and I didn't contradict him. Greg went then, and said he'd call. I wondered if it was him or me who had lost all contact with reality.

It was him. Over the next few days, Greg began to show up more and more. And people let him in, which was more than I could cope with. He sat and watched television with Finlay, and when nobody was in the room with him, he continued to talk, to shout things at newsreaders and characters in *The Bill.* Once, I came back late in order to miss Greg's afternoon visit, and found out he'd been in my room. I was furious. There was a long note on my bed, which contained a mad, ranting apology for all his behaviour. In capitals at the bottom it said: 'HAVEN'T YOU GOT SMALL FEET?' I changed my sheets. Then I went downstairs to shout at everyone.

'He's gone fucking mental,' I said. 'He's your friend, Finlay, why don't you deal with him? Who let him in my room?'

'He is getting worse,' Finlay said, as if nobody could take my word without his confirmation. As if I were the lunatic. 'He's always round here, he's full of shit about who he knows and he never stops talking. He's, er, fucking cracked.'

'It's you. You're always leading him on,' I said. 'You invite him in, you talk to him. You're like his best mate or something, and I can't even come down and make myself coffee because he's in the kitchen all the time now.'

'I – *lead him on*?' said Finlay. He got a laugh from his delivery and the accompanying expression of horror. 'Are you calling me a tease?'

'Yeah, this is hilarious, isn't it?' I said.

'All right, Grace, calm down,' said Richard. 'Come on, you're, well, you're taking it all a bit seriously, aren't you?'

There's nothing you can say to this. You don't want to look like you're missing the joke, do you? I waved the note at them, losing conviction. 'Well, any more of these, and I'm going to turn ugly,' I said.

The next day, and Greg showed up in the early afternoon. Finlay was working upstairs, Heather and Mandy were on the top floor. I made the mistake of getting the door.

'Greg.'

'Grace!' he said, looking astonished. 'I didn't expect to find you here.'

'I live here. I'm usually hanging about.'

'Yeah, of course,' he said, laughing, as if I hadn't just said this through a scowl and clenched teeth. 'I was looking for Finlay.'

'He's upstairs.'

Greg came in, went into the living room and switched on the television. He sat down and put his feet up.

'Finlay's upstairs. Working,' I said. There was a pause. 'I'll get him.'

'Hang on. Is it true what Richard said?'

'What did he say?'

'Are you and Fin – you know?'

'Yes. Well . . . yes. Well, it's complicated. Sort of. Sometimes. Yes. I suppose . . .' I have no idea why I was finding it so hard to lie. But I resented having to. I was pretty much saying all this to myself, anyway, having started up the stairs to Finlay's room.

I knocked and whispered, 'You have a visitor.'

'Oh, fuck. It's not?'

'Who else?'

'And you just let him in? That's a bit like leading him on, isn't it?'

'It just gets *funnier*. He's downstairs and he wants you.'

'Wait a minute.' Finlay opened his door and looked shocked. 'Oh, hi, mate.' Oh, my God he was behind me. I put both my hands in the air in exasperation, made fists, pummelled my temples.

'I'm going to do some work,' I said, and started to unlock my door. Greg was doing wonders for my revision programme.

'Listen, while you're both together, I just wanted to say, I'm sorry I got in the way. I didn't want to come between you. I know you're like an item, and I think that's really cool,' Greg said.

'That's okay, man. It's cool,' Finlay said, using his street-cred mockney voice that I found alternately hilarious and obnoxious. Guess which, this time. My mouth was open; I couldn't speak.

'Do you fancy going for a pint tonight? Just the three of us?' Greg said.

'No,' I said. 'We don't.'

The phone was ringing.

'I'm not getting it,' I said. 'It'll be Greg.' Heather picked it up.

'Oh, hi, Greg,' she said. 'Who did you want to speak to?' Greg had taken to calling eight or nine times an evening, when he wasn't actually already round here. He usually, but not always, asked to speak to me or Finlay. 'Sorry, Greg, she's not in now,' Heather said, watching me frantically semaphoring at her. 'No, he's not in either. No, neither is Richard.' She carried on talking to him for about another ten minutes. We eavesdropped in silence, whispering, 'Jesus!' every so often, in stagey disbelief. Being the chief objects of Greg's attention, Finlay and I traded almost matey looks. We'd spent a lot of time lately talking together because Greg was apparently as fixated by Finlay as he was by me, and we had something in common that nobody else would take seriously. The others, especially Mandy, thought we were overreacting to the excitement, and she even hinted that we were pathetic, glamour-hungry types who exaggerated everything to get respect. It was real pot/kettle stuff and, together, we choked on it.

The world still turned, even though Finlay and I were being

pestered with increasing reliability by a madman. I had my tutorial with Jim McFadyean and although the Greg episode had put me off doing the swotting I intended to that week it went very well. Too well. He seemed to be watching me a lot, and looked deeply into my eyes when I said something, his own dark irises making his pupils sultry, like black ink blots bleeding into navy blotting paper. He became very animated when I mentioned that I'd written an article for a local listings magazine and asked me if I could bring it in. I said that since it was a pile of unreadable crap I most certainly couldn't. 'It would give me immense pleasure to read something you've written,' he said, and held my gaze for a lifetime until somebody coughed impatiently and I flushed and didn't say anything else until we started talking about *Brookside.*

This had been what I wanted, some real kind of sign that he returned my feelings, but when it came I just wasn't so pleased. I was suddenly noticing how skinny he was. I wondered what he'd look like naked. I wasn't sure I'd like it. I wondered if I'd be terrible in bed. I wondered whether I'd have to keep lying about films I didn't like to impress him or whether I'd ever be myself. I wondered what we'd find to talk about if we were alone together, and I suddenly couldn't remember him actually being very funny. He's a bit of a dick, I thought, for an astonishingly lucid but brief moment. I tried to chase this thought to a conclusion but it slipped away from me. I thought, What if I've encouraged him and now I have to turn him down? Then I thought, Jesus, he only asked to read your article. Stop being a bloody Greg. (Our new word for a mad person.)

'Grace, could you spare a few moments at the end of this?' he said, dropping it casually. I was a plastic snowstorm of turbulent and conflicting emotions. He's going to ask me out, oh, my God, I thought first. Do I want to go out with him? I don't even know if I fancy him any more. I could see my knee shaking as the rest of the class filed out. Shit, I was thinking, this is it. He waited until the door closed and smiled broadly. The suspense was unbearable. 'Do you have any problems, at the moment?' he said. 'Work getting on top of you, social life a bit intense?'

'None at all,' I said, a little surprised. 'What, is it the coursework?'

'Yeah, you're going to have to do it, I'm afraid,' he said. 'I'm pretty patient about these things, but I can't remember ever having anyone do so little work. Unless they went on to drop out. And I wouldn't want to see you do that.'

I was so disappointed and so relieved. Not a date after all, just a bollocking. I pouted and simpered at the same time. 'Yes, fair enough. I've . . . had some crazy stuff on my mind recently, but it's no excuse, nothing I can't cope with. I'll make sure you get it first thing tomorrow,' I said, with an impish wink.

'I'm looking forward to it,' he said.

That afternoon Greg came to the house and asked for me. The new rule was that I wasn't to be disturbed for any Greg business, but he had come armed, bearing a bottle of Chanel No. 5 and Mandy, who took French scent seriously, and additionally, didn't like being given instructions, and crucially, couldn't care less, let him through.

'What's this for, Greg?' I said, as he stood holding it out.

'It's just a present,' he said.

'I can't take it. I'm sorry, I don't want to seem rude, but it just seems – inappropriate. Give it to your mum instead. But listen, thank you. It's very sweet of you.'

'Don't you like it? Fin said you probably would . . .'

'Finlay? You mean you discussed this with him? What is wrong with the pair of you?'

Greg had taken to blinking a lot and sort of drooling without releasing the saliva at the corners of his mouth. He had been fairly weird the first time I met him, but this was new. I'd have spotted any rabid tendencies if he'd had them when I gave him a lift. He was simply getting worse.

'Well, we didn't really, like, plan it together. I just said to him, does Grace like Chanel, and he said probably.' Greg's eyes were all over the place, flicky and jittering like someone watching a tennis match in fast forward. I got rid of him as quickly as I could, making excuses that didn't make sense.

I gave Finlay hell, of course.

'Shut up a minute,' he said. 'You know what he's like. He was round this morning, when you were out, and he was just talking at me and he wouldn't stop. I have no idea what he said. I wasn't listening. We don't sit around and talk about what a fantastic bird you are. It's not locker-room chat. He's gone. He's lost it. I don't want to see him any more than you do. And sometimes – just sometimes – it's not all about you.' I calmed down, a little humbled.

The day after that, when Greg rang the doorbell we hid in the kitchen with the lights off and pretended we weren't in. He shouted through the letterbox – normal conversational things, but shouted through the letterbox. We should probably have been nicer about it, more mature, more understanding, and behaved responsibly and rationally instead of hiding in the dark.

'What are we going to do?' I whispered.

'The guy's, er, off his trolley,' Finlay said.

'He's round the bend,' Heather said.

'Looped the loop.'

'He's stark staring maaaaad!' Richard said, in a supremely amusing voice, and we fell about, shushing each other hysterically when the bell rang again. Then we heard the pungent tone of an angry Mandy, as she stamped downstairs complaining to herself and to us, getting louder and nearer to the door.

'You're acting like bloody kids,' she said, and swung the front door open. 'Hello, Greg. What do you want?' Her voice was flat and angry, consonants like bullets. I almost felt sorry for Greg, on the receiving end of what would have been a very mean stare.

'Is, er, Fin around?' we heard him say.

'No. *Everybody*'s out. The house is empty.' All the subtlety of a pantomime, but you wouldn't have argued with her.

'Can I wait?'

'I don't think that's a good idea.'

'Oh. Okay, then. Night, Mandy.' The front door crashed shut.

Mandy came into the kitchen and switched the light on, meaning it to sting. 'That's the last time I lie for you lot,' she said. 'You're being ridiculous. What's he going to do to you all?'

Perhaps all we'd needed was a dose of common sense. With the fun over, the solutions began.

'Look, I've had a word with Marco, who lives with him. He says he's like that all the time now and they've been on the phone to his mother. They're going to try to get him to go home to see someone,' Finlay said, reasonably. The thought of adult interference made it all seem a little more serious. I felt bad for being dismissive of his madness. We all started using more sensitive terms when we talked about it. I called my dad, who's a GP, and asked him what was going on.

'It sounds like some sort of mania, that's all,' he said. 'It's pretty harmless. Don't let it worry you. Just don't let him in.'

'Do you want me to send your brother over to warn him off?' shouted my mother in the background.

'Tell her no.' It felt good to be talking to a familiar voice. I had let myself become like the others, a self-obsessive who treated everything that happened as if it mattered, who was getting flustered about a mildly deranged boy who came to visit, and a date with a tutor that wasn't going to happen. Get real, I told myself. Life's not that big a deal, and you should never upset yourself over something that you'll forget in three months. Words of wisdom borrowed from my father. We were big on not giving a shit, as a family.

My mother came up at the weekend to visit me. Her sister lived in Liverpool, and she could spend the day with me and stay there. She did this a lot, although I concealed it from the others so that I didn't look childishly attached to my parents. In fact, I was independent from the moment I left home. I could go to the pictures alone, eat out alone, sit in parks and read alone, and

I was always perfectly happy about it. The other students were frantically pleased to be away from home, but most of them still had to travel in big packs and do everything together. So although I needed to see my mother a lot, I didn't think it was any measure of my immaturity, or lack of self-sufficiency. I just missed her. I could really talk to my parents. I don't think it had so much to do with the way I was brought up, because my brother was the opposite; brooding, secretive. I suppose he was out of the house a lot more when we were growing up, whereas I never got to cut the cord, illness always pulled me back. But I know that's not the reason: I just liked my family. Because I was always pretending to be something I wasn't with my student friends, I really went nuts when I got to talk to my parents and gushed solidly for hours. When they came separately I had to tell the same stories twice, because I always wanted both their opinions. My father, the optimist, could always be relied on to tell me what I wanted to hear. And my mother, who would have been a pessimist if she hadn't been proved right so many times when things went badly, could always be trusted to present the truth, with no frills.

As things stood then, my father thought it sounded like Jim McFadyean fancied me, and my mother asked me if I'd ever considered the possibility that he might just be friendly. My father thought Greg was no cause for concern, and wouldn't get any worse now, and my mother suspected he could be a violent sex offender. But I didn't talk to my mother to get sugar-coated happy thoughts. I just craved a bit of no-holds-barred love and affection from time to time. It had been my choice never to mention that I was disabled to anyone at college. I didn't want them to sympathize, because that would have been the same as them noticing, and at that stage I was still in denial, pretending to myself that I looked the same as everyone else. Every so often, though, when I was trudging across Albert Square with heavy carrier bags and the pain felt like a long raw nerve being stretched until it snapped, I felt so sorry for myself that I needed someone else to. It never occurred to me, in those days, to walk less. My mother was always tied up in knots over it, always worrying and hurting along with me. She used to say she'd take the pain herself if she could, and I liked to hear her say that. It felt like it could almost happen, the way people feel happy when they make plans to spend the money they'll win on the Premium Bonds. She was so exhaustively maternal that just being with her was like analgesic.

I ended up going with her to her sister's and staying the night there. I called the house to say I wouldn't be back that night, then took a long, hot bath. It was bliss, with no one to tell me that a bath used seven times more water than a shower, or that the energy saved by showering would have saved four rainforests and a tiger family. We went out for Thai food that melted in the mouth, and we ordered more than we ate, and no one got agitated or asked for the menus back so they could calculate their share of the bill and then pay with a cheque for £3.91. And we watched television and nobody quoted the last *Guardian* article they'd read, about the subtext that ran throughout all American cop-concept shows. I felt like I was in one of those ads where someone drinks whatever they're selling and the colour comes back. I felt ready to face them all again.

Well, except for Greg. I could have done without Greg. When I got back, late on Sunday, all the girls were out at the pictures and Richard, who had a new girlfriend, was somewhere with her, and only Finlay was in. We were still getting on very well. Not only were we united in our Greg-related persecution feelings, it also gave us a chance to be on the same side about something straightforward. We had got so used to trying to impress each other with clever analysis of popular culture or house politics that we'd forgotten what it was like to just talk, without effort, without artifice, without that disinterested loftiness we had honed down to an art. It felt pretty good. But Finlay was going out that evening, with some friends from his course, and, reluctantly – yes, I'd admit to that – we broke it up. I went into the hall with him; I meant to lock the door because I was going to shower, and I was always a bit edgy about showering in an empty house. Hitchcock and that. When he opened the door we were both shocked, no, shit-scared, to see Greg standing in our garden. His lips were very, very pink, and he licked them constantly, his tongue sweeping in a large wet circle.

'Oh, hi,' he said. 'I was just going to knock.' Bizarrely, we acted as if he couldn't really hear us, by having a loud argument about him just inside our hallway while he stood just outside the house looking at us through the open door. He held on to the threshold with both hands and rocked.

'I've got to go out,' Finlay said. 'I told Donna I'd meet her at the bar at nine.' So now he pulled the Donna card. Not only did I really not want him to go, but it had to look as if I didn't want him to go and meet her.

'You can't leave me alone with Greg,' I said simply. Standing in my socks, with him in his big shoes ready to go out, the already substantial gap between our heights was emphasized. I looked tiny. I used that. 'Look, I hate saying this, but I'm . . . I'm scared of being here alone when he's here.'

'Don't let him in,' Finlay said.

'He knows I'm in. He's standing right outside looking at us. How can I ignore him?'

Finlay exhaled, as if making a huge decision, and torn. He made me wait a long time before he finally spoke: 'I have to go.'

'Please don't leave me alone with him.' There, I'd said it. I looked at my fingers and waited for him to change his mind. But when I glanced up again, an almost indecent look of pleasure peeked out from behind the understanding expression he struggled to keep on his face. He's enjoying this, he's bloody enjoying this, I thought. I saw red, then I saw sense. I grabbed my shoes and my car keys and walked grandly past both of them. I *may* have tossed my head.

'Wait, where are you going?' Finlay said.

I stood in the road in my socks. I was still shaking with fear from seeing Greg and nearly being left alone with him. I felt the cold soak me through my feet, and allowed myself a moment to inhale the freedom. My mother would be half-way across the Pennines by now. Perhaps I could catch up.

'I'm going home,' I said.

Friday

I'm not always so wretched. So tiresomely insecure. Sometimes, if I go out with Alice and we meet men, I almost expect them to fall for me. I'm really that arrogant. I can see the humour in it, because it seems so implausible, this double life, this schizophrenic self-esteem: by day, on the streets, I feel ugly enough to stop traffic. In a bar, shiny fingernails wrapped around a pink gin, I don't consider anyone to be off-limits. Confidence, as we all know, is the most efficient aphrodisiac known to man, and I never completely shrugged off the ego I got out of my time with Finlay. I have no illusions about my looks, but they'll usually do, and I'm funny and quite sexy, and I've paid enough attention to know that men will fancy any girl until she gives them a good reason not to. Sadly, most women don't know this – they try too hard, which is a waste of energy and often self-defeating. I don't follow matters to a conclusion, because I think, impossible as it may be, that they haven't noticed my walking. There are tricks I use to disguise it. When I get up I'll lean to one side, stumble a little, pretending I'm adjusting my bag and putting on my coat, or I choose the trickiest path through a cluster of tables so I can support myself and have an excuse for negotiating them awkwardly. I don't really believe it works, but I do it anyway, for just long enough to make a getaway. I don't trust anyone with knowing about my body. It would kill me to reveal more of myself and watch someone change his mind, and despite my surface confidence, I can't believe they wouldn't. Frankly, nobody has attracted me enough to make it worth the gamble. Except . . .

Oh, Jesus, I don't want to think about him now. I have to try to get over him.

So, I believe I'm a master of cunning and concealment. That because I'm not talking about my flaws, not drawing attention to them, nobody else will. This'll work to an extent . . . at least, people tend not to talk about it to me and I can assume they don't know and that suits me fine. I just can't decide how to react when I'm forced to discuss it. For instance, just over a year ago, when I was working at the newspaper library, there was a man there I quite liked, Philip, who I thought, assumed, was interested in me. He used to come over and talk, and blush and stammer like someone with a crush. A few days after I'd told the librarian that I couldn't walk as far as the warehouse and explained why, Philip came over, as usual, to stand and waste time with me. But that day he was trying too hard. Then he said, 'Are you all right doing all this filing?'

I said, 'Yes.' I could sense what was coming and tried to zap it in mid-air. My tone was taut and brisk and conclusive. It was a don't-go-there yes.

'With your bad legs . . . What is it – polio?'

I was horrified. I didn't know what to say or do. Primarily I was really, violently angry. To me, it's a very personal subject, too personal to be mentioned. You don't talk about somebody's port-wine stain, or baldness or obesity or anything like that. And because it had come so soon after my talk with the librarian I felt a head rush of paranoia, and the nausea that fear brings. It was as if I was suddenly being discussed by everyone, but instead of being the sexy little chick with the tight skirts I was that poor girl with the bad legs. All our previous chats were contaminated, retroactively, by this one snatch of well-meaning. Polio. It sounded so Victorian, so historical, like rickets or scurvy or the plague. And that one little word – bad – hurt so much. I wanted to say, 'There's nothing bad about my legs. I have gorgeous legs: slim ankles and wonderful knees and chewable thighs. They just don't happen to work so well.' But I couldn't say this and, anyway, by that time he'd realized that I was upset and I'd seen his embarrassment, and I had to put all my energy into minimizing that. But I couldn't; there was a terrible silence. He lost himself in the maze of bookshelves and we didn't speak again for days, and we were never the same afterwards. Some days later, a woman who worked with us both pulled me aside and said Philip was afraid he'd upset me.

I took a breath and steadied my voice and turned on my simper: 'No, not at all.'

I just called Alice back to panic about the reunion. She says I should lie. Say that Random House offered me an advance. Say I'm engaged to a sheikh. I didn't discuss the legs thing with her, but I've made my mind up not to. It's still the big thing. I can't really fool myself that it can be hidden any more. And why did I eat those crisps? I have twelve days to lose twelve pounds. Minimum. I should drop twenty if I'm going to be thinner than I was when we lived together, and I ought to be thinner. I could make something up, closer to the day, and not go, but I want to see Mabel. And Heather, I suppose. Richard. If I'm going to be honest, I want to see them all. I just don't want them to see me.

1992

5

The sole purpose of faculty balls was to pretend we didn't go to a redbrick university. Balls: even the word is onanistic – was I ever young enough to be impressed by it? I was as much a sucker for getting to wear a pretty frock as the next girl, but they were always excruciating, miles beyond disappointing. This was because of the boys who went to them: the mere act of putting on a starchy white shirt gave them ideas. They strutted about like dandies, believing all that blue-collar crap about men in black tie being irresistible. The girls only encouraged their delusions, saying, 'Ooh, I could really fancy you like this,' to them, and the result was they spent the first hour or so getting off on how sensational they were. Then, after they'd smoked a few fags like they were George Sanders, the would-be sophisticates would sit down to dinner and fill their wineglasses to the brim, and take the bread from the person on their right, split it down the middle with their knife and butter it all over, as if they were preparing four rounds of sandwiches for their ma's café. The posh kids would start up a contrived food fight to show that they were at home with all that Oxbridge high-jinks nonsense, even if they were Oxbridge rejects, as we all were, and I'd just want to go home. But it was like childbirth: there was an internal mechanism that caused selective amnesia, preventing me from remembering the really suicide-inducing moments of the previous ball, and when the next one rolled along I was ready to do it all again. I was fully signed and paid up for this season's shindig. The added incentive this time being the appearance of Jim McFadyean. He'd been a little cooler towards me in recent weeks, and this convinced me I was once more besotted with him. It wasn't that I had any subconscious desire to go out with someone who treated me dismissively. It's just that the more a man ignores you, the less likely he is to want to sleep with you, in theory, although in practice that's not always the case.

The other reason my crush on him was looking a little healthier was that life was feeling almost too quiet again, particularly my interaction with the opposite sex. All of a sudden, Greg had gone. He'd been diagnosed as a manic depressive and left university to recover. He made one final appearance before he went, when he showed up at our door one morning with six packets of photographs that he'd taken at the Granada Studios Tour. He'd gone alone, but the photographs – seventy-two in all – were almost exclusively of him. Heaven knew how he'd managed that. There he was in Coronation Street, outside the Rover's Return, sharing a joke with a tourist at the Kabin. There he was shaking paws with Sooty and Sweep in Sooty World. And there again! Greg posing in Baker Street, a plastic pipe in his mouth, an enigmatic expression in his eye. There was something almost great about this extraordinary series of photographs, so disturbing, but somehow epic. We'd passed them slowly around as Greg talked us through them. He had bounced about in excitement as he made plans to return there with all of us.

Then one day Greg didn't call, and the next, and after that he never came round again. We felt the loss with relief, but also a tangible emptiness, especially in the early days when the doorbell rang and we flinched and laughed, and then remembered where he was. With him went the spirit of togetherness he'd forced on us; that must be what old people are talking about when they remember the war with fondness. Indeed, we talked about Greg still, in an attempt to recapture that lost closeness. Life may have been less eventful now, but the coldness and sarcasm had returned to number 52, like a family relaxing into a routine of bitterness when visitors have gone home. Strangest of all, I discovered that part of me regretted the break-up of my sham affair.

The absence of our Greg-era camaraderie was not improved by the fact that Mabel would soon be leaving for her wedding. For her marriage, for God's sake. It seemed like such a for ever thing to do, in a really bad way. I was having second thoughts, whether it was my business to or not. I lay awake feeling guilty about approving, as if I might have been able to change her mind. Why lie to myself? I probably could have changed her mind. It wasn't even as simple as committing to one man, it was the leaving college, giving up her education. When I slept I had nightmares, set in the future, in which Mabel screamed at me in tears that I had told her to go ahead, and her life was ruined. Usually she was heavily pregnant in these dreams, and I would tell her to have an abortion and her waters would break right there, splashing around my feet in gushing, incessant waves, and I'd offer to bring up her children for her while she panted and shrieked in pain. I couldn't tell her that I had started to regret my past enthusiasm. But I told the others and they gave me the bollocking I deserved.

'I told you this, Grace, just before you started shopping for wedding dresses,' Heather said. 'I just said she should wait. I didn't say she couldn't marry him. I just said she should wait. If it's really true love, if it's really for ever, he would have waited a year and a half for her to do a couple of exams.'

I hung my head in shame. 'I thought you'd changed your mind, and you thought she knew what she was doing now,' I said, limply.

'We didn't say that. You were just whipping her up into a frenzy about it, and we didn't want to come across as the big bad heavy mob who couldn't understand true love. So we laid off her. But I've always thought it was a bad idea, you know that, and so has Sara.'

It was true, then. I had helped a twenty-year-old girl seal her miserable fate with a couple of glossy magazines and some over-romantic views on a subject I had no possible hope of understanding. Heather and Sara said it was never too late, and thought I should have a word with her now, explain my reservations. If I could change my mind, they said, maybe she could too. I *wanted* to, but every day I just chickened out. I started going to the pictures daily, and saw the worst films I'd ever see in my life during that time, pictures like *Son-in-law.* If you ever get a chance to see it, I think you should, to get some idea of my desperation. Or I went to gaze at a dress I had fallen in love with, a glitzy little frock with a champagne skirt made of heavy dull satin that was little short of architectural. It stood in the window of a ludicrously expensive dress shop in the city centre, and I walked slowly past it, or stopped to ogle it, covetously, like a Victorian urchin outside a hot-pie shop. I desperately wanted to have it for the ball, but I never dared go inside, just looked. It was my means of escape. I knew that when I got home the accusatory eyes of Heather and Sara would be fixed on me, and the optimistic, vulnerable figure of Mabel would be there to torment me. It was all too much.

Had Mabel changed her mind? Certainly the thrill was fading. Sometimes I spoke to her when we were watching television together and she didn't hear a word I'd said, just carried on staring ahead of her, the tip of her thumb in her mouth. I asked my mother for advice.

'It's not your fault,' she said, 'but if she's your friend you'll regret it almost as much as she does if things go wrong. Let her talk about it to you, and try to get a hold on the way she's feeling. Then make her feel happy about that. It's still a stupid idea, though. You know that, don't you? And you can get the dress on my Visa card. There's plenty on it.'

'How are you feeling?' I finally said, as Mabel was putting in her lenses at the kitchen table one morning. 'About it.' She looked at me through watery eyes. Good, I thought, I won't know if she starts crying. I don't want to know.

'Oh, you know. Scared. Happy. Suicidal. The usual.'

'Have you spoken to Jonathan recently?'

'Yeah, of course. He's being so lovely at the moment. I really want to be with him. But I'm really going to miss this place.'

'Well, why don't you wait till the end of the year?' Too much advice. Steady, now, take it slowly. Turn it into a joke. 'Sleep with as many third years as you can and get them all out of your system.' Not a good joke.

'I've thought about staying till the end of the year, but what's the point? I'm not going to get my degree anyway, and at the end of the year you guys'll all be getting demented over the exams and you'll have no time for my wedding and everything. Then it'll be end-of-year parties and –'

'Oh, you're going to miss the end-of-year parties? Can't you come anyway, even if you're married?' She looked at me as if I were ten years younger than her, rather than the real gap: ten months the other way.

'I don't care about student parties,' she said. 'I know we all liked them a year ago, but I've changed. I've left all that behind. I know you lot love being students, but I've never really felt that student thing, the way you all do. I've never really fitted in here. I don't walk to the same beat as the rest of you.' She stopped, to smile at her pretentiousness. 'I just feel a bit too old for it. Sometimes I go to nightclubs with the rest of you, and you're talking to new people, or dancing and I just think, What am I doing here? I don't like these people – not you, obviously – and I don't want to be here any more. The world is bigger than a few pubs with cheap beer and a bunch of wankers who all say the same thing and all have the same opinion about everything, and while we're stuck here in this time-warp the world is going on all the time outside us, and we don't feel it. We can't see it. We're too busy looking at ourselves.'

I was completely thrown by this revelation, the way I had been when Mabel first said how miserable she was. All the alienation I felt, and rather arrogantly assumed was my own unique take on things here, a symptom of my sophistication, was what Mabel had been going through, and probably a thousand more of us. It was a feeling of being only remotely involved, like doing the college experience via virtual reality. I wanted to shout, 'Me too! This is my life you're talking about!' and slap my chest with impassioned solidarity. I wished Mabel indulged her frustration constantly like Mandy, who stropped and stamped and kept us abreast of each stage of her emotional/menstrual cycle, or that she analysed the minutiae of every gesture and word of everyone who crossed her path, like Alice did. Sometimes I hardly knew Mabel at all and I wished we'd been closer, that she'd talked to me before. Right now, I didn't feel I had the right to give her any advice. I felt small and insubstantial.

'I know how you feel. Honestly,' I said. 'But I'm finishing it. I'm seeing it through to the end.'

She looked right at me with shiny dark eyes and pressed her lips together. 'Then you don't know how I feel,' she said softly.

'You won't lose touch, will you?' I said. It was only when she smiled and shook her head that I started seriously to believe that she would.

Finlay was absolutely dating this Donna girl. The feminine one. He conducted it furtively, never bringing her home to meet us, never mentioning her to me, but everyone else in the house got to hear the details. The swaggering indiscretion that I'd explained away as one-night-stand male bastardness wasn't diminishing, even as the affair matured. I was appalled. I thought he showed a complete lack of affection and respect for her, and although I obviously hated her for being so much more feminine than me, I didn't like the implications of such behaviour. I thought I'd had a narrow escape, but I felt almost violated as well. Either I overheard loud conversations on the landing in the small hours of the morning, or the gossip filtered back to me through the other people in the house, but I already knew far too much about this poor girl. Things she must have thought nobody knew. What her breasts looked like naked, and how much hair grew around her nipples. What she cried out at the moment of her climax. The emetic account of her attempt to zhoozh things up with a vanilla-flavoured edible massage oil. Worse things, things I couldn't bring myself to remember. I didn't really know what men said to each other in a locker-room context, but by any standard, Finlay was going far too far. I knew that I knew nothing about any of Richard's girlfriends, for instance. Unprecedented empathy needled and made me vulnerable, but it was hard to look disapproving without looking jealous, especially when I was jealous. Against my will I still resented the withdrawal of his attention, even though I now knew how despicable he was. I missed being thought of as an object of desire. Only recently I had been the hypotenuse of a bizarre triangle, dealing with simultaneously ardent declarations from one boy who was mad about me, and one who was just plain mad. Now we were three days from Valentine's Day and I would be lucky to get the phone bill in the post. Frankly, it sucked.

Heather was baking again. Biscuits, this time, for Valentine's Day. I sought the comfort of her floury kitchen. I behaved a little tentatively towards her these days, because I knew how irresponsible she considered my part in Mabel's wedding plans, even though it was all okay on the surface now. But Heather never bore a grudge. She was very sweet, really. Generous and warm and much nicer than me. This made me even more ashamed to spend time with her, but it made it easier.

'So what plans have you made for the fourteenth?' I asked. I was never jealous of Heather's relationships, and liked to hear about them. I'd met her boyfriends, all nice boys, but nothing I'd even remotely consider for a second. This meant I could be sincerely pleased for her, without being eaten up by petty, unsuitable side-thoughts. 'Ahh, how adorable!' I picked up the little heart-shaped biscuit cutter that Heather had bought for the job.

'You don't think it's a bit twee, do you?' Heather's round eyes looked genuinely concerned, as if my reading of the situation was important.

'What else are you going to give him on Valentine's Day? Round biscuits? Gingerbread men?' I said. 'Of course it's a bit twee. He'll be thrilled. You're such a nice girlfriend.' That made her happier.

'Okay then, we're going to see *Romeo and Juliet* at the Royal Exchange. How corny is that? Then he's just going to come back here and drink some wine in my room.' I made the obligatory double entendre face, and we smirked about that.

'God, I have to be somewhere else, then.' I rested my chin on the table and looked despondent. 'I don't think I can stand to see you being so perfect together.' Another little bone I could toss her way, and she appreciated the jealousy routine. Every girl wants her boyfriend to be a real prize, the envy of her girlfriends. I could be big about this.

'Oh, have you not made any plans, then?' she said, knowing full well that I hadn't.

'Nobody in the whole damn world fancies me any more,' I said, 'and the last man who did was committed.' Not very right-on, but it dragged a smile from Heather.

'Grace, I've never known anyone have more men chasing her than you,' she lied, out of the goodness of her heart. She greased a tray as well, and looked happy with herself. 'You'll probably end up getting as many cards as the rest of us put together.'

'Do you think I should send one to Jim McFadyean?' I said. 'Or is that really pathetic?'

'Well, you're interested in the guy, so why not? You're not going to sign it, are you? Maybe it hasn't occurred to him that one of his students fancies him. Maybe he's waiting for a sign. Oh, Jesus, what can it hurt?'

Suddenly I was fifteen again, twirling my skirt into a lumpy knot in embarrassment. 'This has to be the most tragic I've ever been in my life,' I said, in squirming falsetto. 'You're baking biscuits for your proper boyfriend, with whom you're going to watch culture – Shakespeare, no less – before going home and having serious, grown-up, monogamous-relationship, proper sex, and I'm asking you if I should send a valentine to my teacher. Why do you even speak to me?'

'Oh, for God's sake,' she said, pleasingly straddling humour and exasperation. She chopped with her little heart cutter through the squidgy oval of dough. 'Send him a bloody card.'

It was a fabulous card. I bought it in an arty shop in the craft centre up past the market, which sounds awful, but it wasn't made of clock parts or anything. I didn't leave any clues, just a question mark, and I got Heather to deliver it for me, in case he spent his days looking through the keyhole at people who left stuff in his letterbox. I wasted at least five hours of my life worrying about it. Then I used the adrenaline to march boldly into the dress shop and buy the champagne frock. When I tried it on I knew I couldn't live without it. It didn't even fit, although the shop offered to make alterations, but it could have been made for me just as it was, fit or no fit. Something in the shape of the skirt, the crunch of the petticoat, the immovability of the corset expressed my personality. I stuck it on plastic and sent a card of thanks to my mum.

It was an astrologically designated day for buying occasion-wear. Mabel arrived home shortly after I did with her real live wedding dress, a little white frock, that she'd eventually picked up in a second-hand shop. She'd found it with Mandy and they'd known as soon as they saw it that she couldn't wear anything else. This dress had come from the point where tailoring meets legend; it was an original sixties Givenchy, with geometrically implausible lines, and confidence sewn into the seams.

There was much conversation about dresses for days, and the boys took the piss out of all of us, parodying our obsessive behaviour with atrocious faux-gay accents (Northern, of course) and silly made-up designer names. I liked that kind of thing. While we were living with men, the lines between the sexes blurred, we were all just the blokes in the house. I liked it when they bothered to remember the difference.

On the morning of the fourteenth a large van pulled up outside our house and a man carrying about a hundred pink roses knocked on the door. I watched him through the window. There was no way I was answering it. Mabel went, because she said if they weren't from Jonathan then he'd have some fucking explaining to do. She wasn't disappointed. The card said: 'I don't deserve you, but you have only yourself to blame. You kissed me. A man doesn't get over something like that in a lifetime – J.'

She sat with the roses in front of her and cried for an hour. Then she managed to get her voice back to normal and called him. As soon as he answered she started crying again. We left her on the stairs, hair in front of her face, finally crying over him for the right reason.

The ordinary post came later. There were three cards for Mandy, two for Richard and one for me. The front read, 'Valentine, I know you haven't got much time for me,' and inside the joke was revealed: 'So how about a quick one?'

I looked at the card for a few seconds, then read it aloud to the other girls, including Mabel, who had hung up and was sitting with her roses looking ethereal and beautiful. 'Well, I may as well just kill myself now,' I said.

'At least you got a card,' sniffed Sara, who hadn't.

' "You kissed me. A man doesn't get over something like that in a lifetime."' I quoted. 'Now that's a *card.* What I have here is . . .' I sat down and stuck out my lower lip. '. . . It's evidence that the missing link had a rudimentary writing system. It's what Stig of the Dump sends to his valentines. Do you see the difference?' But so resilient was my vanity that I spent the day expecting more. I went into the damn faculty building just to see if someone who didn't know my address had bunged something into my pigeonhole. Some shy student, or Jim McFadyean. There was nothing. Who sent that piece of shit card anyway? The only person I could even think of was Finlay, but he was cleverer than that, surely? He had more taste than that, didn't he? Oh, yeah, and he had a girlfriend, I was forgetting that. The postmark was Manchester, so it couldn't have been from Greg. Either I had a secret admirer, or it was a sympathy gesture from the girls, but they would have got a girl card, something arty with hearts and design. No, I had to face the truth. I appealed to someone with no sense of style whatever. Happy Valentine's Day.

Three days later I went to a Jim McFadyean tutorial and was confronted with the sight of my card, standing in pride of place at the front of his desk. My heart was pumping like crazy. I tried not to look at it, in case he saw and made the connection. I couldn't speak, I was in such a complete lather about it. I wondered if he had guessed. And then the girl next to me pointed to it, and he smiled. 'Isn't it fab?' he said.

I hoped I wasn't actually as pink as I felt, but since my cheeks were throbbing in time with my pulse, I expected I'd be puce. I stared into the middle distance and tried to look like I had other things on my mind. I was using a meditative technique that a Hare Krishna man had taught me when we started talking in the street one day, before I knew what drapy orange clothing in a public place signified, and I couldn't get away. As it happened, the technique was really quite effective. Not everything they say is insane. So I was omming internally and doing nicely, too, when Jim McFadyean said something that nearly made me faint.

'Are you going to the ball, Grace?'

My voice didn't work. Why me, for crying out loud? Had something happened? Had we reached an understanding now? Was he asking me to go with him?

'Uh, yeah, I am,' I croaked. I looked up, and he was looking at me with the smug twinkle of a man who knows he can whip up crushes as easily as cream. He knew, all right.

There was a slight pause, and then Tara, a posh girl I liked, said, 'I thought you were going to ask her to go with you, then,' and everyone laughed. Except me and him; we just smiled. But I wondered what his game was, and if he meant to torment me as much as he was doing. I was once again hurled into the usual frenzy of worry and doubt. Shit, it could really be happening now, I thought. I hoped I really was as attracted to him as I'd thought I was a week ago. I also started hoping he *had* sent the godawful card, and that it had an ironic subtext that was vaguely referential to a Truffaut film.

Also at the tutorial, but lurking silently in the shadows, had been Michelle, my 'townie', as students say, because for all their left-wing sensibilities they tend to be incorrigible snobs, friend. Being working-class at college is a good thing, as long as you don't have a pleb's outlook and taste in clothes. Heaven help you if you do. I had lived with her in halls for the whole of the first year, and because we did the same course, Michelle had been my best friend there for the first few months. Needless to say, I couldn't stand her then. She was so odd, so adult, like the girls from my home town who I sometimes met in the holidays, pushing prams and talking like their mothers. I felt if I hung around with Michelle I'd never meet the fantastic and interesting people I was destined to meet. She drank seemingly endless quantities of gin every night and kept about half a dozen litre bottles of Gordon's in her room at any one time. Her walls were covered with Athena posters of half-naked beefcake, with slogans underneath like 'A Hard Man is Good to Find', and her bed was buried beneath the whoomph of furry toys her boyfriend had given her. She said, 'I'm not being funny but . . .' just before she insulted me, or anyone else, which was often. She was obsessed with having her sleep interrupted by the other people we lived with. Early on Sunday mornings she'd play her music (*All Time Great Rave Hits* or Lisa Stansfield) at maximum volume to teach everyone a lesson for disturbing her the night before – she'd actually set her alarm clock so she'd be up in time to wake everyone. And she'd complain to me constantly about all the other students in her rasping, cigarette-grazed voice. I was desperate not to be associated with her, but I knew I was. She never went to lectures, and if I did, she asked if she could photocopy my notes. With all due shame, I'll admit I sometimes falsified those notes, putting in deliberate mistakes and malicious nonsense, I so resented her taking them. But she got vastly better results in the essays she handed in than I did. She was so skinny that she had to drink Slim-Fast shakes to gain weight, because she forgot to eat and her only other calories came from the gin. There wasn't a thing about her that didn't make me insane with rage, nor a word she said that didn't make it into my diary of ranting depression that night (*Angst and Anguish*, vol. I), and I thought at one time that she was the only person I'd ever really go around with the whole time I was at college.

'She'll be your bridesmaid now, you know,' a nice bloke had once said to me, when I confessed these fears to him in the middle of an alcohol-drenched panic. For a long time I believed that, and it was the only thought that consoled me when I worried that I would probably never fall in love and marry.

That all changed, of course, and now I rather liked her. In theory I was a nice person, with a warm and tender heart, but in practice, I simply wasn't. Circumstances usually got the better of me, and I was insincere, mean-spirited and anti-social. I was never actively nasty, though. I never did anything that would have hurt someone's feelings or made them cry. It's surprising how many people with high morals are prepared to do just that in pursuance of their honourable code. Being apart from Michelle now, I could be as nice as I wanted, and I didn't suffer internally for it. It was a problem with commitment that had bothered me, not a problem with her. When we weren't expected to be everywhere together, I found her refreshing, a nice switch from the students with their intensity and middle-class idealism. For all my two-faced, self-interested superficiality, I wasn't a snob.

Michelle waited for me as we came out of the tutorial. She didn't normally go to the same ones as me: he took classes on alternate weeks, but she'd missed her session with him and was making it up today.

'What a bastard!' she said, as we got into the lift, still terrifyingly within earshot. I stabbed at the button to close the doors.

'Who?' I said quietly, my neck prickling.

'Jim McFucking Wanker, obviously. Did you see the look he gave me when I came in? I hate him and he knows it.'

'I didn't know you hated him. Why, what did he do?'

'Everyone hates him. He is *such* a bloody perv as well. Didn't you see him coming on to that girl today – I don't know her name, the one with the blonde bob?' And me! I thought. What about what he said to *me*? That was coming on, wasn't it? Wasn't it? 'He is *exactly* like that with my group. There's this one girl called Karen, she's such a bloody . . . She thinks I'm terrible because I never go to lectures, and she *types* her essays, can you believe it? She actually *types* her essays. And he's always smiling at her and he absolutely *hates* me.'

'Well, he can be a little sarcastic, sometimes, but I quite like that, and anyway I don't think –'

'Isn't he? He's so bloody sarcastic. But he is *such* a loser. Apparently he was asking that mature student where you can pick up women around here. I nearly bloody *puked* when I heard. And he went on one of those Law Society outings, and apparently he got off with one of the girls. She must have been *blind*!'

'Yeah,' I said. I didn't, however, treat this as bad news. I was thinking: Well, if he's done it before . . .

'And did you see the valentine card? Well, how could you miss it? I'm surprised he didn't photocopy it and include it with the hand-out. Somebody likes me! I bet he bought it himself. Sad bastard.'

We walked up Oxford Road together, past the usual circus show: the fat woman with wild hair and a neat grey goatee who shouted, 'Whore! Prostitute!' when I walked by, the colourfully dressed young man who sold the *Big Issue* with a sense of humour ('Please buy the *Big Issue* before I turn into a giant pineapple'). I could have told him his marketing gimmick was grossly misjudged, that everyone who paid enough attention and slowed down as they passed was thinking, No, I'd kind of like to see this pineapple thing. Michelle bought a copy.

When I got home, Adam, our next-door neighbour, was standing at the gate with one arm in a sling and the other hand bandaged with a splint.

'Oh, my goodness, what happened?' I asked him.

'I got knocked off my bike by a lorry,' he said, smiling. 'This is just a sprain, but my bike's completely knackered. Anyway, how have you been?'

'We're all fine. Does it hurt a lot?'

Adam shook his head. 'Actually, I popped round to ask a favour, but you were all out. The thing is, I can't open tins with this on, which would be fine except I can't feed Mouska.' A glossy black Persian seduced his ankles as we talked.

'Oh, *baby*,' I said to Adam, looking at the cat.

'She's lovely, isn't she? I just wondered if you'd mind coming in and opening a tin for me.'

'Sure,' I said. 'I love cats.'

Adam's flat was on the first floor, which was how his living room came to rest alongside my bedroom. The houses were identical from the outside, and I was expecting it to look the same inside. Our house was painted in cold blues, with cheap patterned carpet and woodchip paper, and filth in every corner. Toadstools ran rings around our bathroom floor, and large sheets of curly orange fungus like papyrus scrolls poked out from the gap where the sides of the bathtub didn't meet. Our kitchen floor was covered in the kind of lino that looked grey and dirty even when it was clean, although I only knew that from memory since we never really cleaned it. And the whole place smelled of toothpaste and soap and fags and lavatories and Finlay's tinned

Fray Bentos curries every day of the week. I climbed Adam's stairs, following him up. When I got to the top I felt like I'd stepped over the rainbow.

Adam's living room was the equivalent of my bedroom and Heather's together, with no dividing wall. His floor was a rich, real, mahogany-coloured wood throughout. His sofas were a pale turquoise; fat, faded and velvety and covered with expensive-looking cushions. His bookshelves groaned with the weight of about a million paperbacks, and his curtains were swagged, overlong and exquisite. The light flooded through the arched window that I wasted, sparkling on the most fabulous furniture I had ever seen. There were a couple of tall lamps that looked like they'd come from Toulouse-Lautrec's favoured brothel. Style magazines and large LP covers were scattered decadently on the floor. It was so clean.

'The catfood's through here,' Adam said.

'This place is so beautiful,' I said. 'I'm so ashamed of our hovel.'

'Oh, come on, student flats are meant to be disgusting, aren't they? And you can't make any place you rent really feel like home.' He was so kind. I opened the can of catfood – salmon and prawn flavour – and he reached for it.

'No, let me,' I told him, 'or you'll just flick it about.'

'I have been,' he said. 'Not the nicest experience, getting catfood in your mouth. Although the cat seems to cope.' I laughed and made an icky face. 'Listen, would you like to make yourself some tea, while you're here? I'm sorry, I'm not so good with the kettle, either.' So I did, using Adam's Orange Pekoe teabags, although I never drank tea myself and didn't think I'd like it. I sat on one of his sofas, and he sat on the floor with his legs together, stretched out in front of him. He rubbed his chin with his good hand, and I melted to the scratchy whisper of his stubble. Mouska, who had eaten enough, came in and sat on him.

'Are you enjoying things, then?' he said. I thought for a

moment he meant the tea, which was nice. 'How's the work coming along?'

'I hate my course, I love my tutor,' I said.

'Hmmm. That's not always a good idea. I was in love with one of my tutors once,' Adam said.

'Really? What happened?'

'I slept with him, in the end. But he wasn't really interested. I wouldn't advise it. You're young, and they're not so young, and they can persuade you you knew all along that it was just a bit of fun, and you're forced to be as mature as you want them to believe you can be, and you can end up being hurt.' He stopped and laughed. 'I say "you" and it's obvious it was just me. Don't listen to me. I'm a bitter old man, who once had his heart broken. What's he like, this tutor of yours?'

'He's Scottish, clever, with it, d'you know what I mean?' He nodded. 'He makes the students call him Jim.'

'Yeah, you have to watch those ones.' Adam smiled. 'They can be very hard to work out. They act like your friend, but they're still your tutor. What about those guys you live with? Don't you fancy either of them?'

'They're just kids,' I said, the way very young girls in films always do, before they're cruelly let down by older men. 'I don't think I could date anyone who wasn't at least ten years older than me. Twelve is perfect, I think.'

'I don't know, a big age gap can make things difficult.'

'You sound like you speak from experience,' I said, provocatively, or as close as I got to provocatively in those days.

'Well, yeah. The man I'm seeing now's very young. Very sweet, but very young. He's just come out, and he's really happy about it, you know, really . . . excited. So when we go out to pubs, he wants to sit holding hands, and I get the feeling it's more for show. More like a gesture. And I'm feeling a bit old for that. I don't want to work hard at that sort of thing any more. I just want to get on with my life, you know?'

'Do you think we ever stop wanting to get on with our lives

and actually start getting on with them?' I said. I'd heard so many people saying it recently: Mabel, people in soap operas, me in my own diary.

'I doubt it,' Adam said. 'My life always feels like the trailers. I keep waiting for the film to start, but it's always just another trailer. Do you want some more tea?'

We talked for a long time. I stopped fancying him, eventually, but it wasn't because of anything he said or did that was wrong, or that put me off. It's strange, but when you know someone won't fancy you, when you know you haven't a hope, the attraction just vanishes. Even with movie stars, and untouchables like that, I always feel, ludicrous as it is, that if they got to know me there just might be a chance that they'd be on the same wavelength or something, and find me slightly attractive. And I never fancy your Tom Cruises anyway, but the ugly friends, the character actors. Still, most people claim to find unrequited love more of a torment. I don't see how. If someone isn't interested in you, deep down you know you couldn't really like them, not if you like yourself. If someone doesn't get you, doesn't love that thing about you, then you're missing the point with them too. I knew that part of the attraction with Jim McFadyean was that his behaviour gave every impression of validating my crush. It was true that I usually felt scared when he seemed to want to do something about it, and keener when he seemed to lose interest, but that was just a fear of relationships, I thought. There would never have been any original interest if I hadn't felt something there, something from him.

When I got back, there was only Finlay. He was in the kitchen, filling the kettle. I skimmed my bag across the table and sat down.

'The others went to the pub,' he said. 'Where did you get to?'

'Why didn't you go with them?'

'I've got some work to do. Where have you been?' I toyed with ignoring the question again. I had felt sorely neglected by him recently, insensitive bastard that he was.

'I've been at Adam's. Feeding his cat.'

'Hungry cat,' he said, and sniffed. 'So why can't he feed it? Has he gone somewhere?'

'No, he was there too. What, you think I just sat alone in his house for four hours? He's broken his arm, or something. Can't open the can.' He tilted his head back to show he understood. 'So, how's your life?'

'Oh, you know. Pretty good. I've got a shit load of work to do, but otherwise . . .' We were strange together again. A lot shyer than before the thing with Greg, shyer, even, than we were when we first met. He was acting as if he felt guilty, too. There was a gentleness about him that was quite touching. After the months we'd spent being bitter and facetious to each other, we'd seemed to settle on a tenuous plateau where neither of us knew quite how to behave. 'Tea?'

I pressed my lips together and shook my head. 'Don't drink tea.'

'I know.' We didn't speak while the kettle bubbled noisily. 'I hate the dramatic silence just before boiling point. The anticipation,' he said, smiling slightly, looking down.

'No, you don't. You love it.'

'How well you know me,' he said, and made a cup of tea. He started to walk upstairs to his room. Then he turned and looked at me without saying anything. It made me a little nervous, but, for the first time in a long time, a little thrilled. He leaned on the banister and swung slightly.

'Did you ever find out who sent you the valentine?' he said at last.

'It's a mystery,' I said.

'A secret admirer, eh?' he said. He went upstairs. When he reached the top I heard him chortle softly. I was supposed to.

6

I was ovulating. This was good news. During ovulation the pheromones are giving it all they've got, the ankles are slimmer, the breasts are back to normal after their premenstrual football stage and the complexion's just dandy: date climate. Although, I have to say, I don't think you can beat the actual menstruation days. I'm one of those women who loves all of that, the kind you see in the ads. See, they do exist. So all was well physically, although I felt, as always, on the chubby side, and nearly gave myself a migraine trying to steam off a few extra ounces in a dangerously hot bath. I made the usual mess of my stupid kinky hair, the way I always did before a ball, or whenever I needed it to look good, putting enough products in to render it limp *and* frizzy, which takes some doing. As I backcombed I played Henry Mancini, the soundtrack to *Breakfast at Tiffany's.* Soundtracks are mood enhancers: more than other music, they adhere to your emotional state until you can't really tell where one begins and the other ends. There was a particularly raunchy little tune that sounded like a striptease and it was marvellous to walk around in my underwear, swinging a pair of tights and shimmying. I hoped Adam would hear the music through the wall and think I was as cool as him. Then Mandy knocked on my door.

'Haven't you got it on yet?'

'I'm not going out for another three hours,' I called back, not a little narked. Her disappointment was almost hostile, as if I were inconveniencing her. There was a definite hmmph, I heard it.

'Well, I'm going out in ten minutes. Couldn't you just sling it on?'

'Well, not really. I'm waiting for my perfumed *crème de corps* to evaporate and I'm kind of completely undressed and still fairly sticky.'

'I'd like to see that,' shouted Richard. The pet.

'Oh.' Mandy sighed. 'Well, never mind.' She was more inclined to participate in female bonding rites than Sara, who found them alienating and was staying well away, but in practice, she thought them tiresome. I didn't want to give her the opportunity to comment anyway, because Mandy gave the sort of compliments that made you want to commit suicide. I hoped she'd be gone long before I'd finished.

The music ended and I didn't put anything else on because I could hear shouting in the kitchen. I opened my door a fraction to listen.

'For fuck's sake, Finlay, that's my orange juice you're finishing,' Mandy yelled.

'Oh, don't be so fucking tight.'

'Except you're always drinking my stuff and you never buy anything yourself. I wouldn't mind you taking it if you ever had anything to nick.'

'I'll get you some more.'

'You won't, though. You never do.'

'Look, I'm going to the bloody shop now. And how about I get you a personality while I'm there? You seem to be all out of that too.'

'Fuck you.'

'Come on, mate. That's a pretty shitty thing to say,' said Richard. 'You're always taking her stuff, she's right.'

'I'm going. To the fucking. Shop,' Finlay said. I smiled, and turned the tape over.

After curling my eyelashes I felt prettier. The reflection in the mirror was pleasing enough, although the pleasure wouldn't last. My confidence in those days was like a child's imaginary friend.

It flirted with me when I was alone, saying the right things and winking knowingly. But as soon as anyone else came on the scene it vanished, and I was left talking in an awkward, strangled voice, feeling ugly and out of place. So, although I could leave the house feeling gorgeous, it would be for a limited time only, and my glowing cheeks would turn back into pumpkins well before midnight. The people on my course were the most demoralizing of all, because I was supposed to be friends with them by now, and I simply wasn't. Not going to lectures and tutorials couldn't have helped, but it went deeper than that. When I did go into the faculty building I lurked in corners or sat at the back with a crossword, trying to look as if I didn't mind being alone. The trouble was I was very shy but felt I deserved the life of an extrovert. Inappropriate social ambitions will always lead to insecurity and disappointment. I was ashamed of not being popular, so I behaved as if it was a choice, which left me at an impasse, maintaining a permanent bluff of self-possessed contentedness. It was a self-fuelling insecurity. The only time I minded being alone was when other people were there to see it.

I popped on to the landing to take a look at myself in the long mirror, just as Finlay stamped upstairs for some money. He looked at me and I looked back at him. We didn't speak. I went back into my room to finish the job.

I was meeting Michelle at the halls of residence. When I got to her room, on the evening of the ball, the door was open and she was sharing a fag with the cleaner. They were complaining loudly and grumpily about the new batch of girls. Michelle was sitting in a strapless cocktail dress with an ashtray on her knee, a tall gin to her right and her legs in that knees-together, heels-apart gawky position she adopted when she was wearing a skirt. I was pleased to see her. We air-kissed, I met the cleaner and we went. Michelle had insisted on getting a mini-cab, saying black cabs were a big fuss about nothing, but unfortunately, the last passenger had been some kind of gigantic mohair dog and when

I got out, my long black coat was grey with hairs. I was too happy then for it really to bother me. Michelle and I made our way into the hotel and joined the party.

We arrived. Inside, draped elegantly around the foyer and the stairs, were all the people on my course that I was so scared of. I joined in the compliments, downed a glass of champagne in one graceful, arched swallow, and looked for the handful of people I really liked. That was another thing about balls that I always conveniently forgot: I never really felt there was anyone I could talk to. The people I did know here, I mostly knew through introductions by other people I knew, from different courses. In a ball situation, one consolation is that it's easier to live with knowing nobody. There's so much to do. You can fluff about with your skirt, or reapply make-up, or find drinks. The uniform-imposed anonymity of the black and white men means you can talk to anybody, especially if you don't know them at all, and not have to acknowledge that you wouldn't normally be talking to them. The girls all tend to look so beautiful, and know it, that they're forced to be nicer, to show a lack of arrogance in their gorgeousness, and an absence of jealousy of other girls; it's the Miss World sisterhood effect, where the winner is obliged to say what a great time she and the other girls have had backstage all night. Added to all this is the fact that everyone has paid so much money and made so much effort for one night that they're determined to have a great time, and nothing short of tragedy will get in their way. A good tragedy, in fact, would only increase the feeling of value for money. You're not paying for what happens on the night, but what you can say about it later.

It was just a party, though. I may have been wearing more expensive clothes than I usually did, and showing a bit more anaemic bosom, but everything else was the same. The conversation hadn't changed: once you got beyond the 'don't you look nice?' and had eaten, it was just the same as any evening in the union bar. I sat with Michelle, wondering what I was going to do with myself next, and how I was going to lose her. Like

Tabasco sauce, a little of her went a long way, and I'd had plenty. And then I saw him.

Men love to put on black tie because it makes them look bigger, cleaner, richer and more like the man standing next to them. Curiously, it did none of these things for Jim McFadyean. He was definitively scrawny in a stiff shirt; it swamped his neck like he was Charles Hawtrey, or something. Black was not a good colour on him: it drained his complexion. His chin was stubble-free for the occasion and seemed to lack definition; despite his gauntness the skin under his jaw was loose and slightly flabby. And he had chosen to wear an 'amusing' bow-tie and matching cummerbund, brightly coloured and bubbling with personality. For the first time, I saw that he was balding. It sort of hurt to look at him. It was like a replay of the situation with my first-ever boyfriend back in school. The deep attraction I'd felt for him rested heavily on the fact that his hair curled and flopped over his eyes, but on our first date he'd shown up grinning broadly, and pointing to a freshly shaved skinhead. It had been a horrible night; I felt its resonance in my reaction to Jim McFadyean. If he had come in a kilt I couldn't have been more distressed. I bet he'd thought about it, too.

But he was the reason I was here. This was my chance, I thought he'd made that clear enough. I wanted him to see how well I cleaned up. I teetered over and he looked pleased. He asked me to sit down, offered me some nicotine chewing-gum and started chatting. And I was in love with the idea of seducing him all over again. The nicotine made me wide-awake and perky, the alcohol made me relaxed and stupid, and for once I wasn't scared of him fancying me; I wanted it. I can't remember what we talked about, but it wasn't films and it wasn't my essays, and that was enough. The bow-tie set, so energetically bad, made me self-assured and scornful. Why, I was thinking, he's not even good enough for me. I can do better than him. I may just play with his heart and move on. I had the specific confidence that I'd lacked before, the confidence that made the idea of a relationship with him viable – I finally felt good enough to turn him down. And as my presumption began to spread out and make itself comfortable, he decided it was time to introduce his girlfriend.

'Have you met Brittany?' he said, and gestured over the table to a small, slim girl with cascading primrose hair and the patience of a saint. How many other would-be temptresses had she had to endure over the evening? She was as sweet as candy-floss, but I could see in her eyes that she wanted to give him hell. I should have sympathized and laughed at him with her, but I didn't. I treated her like the enemy. I kept on talking to him, monopolizing him. Where was my smooth, aloof exit? I couldn't do it. I just sat there, looking ever more desperate, being ever more annoying. His syllables got sparser, he tried to involve his date, he tried to change the subject to one I didn't feature in, and I kept talking, until finally, Brittany stood up. 'I'm getting really tired just sitting, Jim. Can we go and dance, now?' He looked at her, then me, then got up and excused himself.

I went back and found Michelle.

'Why were you talking to that dickhead for so long?'

'Well, I just thought I'd –'

'You want to watch him. Remember what I told you about him? He'll probably get pissed and try to come on to you. *Do* not go near him.'

I glanced over at the dance floor, where he was whirling his girlfriend around in a so-uncool-it's-cool manner. 'That was sort of the idea.'

'You *are* kidding, yeah?'

I mussed my hair until it looked terrible, smiled feebly and put my feet up on the next chair. 'Yeah.'

I felt better in the morning. Part of me was glad that I'd been so preoccupied with Jim McFadyean, rather than selecting some undeserving, pimply youth to suck face with as I normally would have. There was no rash on my skin from the proud stubble of a juvenile chin, something I woke with far too often, and I'd got to go home alone, which was nice, and to thrash out the issue of rejection in a way I didn't normally, and that hadn't been an altogether unpleasant experience. I'd always sort of liked rejection, anyway. There's something empowering about it. What is rape, if not rejection? And yet we're told that rapists do it for power. It's a pretty horrible comparison, I know, but you see what I mean. The point is that there's nothing intrinsically weak about being rejected. You don't have to curl up and die about it. A romantic suggestion didn't come off, that's all, and the rejecter usually feels worse. Also, when the air is cleared, there's that marvellous feeling you get from knowing that it's safe now, that neither of you has to take it seriously. They know you know they don't want you and you can carry on throwing yourself at them without the fear of acceptance, which is the only consequence to be really worried about. That's when things get scary. The embarrassment from exposing my intentions lingered, throbbing away at the back of my mind like a hangover, but I knew it wouldn't last for ever. Let's face it, I could pretend I didn't remember, which was as good as it not having happened at all. In those days, I recovered quickly from emotional turmoil. But it's not really ever very serious, is it? I told the story playfully to everyone as I crushed paracetamol between two teaspoons and stirred them into a glass of Coke, and built up the 'I'll never live it down' factor, because I knew it would be expected of me.

'That's soooo unfortunate,' Sara said. 'Did you know he had a girlfriend?'

'I think she was a date rather than a steady girlfriend, at least that's what somebody told me. But they were obviously going to have sex last night, they were an item.'

'God, and he's been flirting with you for months. What a bastard,' Heather said.

'Well, I don't know if he has, now I think about it. I think I might just have been reading things into things. He's just a trendy teacher, isn't he? He likes to be down with the kids. Perhaps I just read the signs wrongly. Jesus, what a dick I was.'

'But he wouldn't have gone to a ball alone, would he?' Sara said, kindly. 'He had to take a date. He'd have looked a real arsehole just hanging around the students trying to join in their conversations. And you said she's not his proper girlfriend . . .'

'Someone said that to me. She might be, I don't know.'

'Well, it's probably true. He had to go with someone, and then he could hardly ignore her all night. He probably does fancy you.'

Girls are so nice, aren't they? They really support each other when they're down. I was going through a period of losing my patience with Sara, and she was still sitting with me, trying to talk me out of humiliation and disappointment. I'd have done the same for her, too. And, really, when we were together and just talking or cooking I liked her. I liked them all as long as we stayed in the kitchen. Out of the kitchen they developed their own personalities and irritating tics. In the kitchen, we were always more in synch.

Mouska was getting used to me. She pawed at my leg as I prised the lid off a can of food. 'Shut up, cat,' I told her. 'I'm opening it.'

'How's your sexy tutor?' Adam said, stretching like a cat himself, as he leaned against the fridge.

'Oh, God. Well, he didn't want me at all, he produced some tart out of nowhere and I spent the evening stalking him. Your basic student ball, really.'

'Just as well,' Adam said. 'You wouldn't really have wanted to get involved with him. They still frown on that kind of thing, I believe. And teachers are a very dull lot.'

'You're not dull.'

'You're very kind.'

'You're not, though.'

'Well, speaking of your kindness, I'm having this thing taken off today. I'll probably be able to feed the cat now.'

'Oh. That's good.'

'But still, come round for coffee whenever you want to chat.'

It was slightly embarrassing that he had to say so, that he sensed my disappointment at the end of his disablement. It was out there. I knew I wouldn't see him so much now. I'd liked having an excuse. I didn't feel we were on popping-round-for-coffee terms, even now, even though his cat trusted me and we knew each other's relationship histories. I'd ruined plenty of friendships that way, being shy and making no moves. When people said, 'Call me,' I couldn't be sure they really meant it. For now, I nibbled on a muffin and drank instant coffee and made the most of the last cat-feeding. Françoise Hardy was singing about broken hearts. It was one of my mother's favourite songs; she used to play a fragment of it that she'd taped from the radio. Hearing it now brought tears to my eyes.

When I got back to our house, Mabel was wearing her wedding dress in the living room.

'It's amazing how well it fits you,' I said.

'Well, people were shorter in those days,' she said. She was trying to look at her bottom in the long mirror that was fixed to the door. 'How's the cat?'

'The cat's fine. How are you? I haven't really spoken to you in days.'

'I spoke to Jon today. This morning when you were out. He's coming over for a few days to talk. Do you think he's changed his mind?'

'Why? What did he say?'

'Nothing, just that he missed me and wanted to see me. But he hardly ever comes up here.'

'I don't think men think as much as women. And if they do they want you to know about it. They like the idea of subtlety, but they're afraid nobody'll notice them doing it. If he says he misses you, that'll be what he means, I think. I think if he wanted to change his mind he wouldn't have been able to resist hinting.'

'Maybe he did and I missed it.'

'Stop worrying. Have you bought white shoes yet?'

'Nobody wears white shoes, do they?'

'What were you going to wear, your Doc Marten's?' Mabel looked down at her feet; she was wearing stripy socks with a hole in one toe.

'I hadn't really thought about shoes. Shit.'

'I fancy going shopping. Do you want to come and buy some shoes and have a makeover?'

'How do we do that? Where? Oh, I can't, I'm broke.'

'There's a bargain bin sale,' I pleaded. 'We'll just look. Oh, go on, let me get them for you.' I was already flicking through the phone book for the department store's number and ignoring her objections. You could tell I'd been fairly spoiled as a child. I believed that new purchases and presents made everything better. Where Heather would have sat her down and listened and counselled and generally been wise and right, I just took her to the shops.

I dropped Mabel off at her bank because I couldn't find a parking space, and she said she'd be a long time begging for more money from her sadistic student financial adviser, whom we all knew by now because she made Mabel's life hell. She was called Bev Glendale, and Mabel said she asked lots of rhetorical questions and waited for answers, and she wouldn't let Mabel withdraw money unless she admitted she was stupid, irresponsible, feckless and was making a mess of her life. How old do we have to be before we leave all the teachers behind? I circled my usual fairly secret parking-space places and was dismayed to find them all full. So I decided to wait behind a parked car outside Marks and Spencer, and take the space when it went. This happened quite quickly, usually. I waited ten minutes, maybe more, and by then I was due to meet Mabel at Kendall's in five minutes. A woman came back to her car, and I moved mine to let her reverse out easily. The man who had been waiting behind me for perhaps half a minute slipped into the space like a man with a very small penis into a sixty-year-old whore. At least, that's what I think I shouted at him, when I tore out of my car. I believe I may have lost my grip on reality for a moment.

‘What did you think I was fucking doing?’ I yelled. ‘I’ve waited twenty fucking minutes for this fucking space. You could see me fucking waiting, you stupid sod.’

The man, who had got out of his car now, was standing silently for a long time, looking at me. Oh, Jesus Christ, he’s a crazy person and he’s going to hit me, I thought. ‘I won’t be spoken to like that,’ he said, in a strange, cold monotone. ‘I’ll move if you apologize, but I won’t be spoken to like that. I won’t be sworn at.’ I stood, breathing heavily and wondering what to do next. I was still a little afraid that he might hit me. But I was still hopping mad. ‘I’ll move if you speak to me nicely,’ he said again, obviously aware that he was in the wrong, but looking strange with it.

‘Eat. Shit.’ I said, carefully. Not two separate commands, of course, but a measured delivery of my final obscenity. He locked his car and strode off without looking back. I was furious. I wrote a note and put it under his windscreen wiper. It said: ‘You’re a fucking cunt.’ This didn’t seem enough so I wrote ‘FUCKER’ in lipstick on the back of his car. And then I had to find a parking space quite far away so he didn’t let down my tyres when he got back. Amazingly, I made it to the department store on time, and even before Mabel, who’d been getting the usual humiliation from Bev Glendale. We wasted no time heading over to the Estée Lauder woman. I was still dripping with adrenaline, and I really needed a facial to calm down. Not to mention a new lipstick.

But something has happened to the next generation of make-up-counter staff. Gone are the days when you could put yourself in their hands and be confident that you’d walk away with a flawless amber complexion and the season’s directional colours striped around your eyes. The geometric lines of puce blusher and Joan Crawford lips are distant memories. These girls know all about minimalism and subtlety. They still spout the same nonsense about ‘the delicate skin around the eye area’ and beta-hydroxies and free radicals, but you couldn’t get them to lay on slap with a trowel if you bribed them. The day I went with Mabel, they were still something of a novelty, the new breed of cosmetic consultants, but they were already well into the swing of the sophisticated, natural palette, and when I asked for a heavy eye it was nothing doing. I walked away with a hint of grey shadow, a virginal flush and a whole heap of cleansing products I'd never use. Mabel looked ravishing, but then, she always did. I had to apply two more coats of mascara as soon as we were out of view.

We found some dirtyish whitish shoes in the Shoe Be Do sale, and I bought them for Mabel, after convincing her that they'd clean easily, and that I could afford it. I told her to think of them as an early wedding present. She made me buy something too, another bargain, but something I expected to wear only in the privacy of my own home. They were pink and strappy and shockingly tarty, and so, so beautiful. My walking was okay then, not too painful, not too ungainly, but already I couldn't wear high-heeled shoes if I actually intended to move anywhere. There was too big a difference in the lengths of my legs, too much restriction of movement. I felt the bitter-sweet sting of owning something so perfectly pretty and feminine, but never being able to use them. Long before all the difficulty, I had had a very sexy walk. The boys at school used to laugh at it, talk about it, watch it. It was unaffected, produced by a combination of wide hips and slim legs, as natural and fascinating as those sand snakes that skim across the dunes in infinity bands. Now there was stiffness and jerking and low, soft trainers. But I could still own real girl shoes. Together, both pairs cost twelve pounds. Like all clichés, the one about women and shoes is true: no other purchase compares. The fact that they give you boxes, I think, is one of the chief components of the pleasure.

We smuggled them into the house. I didn't want the other girls to know I was pushing the wedding as usual, and I didn't want anyone to see the shoes I'd bought myself. They had a furtive, vaguely pornographic feel to them, as I'd bought them for fun, rather than function, for slipping on in my bedroom when I wanted to fancy myself. It felt too personal to show anyone else. I told them the story of the man who'd parked in my space, and coasted along on the buzz of the new image I was defining for myself, someone who swears at strange men. I enjoyed revealing that I could be so feisty. They all thought I'd been amazingly brave. Richard said, 'Jesus, Grace, I wouldn't like to meet you in a bad mood.'

'Oh, come on, I'm a pussycat. You know that,' I said, with a smirk and a cute little shrug of my shoulder. Finlay straight-manned me with a 'huh'.

'Your boyf– your fiancé phoned when you were out,' he said to Mabel. 'He wants to know if you'll be able to meet him at Piccadilly station tomorrow. Call him back.' Mabel went to phone him, and we began whispering about her as soon as the door closed.

'What's he like, then?' Richard said.

'He sounded like a complete prick,' Finlay sneered, folding a newspaper efficiently to convey how tidily he disapproved.

'How can you tell from just speaking to him on the phone?' I asked, snootily.

'Yar, is my beautiful *intended* able to come to the phone, mate? Hyar hyar hyar,' he said. It doesn't sound very funny, but Finlay was a brilliant mimic, and this was inexplicably hilarious. We were all falling about, me reluctantly, at the imitation of Jonathan's laughter, even though most of them had never actually heard the real thing. I'd spoken to him on the phone once, but only exchanged a word or two, and never a hyar hyar hyar. We covered it with coughing when Mabel got back in.

'Oh, my God, you lot are going to meet him tomorrow. I'm so nervous that you'll think he's a complete arsehole.'

'Of course we won't,' Heather said. 'You wouldn't be marrying the guy if he wasn't fantastic. The number of men who've been after you since you got here. And some of them have been amazing and you've still turned them down for this Jon of yours. I can't wait to meet him.'

'And you'll all be nice to him?'

'Mabel, my love,' Richard said, in his mature, responsible voice, 'we'll treat him like one of the family.'

'You'd better be nicer than that,' Mabel said, looking stern. 'I mean it.'

'He sounds like a funny bloke,' Finlay said, cattily, 'hyar hyar hyar.' We all sniggered silently, until Heather squeaked and we couldn't contain it.

'Is that meant to be Jon?' Mabel said. She was amused, but still stern. 'Well, he doesn't sound anything like that, Finlay, you wanker. And you'll all see that tomorrow when you get to meet him.'

Wednesday

Today I gave up. Everything: the diet, the laughable attempts at exercise, the vain hope that I can conceal any of the disaster that is me, now. And the self-delusion that my life is ever going to be anything like it could have been. If.

I spent all day crying, which is nothing new, because the slightest, corniest things still toy with me, ruthlessly. Even the despair is nothing new. I've done all that already, I just hoped I was past it. It had stopped physically hurting when I thought about him. I thought the worst was over. The truth is, it'll never be over. Thoughts catch me, at the stupidest times, like a surprise, like finding out for the first time all over again. I didn't call Alice or my parents today because I didn't want them to know I'd been crying. Officially, my period of reasonably being able to cry about this is over, something that hasn't gone unnoticed. My mother does her best. 'I know what you're going through, I think about you all the time,' she says, and I think, Sure you do, except when you're paying the gas bill or buying potatoes or parking the car or watching television, or just *living*. The times I think about it, in other words. It's wrong of me to say this, I know that, because it is my life, these are my problems. I just resent it when people, even my mother, say they understand. They think I really should be pulling myself together by now, because it's not like it was even real, ever. They think I only feel it so badly because I'm using it to express my real sadness. That this is the cover under which I'm venting my frustrations about my physical condition. The truth is, it's the other way round. When he was here nothing bad mattered, and now he isn't, nothing matters. I can't stop thinking about him, not for a single day. I want everyone in the world to know about it, I want to justify the pain.

It's the worst kind of pain because it comes from nowhere and everywhere all at the same time. I never stop wishing and trying to change things and hating myself when I can't. There's so much help and advice out there, in magazines and papers, and on television, and it's so alluring when people start to talk about their own experiences, similar situations, except their problems never seem as bad and none of it helps; as a result of all this I've become nicer *and* nastier. That's how it works.

So now, with this, this *grief*, I've acquired a double standard. I seek out stories of true-life heartache and weep as hard for them as I do for myself. I need to hear about death. I buy depressing books, see depressing movies, listen to sad songs until I think I've peaked, and then go through the hangover the next day. But I couldn't care less about problems I don't have. I sit watching *Oprah* and think: Pull yourself together. The worst are the people who are depressed for no reason. 'I just can't seem to shake it,' they say. 'Although I know there's nothing wrong with my life and I should be grateful, I just can't face the mornings.' I hate these people. My one consolation is that they make themselves miserable. I'm incapable of low-level pity and can't endure the people who complain when there's nothing left to complain about, even though I can see how I'm probably one of them. This is what I tell myself. It happened. Your life has changed. Move on. It doesn't work.

With the legs problem, although it isn't on the same scale, I've the same reaction. Sometimes I watch real-life stories of real people and it tears my heart out to see what they've gone through, children who've had fifty operations and smile because they had ice-cream today, the journalist with cystic fibrosis who breathes through a ventilator and can't ever leave his house again. I find myself crying until my eyes nearly bleed, although, no doubt, there's a hefty dollop of self-pity helping things along. To counter this, just as often, there's another, horrible, unsympathetic side. No one is allowed to be sad or suffer unless they're qualified to, which means their problems are comparable to mine. And even if they are, they're not allowed to complain, because I'm not.

As a proportion of their population, there are more disabled bastards than there are able-bodied bastards, and okay, perhaps they have an excuse of some sort, but that doesn't make them any less intolerable. I was on the tube the other day, which is something I rarely do, what with the stairs and the station being miles away. A woman got on, as efficiently as anyone else, and shouted that she needed a seat because her leg was very painful. A few people got up straight away and she sat down. Then she shouted again: 'Does anybody know how far the Circle Line goes?' There was silence. The next time she opened her mouth it was a scream. 'Does anybody know how far the Circle Line goes? You can't ALL be stupid!' Still no reply. At the next stop she got up and pushed her way out of the carriage, using her bag and elbows viciously. 'DON'T touch my leg!'

I sat and grinned. It was funny. I was glad that nobody had helped her, and enjoyed seeing her getting angry. Because she was one of the bad disabled people, the kind who give the rest of us a bad name. Only they don't. They're accommodated and pitied; they make people feel ashamed of their physical normality. There are plenty of them. There was one in the solicitor's where I did some work experience when I first moved here. He was always groaning and puffing and making people move for him. It took him half an hour to sit down, longer to get up again. I used to think, Come on, modern medicine's not that bad. They wouldn't let you out on the streets if you were in as much pain as you're making out. Because, even when it feels like hell, you never *have* to let it show. Once he fell over, and everyone rushed around to help him up. I looked the other way. Attention-seeker, I thought. I bet you did it on purpose.

This is so hypocritical. Because some of me would be the same. I want to shout at men in the street when they nearly knock me over, to accost people for their compassion. I'm jealous of the people who do. The truth is, how you deal with disability has a lot to do with vanity. The only reason I cover mine so well, with such tired persistence, is I'm desperate for it not to show. To some people, that matters less than sympathy. Of course, I want both. It's not an option.

So in the grand scheme of things, if my life is such a congestion of unhappiness, why do I care about a shitty reunion with a bunch of people I hardly liked? I wish it were that simple. This reunion has become the focus of my life, although, let's face it, it's not a very focused life. I have nothing else to think about. It's like a project now, being suitable when I see them again, the ambition that motivates me and drags me out of bed in the early afternoons. I can't explain it. They're not the only people I've ever lived with. I've had other friends; but these ones compel, and I don't know why. I'm not even big on reminiscing. Nostalgia is only enjoyable when it's someone else's past. I run like the clappers from my own, believing it will taint my future if the two ever meet. Now, suddenly, I need to see what's happened. I only want to know that other people have done badly too. I don't want to share. I don't want my own experiences to console.

1992

7

Jonathan Ong wore a suit and was out of his depth. At least seventy per cent of Manchester students, as I may have mentioned, although I'm not at all obsessed with this, are Oxbridge rejects and we share a secret envy and distrust of the erstwhile rivals who made it. We suspect them of having cheated. Jonathan had that Oxbridge aura about him, that Ready-Brek glow of assurance, even on the threshold, and I could tell we weren't going to like him. His smile was synthetic sincerity and his hair was nylon-neat. He came in holding Mabel's hand for support, and plonked himself down in the middle of our big sofa. We had exactly enough seating space for the normal household: seven places. Mabel had gone to make tea, and Mandy and Heather, who wanted to get a look at him, were forced to flank him on either side. They relaxed back into the sofa, and Jonathan leaned forward, swinging his clasped hands between his knees. He looked eager to talk, and to please. When someone new comes into the house, a friend of a friend, it always helps if the linking friend is there too, like an interpreter. Otherwise, the conversation gets a little trite. Particularly when I'm steering it: I can out-trite anyone.

'So, you're a dentist?' I began.

'Dental student, yep.'

'And are you working on real mouths yet, or just sets of false teeth?'

'Oh, real mouths, real people.' No one helped him with the silence. 'Real teeth.'

'That must be good,' I said. 'Unless it's horrible, obviously.'

'Well, you get used to it. It, er, comes with the job.'

'Of course. And you went to school with Mabel? That's how you met?' This was me again. I really had to stop asking questions soon, or else he was going to think I was Mabel's mother. But the others weren't saying anything.

'Yeah, well, we went to the same grammar school, but it was separate. You know, by sex. So I didn't really speak to her a lot at school.'

'Oh, that's interesting,' I said, quite unconvincingly.

'How long are you up for?' Mandy asked.

'A couple of days, probably. You'll all have to tell me where I should be taking Mabel.'

'Yeah, we'll have to do that,' Finlay said, a touch sarcastically, but with the sarcasm not in the obvious places. We all caught it, being used to him.

'Are you looking forward to the wedding, then?' Richard said, brightly. Richard, being a public-school boy, was very well brought up, and good at making people feel at ease. His question was just as rubbish, but his voice was vigorously matey. Jonathan didn't get to answer, as Mabel came in with the tea.

'There's a plate of cakes in there. Does anybody mind getting it?' she said. Five of us stood up, sat down, stood up again, and tittered at each other.

'I'll get them,' Heather said. They were great cakes; Mr Kiplings, Jaffa cakes and sliced angel cake from Marks. You couldn't have assembled more E numbers in such a small space. Heather put the plate down on the coffee table in front of Jonathan and sat on the arm of the larger sofa.

'How's Jerome?' Mabel asked Jonathan, and they started having a conversation about people they knew and we didn't. Nobody could add anything or interrupt, but we all had to listen, and for a moment the atmosphere hovered between really quite funny and really very embarrassing. I could see Finlay storing up ammo for later.

'Where are you from, originally?' Mandy asked Jonathan. She

had spent a year teaching in China and knew all there was to know about the culture. Naturally, this made visits to Chinese restaurants with her virtually intolerable, as she insisted on speaking Chinese to the waiters and explaining the menu to us and muttering under her breath in Chinese as she read it to herself. At the end of the meal, she would pick up button mushrooms deftly with chopsticks, and talk about how the tea had been very Western.

'Chiswick,' Jonathan said. The rest of us smirked. Jonathan offered no more information, but sat munching demurely on a frangipane slice. He was very handsome, very symmetrical, very clean-looking. They made an attractive couple.

Sara stood up. 'I have to go and do some work, now. It was nice meeting you, Jon.' Jonathan said much the same, without the work thing, through cake. I love the sound of people talking with cake in their mouths. On the other hand, talking while you're chewing a piece of meat is a horrible sound.

'Have you made any plans for tonight?' Heather said.

'We could think up something for you to do,' Finlay offered.

'We were just going to go for something to eat in Chinatown, then on to the Zygote Bar,' Mabel said. The Zygote Bar was one of the places we took out-of-town friends to impress them. It was a happening, visibly designed place, and you could sometimes end up queuing for cigarettes with pop stars or footballers there. 'You're all welcome to come,' she lied. There was a cavalcade of overlapping excuses, then a silence as we all ate more cake. It could have been more excruciating, probably.

When Mabel and Jonathan left, most of the house had gone back to their own rooms, pretending to work. I was in the kitchen, pretending to clean. As soon as the door slammed we came back into the living room to discuss him.

'He's really good-looking, isn't he?' I said first. The other girls agreed, and the boys joined in, until we'd all noticed they were taking the piss.

'I don't like him,' Heather said. 'I think she changes when

she's around him. And did you hear her laughing at some of the things he said, and I was, like, did I miss something?'

'He was a bit straight, wasn't he?' I said. 'But he must have been really nervous, surrounded by the whole lot of us.'

'Yeah, you could be right,' Heather said.

'He didn't look nervous, though, did he?' Mandy said.

'Maybe that's how he looks when he's nervous. Maybe when he's relaxed he's even more laid-back.'

'Maybe when he's relaxed he just slips into a coma,' Finlay said. 'Yarrrs, I liiiiike taking out teeeeeethzzzzzz.' Again, he'd captured Jonathan's voice viciously well, and I had to try hard not to laugh out loud. But I had enforced a new rule on myself: no letting Finlay see you find him really funny. The others laughed and I sucked the insides of my cheeks.

'I thought he was a bit of a tool, actually,' Richard said, as if he was the voice of common sense. 'She could do a lot better than him.'

'And he fucks around,' Mandy said. 'I don't get what's the big thing about him. He's good-looking, but so what? He's about as funny as cancer. He's so bland. I was struggling to keep my eyes open when he started on about some of their friends.'

'He doesn't fuck around any more,' I said, pretending to be the devil's reasonable advocate. 'Not since they got engaged.'

'Big of him,' said Heather.

'And he's been so nice to her recently. Remember that valentine. We don't know what he's like to her when they're alone together.' The others looked at me as if I was thick.

'You kissed me. I never got over it. Hyar hyar hyar,' said Finlay, and this time I laughed.

We got bored of having nothing much to say about Jonathan, and everyone went back to study. Except Finlay, he stayed and opened a can of beer. And I stayed, because I didn't want to go back into the kitchen again. We didn't speak for ages and I started doing a crossword to indicate that conversation was neither necessary nor expected.

'How's the, er, tutor?' he asked. I wondered how I should play it, but I couldn't think of anything to make up. And I didn't know how much he knew. Everything, I supposed. There were no secrets in our house. Well, there were secrets, but we all told each other what we knew. We stuck to groups of two or three for spreading house gossip, to maintain the façade of confidentiality.

'It's just like it always was,' I said. 'Nothing's changed. I don't even know if he noticed I was trying to make a pass at him.'

'Are you not really embarrassed about seeing him now?'

'No. Life's too short to be embarrassed. I only have two emotions, actually. Happy and sad. The others aren't worth the trouble.' He took a deep, annoyed breath and let it go, exasperatedly, then started watching television. Finally, he spoke, as if leaving his thoughts unspoken would be morally irresponsible.

'That's such a typical thing for you to say. You only have two emotions. Jesus. Nobody only has two emotions. Jesus!'

'You don't know what I feel.'

'Well, that's certainly true.' He took a cake from the plate Mabel had left and examined it closely, as if he hoped to find something unpleasant. Then he put it back. 'So you thought Jon Ong was okay, then?'

'We were all horrible to him. I think it was really brave of him to sit there while we judged him. I don't see you subjecting your girlfriend to our totty-assessment panel.'

'She's not my girlfriend.'

'Well, whatever she is.'

'Everyone knows who she is, anyway,' he said. I didn't say that I didn't. I was already showing far too much interest. And, besides, he knew that I didn't.

'So what didn't you like about him?' I asked him earnestly. I posed a little as I looked up at him. Looking up is a good angle for my face. He looked back at me for quite a long time. I loved that short-cut intimacy we shared, the knowledge without responsibility. I enjoy that whole sex thing, the attraction that goes on between people even when they don't intend to do anything about it. He was still the biggest romantic deal in my life at that point, even though I sometimes loathed him, and I always infuriated him and sometimes we went for days without saying a word to each other. The charge remained, fizzling a little, like an electric fence in a cartoon.

'You didn't think he was smug?' he said.

'He was confident.'

'And the difference is?'

'It's a matter of degree. And justification. Take you, for instance. Sometimes you're confident. And sometimes you're just smug. And sometimes you're neither. That's when you're most tolerable.'

'Is that what I am?' A smile dressed his lips quite prettily for a few seconds. 'I'm sometimes tolerable.'

'Sometimes.' He pinged the ring-pull on his can of beer. The silence was toasty and orangy and terrific. Then he spoiled it.

'She really isn't my girlfriend,' he said.

'It really doesn't matter, does it?' Perhaps I spoiled it. This annoyed him, anyway. He stopped smiling, and the silence was edgy this time. I reached over, took a jam tart and began to eat it delicately.

'She talks about clothes all the time. It's not exactly stimulating.'

'Mabel and I talk about clothes all the time. It's what girls do. Heather talks about clothes all the time. We're not all like Sara. Most of us are shallow.'

'It's not the same. I'll be talking to her and she'll interrupt with a story about what a great pair of flares she found in Affleck's Palace.' He put on what was obviously an imitation of her voice as he said the last part, and it was funny, even though I didn't know her, but he wasn't trying to be. There was something endearing about that. 'She's obsessed with the seventies. It's just so dull.'

'This coming from you. For you, nineteen eighty-three never

really went away, did it? Everything since has been a dream sequence. You watch television from the eighties, listen to eighties music, and that blouson leather jacket you wear . . .'

'That jacket cost two hundred quid,' he said, and I remembered in that sentence the two things I hated most about him. His meanness and his love of his blouson leather jacket. But I smiled, anyway, just to show I still had the edge in the composure stakes.

'Why do you see her, then?'

'She's very attractive.' Did the disappointment show on my face? I was so jealous of everyone in the world who was prettier than me. I'd had enough; I didn't want to talk to him if he wasn't going to be madly in lust with me any more. It wouldn't do. But I hardly ever walked out of rooms first in those days. I waited for him to go. He sat back. He twanged the ring-pull some more. Apparently he thought we were going to have a rich, meaningful conversation and I'd only wanted something low-fat. I chewed my bottom lip and waited for him to say something else. He yawned and tried to sound casual. 'Why are you so interested in her now?' I wondered how I could balance the offence I should have taken at such a question with the nonchalance I should have exhibited if it was really an unfair accusation. I opted for sarcasm.

'Because I'm desperately jealous of her and I want you for myself. I'm just being polite, Finlay. She is your girlfriend. What else are we going to talk about?'

'She's not my . . . bloody girlfriend.'

'So talk to me about Mabel and Jonathan. Are they well suited? Is it going to last? What's your view?'

'If you were really her friend, you'd tell her not to go through with it,' he said, sanctimoniously. I wasn't as bothered by this as you might have thought. The girls had ticked me off enough about the whole affair in the beginning for me to have spent time rationalizing it, and reaching the conclusion that it wasn't my business, and the best thing I could do was just be nice to Mabel every step of the way. And I also knew that, as a boy, he didn't really have the first clue about other people's relationships.

I don't think men are as empathetic as women. He certainly wasn't. Emotionally, he was wholly unilateral.

'Well, obviously I'm not really her friend, then, but I don't see the point in adding to her anxiety by forecasting a terrible future for her.'

'And what happens when the future is terrible?'

'Finlay, marriages fail. It's not my life.'

'That's a really, er, caring attitude.'

'I don't mean I don't care what happens to her, I mean I can't choose the way she lives. I wish some of you thought about that instead of predicting eternal doom for her with no more authority than Mystic fucking Meg. You're not going to change her mind, you're just going to make her unhappy.'

'Oh, I don't want to talk about it any more,' he said. 'I'm pretty tired of all this talk about Mabel, to be honest.' I was still waiting for one of us to move, and I couldn't make myself and he didn't, so we sat in a grumpy silence.

'I'm not seeing her any more, anyway,' he said, some minutes later.

'Who?' I said it without thinking, but it sounded a bit forced.

'Who do you think?'

'Since when?'

'Since whenever. I get enough of women talking crap at home.' And then he walked out, leaving me to contemplate the conversation we'd had and try to work out when I'd stopped understanding it.

Jonathan left late at night two days later, without having to face the panel in its entirety again. Mabel kept him out of our way, or he dragged her away a lot. I wondered what he'd said to her about us. Especially the boys. I saw him once or twice and he was always very nice and friendly, and meeker when it was just two of us. Perhaps his smoothness when he first arrived was a defensive response, and he'd really just been nervous. I could imagine him being very gentle and affectionate and sweet as a boyfriend. I could see what Mabel might see in him. Anyway, when he'd gone, Mabel practically ran into Mandy's room and began talking about him. I wasn't hurt that she went to Mandy, because she wasn't really my best friend or anything, just the girl I liked best in the house, but I was still curious, and wanted to know what was going on. I didn't have to wait long. Heather just knocked and barged in on them, and after a while it was impossible to resist doing the same. After all, they weren't officially talking about something secret and gossipy. Mabel was sitting on Mandy's bed, Mandy was cross-legged on the floor, Heather was sitting at the desk on a chair. I leaned against the wall. The others stopped talking in the way people do when new people come into a room. It's a polite thing to do, but it makes the newcomer paranoid.

'Well, he seemed lovely,' I said, and then realized that this wasn't a fun gossip session but something more serious. 'What is it?'

'It's Jon,' Mabel said. 'No, I can't say it. I don't want to say it again.'

'He's got herpes,' Heather said gravely. Ah, I saw why Mandy had been the first choice. She had had the clap, and treated it rather ostentatiously in the first year. She was our expert on venereal disease.

'Oh, Jesus. Is there a chance that . . .?'

'No. I don't think so. Jon says he knows the girl he . . . got it from and he hasn't slept with me since he slept with her.' It took me a few moments to get the implications of this in order. I wanted to say, 'So what are you going to do now?' but it seemed futile and intrusive. Thank God for Heather, who asked the question for me. Heather wasn't capable of intrusive. She shared too much of her own life.

Mabel buried her face in her hands and her voice was high-pitched and we all thought she was crying. But when she took her hands away her face was the same. 'Oh, the bastard. He told me he wasn't going to sleep with anyone any more.'

'What a cunt,' Mandy said. 'I'm sorry, Mabel, but he's such a cunt. What did he have to say for himself?' Mabel put her face in her hands again.

'Mandy's right,' said Heather. 'He's a shit. He's not worth all this, Mabel. You deserve so much better.' Only I said nothing, too chicken to condemn him, too wise to defend him. Finally, a little surprisingly, Sara came in and sat down. But today she didn't look at all awkward in the femaleness of the moment. She made it complete. The difference this time was that it wasn't some hormone-heady, artificially contrived indulgence. It was a serious thing, and seriousness brought out the best in Sara. She listened to everything and her response was measured and sensible. Her voice didn't get louder, she didn't swear for effect. She just called it like she saw it.

'The herpes isn't what's important now. Obviously don't touch him. But what you've got to see now is that he's not willing to commit, whatever, and that's what marriage is. It's about commitment, not just living together. You can see that, can't you, Mabel? He's lied to you a heck of a lot and you have to ask yourself whether you want to be married to a man who lies to you. Not who sleeps with other women, although that's about as bad as it gets, but who lies to you.'

'And that stuff's for life, you know? Not just for Christmas. It's a good thing you didn't have sex this last couple of days,' I said. I could only contribute at a medical level; I didn't have a view. I was good at cheering people up, which didn't help here. I felt inadequate, like the others were her real friends, and especially in awe of Sara, with her cool, measured wisdom. She sat on the bed and slipped her arm round Mabel's shoulders, not saying anything for several minutes. Sympathy is the most lethal substance for miserable people: it gives credence to their self-pity, breaks down all composure. This one, touching gesture of compassion was too much for Mabel: her whole face mutinied, the eyes becoming glassy and a rosy stain spilling out over her cheeks. Looking at her, I felt almost an out-of-body experience, as if I'd turned invisible and grown very distant, as if I was watching all of this on television and anything I said would be redundant, like talking to a soap opera.

'What are you going to do?' Heather said again.

'Well, I love him. That's the point. If he had any other kind of disease, like cancer or something, I wouldn't stop loving him . . .'

'But you don't get cancer by . . .'

'No, you don't get cancer from screwing other people. But the disease isn't the point. It hasn't changed the point, which is, he's been unfaithful to me at least one more time after swearing he wouldn't be. I've forgiven him before. I can forgive him again. But I want him to change, too, and every time I forgive him he won't change one more time.'

'If he's making you unhappy, I think you should seriously consider breaking it off,' I said, cautiously, feeling as if I should say something useful or I wouldn't belong. Part of me just wanted to test my visibility. 'You can do without grief before you get married, let alone during the marriage.'

'It's not that easy to leave long-term relationships,' Mandy said high-horsily, to me. She, we all knew, found it impossible to disentangle herself from the most casual flirtations and was always being bothered for ever by people she had once met on a bus or boyfriends she'd snogged when she was eleven. Some of them threw themselves off roofs if she didn't return their calls, which was why, she said, you could never afford just to hope they'd get over it. She never missed a chance to overdramatize sex.

'Sure it is. If you don't want to stay with someone you don't have to. It's that easy.' In my attempt to squash Mandy's conceit, I was treading too heavily on Mabel's feelings. I pulled back. 'It seems hard because you love him. But he's not the only man alive who can make you happy. And he doesn't, even.'

'Actually, it's not that easy,' Mandy persisted. 'You can't just say one day that you've changed your mind, it's all over, and you don't have to see them again.'

Mandy was playing on my well-known ignorance in this matter. I'd never had a long-term relationship, not a proper one, and she knew this. I wasn't qualified to speak on the subject, and Mandy had a bloody doctorate in fucked-up boyfriends. It was stupid trying to argue when I really didn't know what I was talking about, she was right. I faded back into the wallpaper.

'You say that every time you forgive him it just gives him a licence to go and do it again,' Sara said. 'Well, perhaps now's the time to be a bit meaner to him. Even if you think you want to go back with him, make him work for it. And not just with flowers and stuff, that's too easy. Make him earn your forgiveness, and then hold out even longer when you think he has. That's if you ever think he has. You might find he can never do enough for you, and that's when to walk away. But right now, don't take his calls, don't take his shit. And don't bloody well marry him.'

'What if I do all that and he finds someone else? What if he doesn't love me enough?' Mabel sniffed. I found that a little annoying, to tell you the truth. It was so . . . pathetic.

But Sara had an answer for this, too. 'If he could find anyone as good as you do you really think he'd still be coming here? Do you think he just proposed to you at random? Mabel. You're gorgeous. You're so gorgeous I feel like shit standing next to you in a club sometimes. And you're so bright and funny and nice. He's never going to find anyone like you and he knows it. But he's a top-of-the-range wanker as well, and, like you say, he's going to do it as long as he can get away with it. If it's a choice between him with the herpes and the other women, and no him at all, you know what you have to do. Don't you?'

'It's going to be tough, sweetie,' Mandy said, soothingly, 'but we'll help you through it.' What, precisely, is so tough about dumping people? You tell them you don't want to see them any more. If you like, you can throw in a little stuff about how fabulous and sexy they are and it's you that's screwed up. Then you walk away, you put the phone down. Anything that happens after that is the icing on the cake.

'Okay, here's what you do,' said Sara. 'You don't phone him until he phones you, and when he does call, stay stroppy, tell him you think you've had second thoughts. Don't say any more, let him work them out for you. And then stand back and let him sort it out. By the end of him trying to make things better, you'll either still hate him or realize that he's still the one. But, if you really want my advice, he's not. He's a shit. That's the last time I'll be impartial.'

'I don't see why we have to be impartial,' Heather said. 'Get rid of him now.'

Mabel gripped her head in both hands and shook it, as if to shake out all her problems. 'Well, whichever one of you I listen to, I have to act the same way. I'll be cool and mean, okay? And if any of you sees me being nice to him, tell me off.'

We didn't tell the boys about the herpes, or even let it slip out, the way most private business usually seeped into our collective consciousness. This was a little too personal, a bit too important as well. But they could tell we were all hiding something because they carried on telling jokes about Jonathan and getting frosty receptions for them. It was the biggest crime in our house, not having a sense of humour, not getting it, and the boys resented us for a while and we resented them for their insensitivity and there were a few petty arguments every day. I wasn't so much a part of it, because I never took anything very seriously and I continued to ingratiate myself to both sides of the split, because I liked being liked. It wasn't very sisterly of me, but what the hell? The boys hadn't done anything wrong. But keeping a foot in both camps means you are treated warily by everyone, and I became more detached, going for long drives to Alderley Edge and Didsbury and coming home late. We were all, I felt, very tired of living together around that time, which was sad, because we'd been such good friends at the start of the year. I hadn't known the boys all that well initially. They'd been Sara and

Mabel's friends and I spent so much time with Michelle in the first couple of terms of the first year that I never really met them. But when the girls asked me if I wanted to live with them we'd started going out together, to Rusholme for curries, to the union bar, always the seven of us and nobody else. We were soon a unit. That was the best time. We were all delighted with how alike we all were, and that was all that mattered. We weren't living together – well, we were in residence halls together, but halls are different. There are lots of other people, you can go weeks without seeing some of them, you never have to eat breakfast together or fight for a tiny bathroom or buy loo rolls. You can't predict from halls what living together will really be like. Now we never went for curries together, or to the union bar at lunch-time. We went to the same parties, and out at night in a big group still, but that was to see other people, and if no one from outside the house was going it tended not to happen. It was sad, but inevitable. When people become your family, however they do it, you don't want to be around them all the time.

Which is why I decided on a girls' night out with Michelle. It was something we were always pretending we wanted to do, but we never sustained the enthusiasm long enough to organize it. This time I called her bluff and started to talk times and dates. I met her on the Wilmslow Road, outside her halls, and we caught a bus into town. She was wearing expensive perfume, loud make-up and heels. I'd put on a checked shirt and my favourite jeans. If you'd subtracted my bosom and hips, there would have been nothing else visible to the human eye: I looked terrible, and she was embarrassed for me. ('I'm not being funny, Grace, but is that what you're wearing?') Too many months living with people who suited the casual look had done nothing for my sense of style.

We went to a cocktail bar, and I lost my sartorial paranoia at the bottom of a citron martini. It was icy, but the alcohol burned deliciously, amplifying my affection for Michelle.

'Oh, God, I needed this,' I said. 'I am so sick of being the only person in the world who doesn't drink pints of bitter. If I have to drink any more pub wine I'm going to get anti-freeze poisoning.'

'Why, where do you go with your house?'

'The union bar.'

'Still? God, poor you. But you live with that tosser, don't you?'

'Which – oh, Finlay. I didn't know you knew him.'

'Oh, God, I'm not being funny, but I really cannot *stand* that little bastard. He is *always* nicking my fags. Every time I see him, he goes, "Oh, could I just skive a smoke off you?" but he has *never* given me one back. And what *is* he trying to do with that hair? What is that all about?'

It was almost uncanny how Michelle managed to censure almost everyone I had considered sexual relations with.

'He's not so bad when you get to know him.'

'Oh, he is, Grace. Anyway, I shouldn't really say that because you live with him. So you already know what I'm talking about. I'm preaching to the converted.' She laughed attractively, and easily, like a kid. Students usually like to make even their mirth sound sarcastic. They reinforce it with non-committal subtext, just in case it turns out they've been laughing at the wrong thing.

'Oh, this is fun. We should do this more often. Mm, this is good.'

'Yeah, well, hurry up and drink it, and you can have another one.'

I was no wimp when it came to alcohol. I could make it to the other side of a bottle of dry vermouth without sacrificing my diction, and still follow it up with a few fingers of vodka, but with Michelle, I was outclassed, outdrunk and out of my head within a few hours. I was clutching the table to stop myself sliding under it, while somewhere high up and far away I could hear her asking me if I wanted another martini.

'Water, just water. Lots of ice. Lots,' I said.

'Are you sure that's all you want?'

I tried to nod, and it hurt. Michelle went to the bar and was gone long enough for me to fall asleep. She came back and prodded me. 'These lovely and generous men bought our drinks for us,' she said, sitting down gracefully. 'Say thank you.'

'Mine' was a children's nurse, a Liverpudlian. He was lovely, but a real-life man with a job, which made him a bit frightening. He had drawn the short straw – I wonder how men decide who chats up whom – but he was coping gallantly with it, laughing at my jokes, only spending a few seconds out of every ten minutes looking at Michelle's tastefully displayed cleavage. I would have been having a good time if my grip on consciousness hadn't been so tenuous – I just wanted to sleep. Then we were moving; I was vaguely aware that the locations were changing, but couldn't remember getting to them. Michelle noticed my eyes closing and told the men we had to be going home.

'I'm sorry to be such a wimp,' I said. 'I don't know what came over me. I must be getting old.'

'It's fine,' Michelle said. 'That Gavin was a little bit too keen anyway, and I would never be unfaithful to Chris.' Her steady. 'But that nurse seems really nice. Did you give him your number?'

'He didn't ask for it. But he was very nice.' I smiled. 'I don't think I was his type.'

I slept dreamlessly on Michelle's floor and woke early to vomit. It wasn't the good kind of vomiting, that makes you feel detoxed and cleansed and better. It was the bad kind, the endless strand of foamy-saliva kind, the kind that makes you feel you've dragged up your liver and flushed that away too. My head was very sensitive to movement and I sat on the floor, moving it degree by degree to the wall, wishing it was tomorrow and this was all over. I spent an hour or so in the bathroom, trying to gauge the risk of repeated vomiting, getting up and changing my mind, holding my head and wanting to cry; then finally went back in to Michelle, who was awake and smoking her morning fag.

'I'm not being funny, Grace, but you look like death, you really do,' she said. 'Cigarette?'

*

Although I was trying to see more non-house people I started having lunch with Richard every Wednesday. We both had a break between lectures at the same time, and it was nice to have someone to sit in the union refectory with. It was normal for him, because he was a big man on campus, popular and seldom alone, and he needed someone to fill in that hour with him to keep things like that. It was unusual for me, because I got far away from the university whenever I had free time, and I almost never went for lunch in the refectory with other people. I always felt inadequate because of this. That's what students do, they hang out together and eat cheap lunches. It had been a mysterious clique that I thought I'd missed out on, so I liked these Wednesdays. We talked about the house in mature and sensible terms and he ate potatoes with cheese or chilli topping – you know, balanced meals – and I ate McVitie's fruit-filled cake bars and chocolate-fudgy no-bake affairs, and we drank lots of coffee and it was nice.

'What's going on with Mabel and Jonathan? Have they split up?' he said, the first Wednesday after the herpes revelation.

'They fell out when he was over. It was quite a big deal. She's wondering if she still wants to marry him.'

'Cold feet, eh?'

'Well, it's a little more than that. Well, yes, I suppose it is cold feet, really. It's a big decision she's making.'

'It's a stupid decision. But anyway, that's why you're all acting like total bitches, is it?'

'No, that's because we're all having periods. We've synchronized like nuns. You'll just have to get used to that. We intend to be having them for several weeks at a time.'

Richard ate his potatoes in a methodical, neat way that drove me a little crazy on one hand, but was fairly absorbing on the other. He was a Virgo, and they do that sort of thing. I suppose if I'd been in love with him I'd have found it angelic, and if I'd married him and then fallen out of love it would have become grounds for divorce. He ate the last perfectly measured isosceles triangle and asked me if I wanted another cake. I said I did.

While he was gone, Finlay turned up and hovered at the table. 'I don't usually see you in here,' he said. 'Mind you, I don't usually come in at this time. My lecture was cancelled. So how's it going?' An unfamiliar environment, this time a familiar environment made less so because I wasn't usually there, always made Finlay more reserved and well behaved. He didn't sit down. I was wondering if I should invite him to, if he was waiting for me to. Richard came back with a bowl of rice pudding and a Black Forest cake bar.

'Oh, hi, mate,' he said to Finlay.

Finlay looked at us both. He obviously hadn't noticed Richard before and seemed surprised to see us together. He looked lost for words and hostile. I felt like I'd been discovered having an affair. He stood for a while running his hand backwards and forwards through his insubordinate hair, then sat down and started small-talking to us. Richard and I, strangely guilty, were quiet and unresponsive. This just made matters worse.

'Am I disturbing something?' he said, as a joke.

'Yes, actually,' Richard said, also as a joke. 'Wednesdays are our special lunch days. We like to talk about the rest of you without you.'

Finlay said nothing, as if he couldn't work out whether it *was* a joke. It didn't make things any easier. 'Well, I'll leave you both,' he said, still friendly, but with a flicker of doubt somewhere just in front of his retinas.

'Don't be silly. Sit down. Have a pudding,' I said. 'We do this every week. It's not a date, ha ha. Stay.'

'No, I've got to get off anyway. I'm meeting Bob in the bar.' Finlay picked up his stuff and went.

'Do you think we offended him?' Richard said.

'Oh, who cares? You were telling me that you don't think Mabel should get married.'

'He still fancies you,' Richard said lightly.

'What about this what's-her-name he was doing?'

'He doesn't do her any more. He just goes round there. She's quite boring, he says.'

'Well, it's not going to happen with me, is it?'

'I've told him that. I know. You could try being a bit nicer to him, though.'

'I thought he and I'd been getting on very well recently. I'm quite hurt to hear you say that. But, then, if we're not engaging in furtive snogs in the kitchen, Finlay says I'm being a bitch to him.'

'Is that what you used to do?'

'Oh, yes, he had me up against the freezer when the rest of you were asleep.'

'Saucy! Anyway, Mabel, yeah, I don't know what this latest argument's about, but I still think it's all a bad idea. And if they're arguing before the wedding that's got to mean trouble, hasn't it?'

'Who do you fancy now?'

'I don't know why she doesn't leave it till after she's graduated.'

'Everyone says that, but she's so depressed she doesn't think she'd finish her degree anyway. Her tutors have been giving her grief for months, she can't get started on her thesis . . . And all couples fall out before the wedding, it's the most stressful time, obviously.'

'I don't fancy anyone now,' said Richard. He never talked about the time he'd slept with Sara at the party, and neither did she. They were the opposite of me and Finlay, who'd never done anything but were constantly rehashing it for everyone's entertainment. But their relationship was strained now, and they never teased each other the way they once had.

'You need a girlfriend,' I said. 'You're a girlfriend sort of bloke.'

'What does that mean?'

'I don't know. You're nice, that's all.'

'That's what girls tell me. That's *why* I don't have a girlfriend. I hate being nice.'

'Don't knock it. And don't believe the hype. Girls like nice men, it's not an insult. And it's more than that, anyway. You're sort of . . . decent, like James Stewart. I think that's what I mean by nice. That's why I expect you to have a girlfriend.'

'I don't want to be nice, I want to be dangerous and sexy. But you're right, I need to be going out with someone. And so, if you don't mind me saying, do you.'

'I'll be all right after a good seeing-to, is that what you mean?'

'That's right. It's what all you post-feminists want, isn't it? Put you back in line.'

'It sucks, doesn't it? Here we are, surrounded by the cream of our generation, and we can't get laid. Well, we can, but not by the people we want. We're never going to be constantly meeting so many eligible people again, who have too much time on their hands, too much cheap booze to get through, and whose sole purpose is to find someone to sleep with. If I can't find someone now, I never will.'

'Well, if you're desperate, love, you can always come up to my room.'

I picked up Richard's spoon and ate some of his rice pudding, which was now cold and delicious. 'You shouldn't tempt me.'

'Do I?'

'Now, come on.'

'Well, *some*body should.'

'Don't you have a lecture to go to?'

'Yes, I suppose. See you next Wednesday?'

'You'll see me long before then.'

Richard had stood up and now looked flirtatiously over his left shoulder at me. 'Good God, if I'd known it was that easy I'd have asked you long ago.'

'We live together,' I said, unnecessarily, but letting the ambivalence hang there for a few seconds before choosing: 'So you'll see me when you get in. Now be off with you.'

*

Jonathan started calling a few days after he'd gone back home. We handled him as a group, with tactics. First, we took turns to tell him that Mabel was out of the house, but we made it an obvious lie, to taunt him. Then, when he got angry and started to say that he knew damn well that she wasn't we said, gravely, that she was in the house, but she just didn't feel like talking to him. Mabel was under strict instructions not to answer the phone. But one day we were all out of the house and she was in, alone and vulnerable, and she picked it up when it rang.

'He says he's sorry,' she said, when a few of us came home.

'Mabel – Jesus – you didn't call him, did you?' said Mandy, in a loud panic, as if Mabel had broken the first rule of dumping people and some sort of apocalypse would ensue. Actually I envied Mandy's histrionic range of emotion. She was so unself-consciously over the top. It looked like fun, but I didn't have the flair to carry off something like that.

'No, he called,' Mabel said, and I wondered if it was true. 'I had to get it. It could have been someone important for one of you. It could have been someone important for me. And, well, it was someone important for me. I've been silent long enough.'

'Maybe,' Sara said. 'What did he have to say for himself?'

'Well, the good news is, it wasn't herpes. It was something else. I can't remember the name. But it's not herpes, anyway.'

'I don't understand. Didn't he see a doctor before he told you?'

'He did now. He hadn't before. He'd just asked this girl he'd . . . She said it . . . Anyway, it's not herpes.'

'Not herpes, just infidelity and an STD. Come back, Jonathan, all is forgiven,' Sara said.

'All isn't forgiven. But, you know, it's good news, isn't it? Maybe it was just one last fling. A farewell to totty before he treads down the aisle of monogamy for ever.'

'Is that what he said?' I said.

'Kind of.'

'And you believe him?' Mandy said, a little too incredulously.

'Kind of.'

'And what if he spots some more totty sitting with the bride's party as he makes his way up the aisle of monogamy?' Sara said.

'Okay, that's enough,' Mabel said, sounding a little unstable. 'If I want to be depressed I can phone my mother.'

The next day we had a delivery of balloons. They all had 'sorry' written on them. I came in when they'd already arrived, and marvelled at them, huddled together on the ceiling like gigantic flies.

'It looks like he's sorry,' I said to Heather, who was the only person in at the time.

'Sorry my arse. Sorry he can't get any more unconditional sex and adoration from Mabel. Sorry his two-inch dick is hanging off with the pox. But luckily he's got plenty of money, so he can make it all better.'

'I suppose . . .'

'Listen, Grace. You'd better not talk Mabel into marrying that bastard again. You see what your approval already did? You already talked her into a full white wedding with fucking Casanova. She's had a lucky escape. And I don't think you should say anything else to her on the subject. I'm sorry, but she's very vulnerable right now. She needs her friends to support her.'

'Well,' I said. I couldn't think of anything else. I wanted to cry, actually. I felt like I'd just been told off by a teacher.

I went to buy some stress medication from the corner shop: good-quality stuff, Lindt Excellence, none of your Cadbury crap. Adam was in there, buying a massive bottle of Jack Daniel's.

'Looks like it's going to be a good evening,' I said. He turned to look at me and I knew instantly that I'd erred, badly. The circles under his eyes were as stretched and dark as the shadows in a Bogart film. I pretended not to notice.

'Hardly,' he said, and managed a smile. He cradled the bourbon to his chest and pushed the door open with his back. 'Listen, you don't fancy joining me?'

I was going to try out something flip and funny, and then I caught his expression.

'If you're busy, that's fine,' he said, smiling. A tiny muscle under his left eye flinched; it looked like vulnerability.

'Yep,' I said, nodding. 'Sounds good.'

Carlos Gardel's 'Tango' crackling on the record-player, whisky like hot honey scorching and soothing my throat, soft lighting, man, me, and no chance of sex. The perfect romantic scenario. Adam poured himself another drink and held the bottle up to me, raising his eyebrows. I shook my head.

'What's stupid, what's so stupid, is it's all my fault,' he said.

'It's pointless blaming yourself.'

'No, it totally is. I started the argument, and it wasn't easy to start. He's so easy-going, so *reasonable*. But I stuck at it.' Sigh. Swallow. The clink of ice. 'And I said there was no point carrying on the way we were. So it *is* all my fault.'

'I suppose you've already apologized. Of course you have, sorry.'

'Of course not. It's my fault. The luxury of apology is only available to the person who behaved well. That's the rule. You apologize to make someone feel guilty. I haven't got the right to apologize.'

'Oh, come on, how does that work?'

'You must be new to this.'

'Do you want him back? Oh, sorry, that's such a stupid thing to say.'

'It's not. It's a good question. If everything was fine I wouldn't have started the argument. I wasn't happy.' He exhaled quickly through his nose and lowered his voice, so he was almost talking to himself. 'Whereas now I'm ecstatic.'

There was a long pause, and I wondered what I should be saying. I wasn't Sara, I wasn't good at this. 'Do you want me to go?' He shook his head. 'Say when you do. I can't be offended. I'm pachydermal.'

'Is that a word now?'

'I think so.'

'Well, I'm jealous, then. It sounds like a good thing to be.' He drank again, and scrunged like Victor Mature. 'Am I a boring, self-pitying bastard? Say if I am. I won't be offended.' I opened my mouth to deny it. 'This can't be much fun. Trapped in the house of the strange old man next door while he talks about his failures.'

'You're being silly, now. If you want to know the truth, I'm sort of morbidly almost happyish to be here. Not, obviously, happyish, considering what . . . I mean I'm flattered you feel you can talk like this, even if it had more to do with the fact that I was in the shop when you planned this . . . And what's really sick is that I'm even a bit jealous.'

'Of?'

'I don't think I'm ever going to feel like this. I've never been in love, I've never had my heart broken and I can't see it happening. I've met almost every type there is now, and none of them has ever come close to making me cry, or even making me angry, not really, and I don't think you can ever be really happy until you've got at least the possibility of being really sad, being really affected by someone.'

'Is that what you really think? You watch too many movies,' Adam said. 'Sorry.'

'It's true, though, isn't it? And you're just playing the hardened cynic because at the moment you're emotional and it worries you. Sorry.'

'We really should stop this politeness. Shall we just take it as read from now on that we're not trying to offend each other?' I lifted my glass to acknowledge this. 'Yeah, let's make it a toast,' he went on. 'To the end of politeness and the beginning of a beautiful friendship.' We clinked.

Wednesday

I write good letters. It's a talent, but as talents go, it won't take you very far. That's how it began, though, with a good letter. He put an ad in the *Guardian*, looking for researchers for his new programme, and I wrote to him. From here, what I wrote looks hopelessly naïve, with jokes about Quaglino's and parodies of pretentiousness that were more pretentious than the real thing. It did. His secretary called to say he wanted to have lunch with me. I was pleasantly surprised, but not drop-dead surprised. Not even surprised, really. It was more like unexpected confirmation of something I'd believed tentatively but consistently. And lots of people are impressed by my letters. I'm good over short distances.

So we met. I knew his face from a couple of late-night television appearances, the sort that nobody but the unemployed and the terribly serious watch, and from photographs at the top of his articles. I hadn't considered him somebody I'd fancy, until we met. It wasn't that he was so different from my expectations, but the final dimension mattered; it gave him depth. I was profoundly nervous. I'd bought a really pretty new dress, but I'd also had a really bad haircut, and I wasn't sure if one cancelled the other out. It had been the stickiest, sweatiest week of the year, and I was praying for cloud. Unbelievably, that day was cooler, and overcast for the first time in two merciless weeks. My dress was perfect, a gasp of white that moved just a moment after I did, like an echo. And when he first looked up to see me, a light breeze announced itself through the window behind me, and teased the folds of my skirt. I couldn't have wished for a better effect.

He asked where I wanted to eat, just to cosy things along with a reference to my Quag's joke, but it almost defeated me because I hadn't really been anywhere in London and I wasn't half as hip as I'd made out. And, I suspected, he wanted to use my answer to supplement what he knew about me.

'I don't know. Anywhere.'

'Ah, come on, that's no fun. Where have you been dying to go and haven't yet?'

'There's nowhere I can think of,' I said.

'Nowhere at all?' he said, wheedling, mock-boyishly.

'This isn't fair. Just anywhere. I'm not going to pick.'

'Hmm, passive-aggressive, eh?' he said. The humour that lit his eyes was like the suggestion of a wink, and I felt fine. So that's how it's going to be, I thought. Less of a working lunch, more of a date. This I can cope with. He mentioned a place I'd never heard of and I shrugged acceptance without admitting ignorance, then he got his secretary to book the table while he swept around his office with bits of paper, and slapped buttons on different computers.

We took a cab, and I braced myself for awkwardness. There was none. It happened that we had a little shared history. A short time before I applied for his research job, I'd worked in the library of the newspaper for which he used to write the restaurant column. I was made redundant when they computerized it all, which was devastating because I'd loved my life there, clipping clippings and doing research on every subject in the world. I even left the place with a passable general knowledge. Remnants of it endure, but the world has moved on and I've slipped back into hostile unconsciousness. Although we worked for the paper at different times, he knew the librarian and I knew a lot of the journalists who came in regularly, and he gossiped about the people we had in common. Right from the beginning, it just wasn't hard work, it was – which cliché is best? – it was as if I'd known him for ever. The taxi bucked over the roadworks on Oxford Street and we were thrown closer, and he noticed I had a smudge of mascara on my face, and I felt gawkish again and jabbed clumsily at my cheek with my thumb. He said, 'Here, let me,' and touched my face very gently, so that the side of his hand brushed against my lips.

'You'll have lipstick on your hand,' I said.

'It doesn't matter,' he said. It was such an intimate, ordinary little gesture, but I suddenly couldn't breathe properly because I'd just fallen in love.

I was reading the menu and he asked me what I wanted, and I told him the artichoke salad, and the red snapper and he nodded, as if it were important and he approved. 'Good choice. What if you couldn't have either of those?' he said.

'Can't I?'

'Yes, but just pretend you couldn't. Choose something else,' he said. So I did, frowning, not understanding where he was going with this. The waitress came and I went with my original order and when she turned to him he asked for my second choices.

'Good grief, you must be very indecisive,' I said.

'I eat here a lot. I just thought I'd give you room to make a mistake.'

'Well, that seems almost too kind.'

'Do you think so? It's just one lunch. Have an olive.'

'I'm not mature enough to like olives,' I said.

'Well, they are an acquired taste, but I think you'll be able to handle them,' he said, pushing them with some enjoyment. 'These are good ones.'

I ate the olive as lasciviously as I could, and delivered my verdict. 'It just tastes like olive oil,' I said.

'What a surprise,' he said, and our eyes met.

If there was one thing I got from my year with Finlay, it was flirting. Ably. Through him, I unearthed the Lolita beneath the comprehensive-school swot. He let me think that nobody would laugh at me. Like riding a bike without stabilizers for the first time, flirting's something you have to believe you can do before you can do it, and suddenly I did, so I could. It seemed useful and I kept doing it. That's the point, though, it's something *I* do. I've been chatted up, propositioned, nudged and winked at, had it tried on, had it pulled off; the full gamut of sexual euphemism, but it all required sustained and considerable effort on my part; whenever I didn't make the first move I substantially facilitated the move-making. I thought that was how things were meant to go, I never looked for problems. And it *was* only one lunch, but it changed everything. Now, like a reformed smoker, I've become sanctimonious about the addiction I once depended on. I tend to think that there's something rather empty about flirting. It's an unnecessary advertisement for your sense of humour and sex appeal. It's exhibitionism. To be able to flirt you have to establish mutual tolerance, to redefine the thresholds of sensitivity, which implies a smug predetermination to events. It's all a bit vulgar.

That day, I forgot to do it. We just talked, and everything I said sounded like a thought, unadulterated. I realized that I didn't like artichokes as much as I'd remembered and he noticed and made me swap, and the manoeuvre hardly even rippled the conversation. We talked, and it was all so plain and grown-up that it would have felt . . . shocking if it hadn't been so easy, if the enticing lilt of his voice hadn't seemed so familiar. We argued and agreed about Orson Welles and Yves St Laurent and dieting and even politics, at which point I thought, My God, I've become Sara, and isn't it marvellous? We talked, and it was like girl-talk with a dash of Angostura bitters. He asked me where the dress was from and somehow that segued into lingerie. And I said it was impossible to buy lingerie in my size – which is just inside or outside the average in most directions – except at Rigby and Peller, and he said that Rigby and Peller was for the Queen Mother and maiden aunts, and I said, So what's the alternative, and he said, Fenwicks is one, and I said they just sold Rigby and Peller bras anyway and he said, Well, there's Agent Provocateur, and I said I'd read about it – it had only just opened – but I'd never been, and he said, We'll have to go. We talked, and it was light and natural. Seamily mundane. Perfect.

We were discussing work, and he asked me what I really wanted, what my greatest ambition was, and I said I didn't have any. I just wanted to get married and get knocked up.

'I want to have babies,' I said, 'because it opens up so many new shopping possibilities.'

'So let's do that,' he said. 'It's a fine idea. Imagine how clever our kids would be.'

'Oh, do stop,' I said.

'I mean it,' he said, with the excitement of someone who has just hit upon the only solution to everything, and the brightness of a washing-powder ad. 'Let's get married. Let's rule London. You and me. Doesn't that sound like a good idea? Wouldn't it be cool – can you imagine?' His eyes caught the flame of his cigarette lighter, and in that flash was danger and fun and the future. I blushed and smiled and bit my bottom lip and he changed the subject breezily and effortlessly, and the ghost of a coquette that had almost rematerialized vanished into the spiral of his cigarette smoke.

Over frozen chocolate petits fours in the now empty restaurant the alcohol was starting to sink in. I still felt fabulously relaxed; we deadpanned without fuss, without looking for acknowledgement, but we'd been having lunch for almost four hours, and it was time to go home.

'So when can I see you again?' he said. 'Are you free tonight? How about dinner?'

'That'd be nice,' I said.

We lingered outside, me feeling soft and swoony, while he looked for a cab. Suddenly he stopped, and swivelled in the street. 'Hang on, we were going to buy you a proper bra, weren't we?'

'We were?'

'Agent Provocateur. It's just round the corner. Unless you have to go home now. It is quite late, and . . .'

'Well, I would like to see it but . . .'

'Well . . .' He mocked my indecisiveness.

'Oh, what the hey.'

'Okay, good for you.'

We walked there. I was walking. Alcohol's a painkiller, and his stride was so long that I had to skip every so often to keep up, so the irregularity was camouflaged, but he must have seen, I couldn't pretend that well. Which could mean only one thing: it didn't matter. I felt slightly afraid of that thought, as if it was massively important. There was something smooth and kinetic about him, and it was infectious. We looked at bras and, my goodness, at knickers, which seemed, later, a scandalous idea, but at the time it was shopping. He didn't lurk near the changing room when I tried something on, or suggest suggestively. And I chose, and I insisted on paying, and he reasoned with me, persuaded me, and it all seemed perfectly fine and he paid.

'Does this mean I have to sleep with you now?' I whispered drunkenly into his ear, suddenly amused by the situation; a near stranger buying me silk lingerie. It *was* funny, and surreal and very probably postmodern.

'I certainly hope so,' he said.

When I got home I called my mother. 'He's smashing,' I said. 'We really hit it off.'

'You got the job?'

I stretched my toes out and threw my head back, girlish for the first time in years. 'No, but he really likes me, and he's fabulous.'

'What? You're kidding. You didn't get the job?'

'The job doesn't matter, Mum. I'm going to be his girlfriend.'

'What are you talking about? Are you mad? Are you drunk?' my mother said.

'I'm not mad. Yes, I'm drunk. It was such a nice lunch. He bought me underwear.'

'At lunch? *What* did you say?'

'Don't worry, it was all very decent, it was very tastefully done.

We were just discussing it, and then we bought it. He bought it. It was actually the correct thing to do, as he'd recommended the shop.'

'I can't believe what –'

'Mum, it was just fine. Don't worry.'

'I'm not worried,' she said. 'But I think you're mad.'

Later, I arrived early and sat at the bar. He swept in, also early, but less, and apologized. 'Oh, you poor thing, sitting by yourself. Have you been here long?'

'Seconds,' I lied.

'I didn't think I was going to be late.' He pulled his sleeve up to reveal a tacky green plastic watch.

'That's your watch?'

'I think it is, yes.'

'But it's so . . . horrible. You have a proper job. You write about style for a living. What on earth are you doing with such an ugly watch?'

He laughed loudly. 'Don't you get it?' he said. 'That stuff doesn't matter.'

'Of course it *matters.* I mean, if it didn't, what would be the point of anything? Well, what the hell does matter, then?'

He leaned over and kissed me gently. He didn't smile when he drew back to look at me; I hate it when men kiss you and then smile.

'I was telling my mother about the underwear and she thinks . . .'

'You told your mother?' he said, laughing again. 'Really? How did *that* conversation go?'

'Of course I told her.'

'I want to know what you said. I'll be your mother. The phone's ringing. Hi, Mum. Hi, honey, how was your day? And then what?'

I squeezed his fingers to put a stop to the impression of my mother. 'I just told her it was fine, and she said if it was fine that was fine but I should pay for dinner.'

'There's no need.'

'Well, at the time . . . but now in the cold light of . . . I feel a little awkward about the whole . . .'

'Don't worry about it. It's not important. Do you always tell your mother when a man buys you lingerie?'

'Do you always buy girls lingerie when you're interviewing them for a job?'

'It wasn't an interview. I told you I couldn't give you the job. You don't have the right sort of experience. And you lied about the experience you *did* put down.'

'Yes, but I told you I lied, so that doesn't count as a lie. I get points for being honest when it was important. Well, I don't get it, then? Why did you see me?'

'I thought you needed to see *some*one. And it was a good letter.'

1992

8

By and large, I had never been very proud of my opinions. Opinions aren't like hairstyles or shoes: you can't check them in private first, in the mirror; you can't get any helpful feedback about them without first exposing them to other people and by then it may be too late to go back. Unlike hairstyles and shoes, it's hard to outgrow your opinions convincingly, harder still to explain that they've outgrown their own usefulness. People expect you to keep them for life. I knew I was cool, but I didn't know if the people I knew dealt in the same currency of cool, I didn't want to lose friends by having the wrong ideas. By and large, then, I didn't admit to having opinions at all, and remained neutral about everything of any consequence. But I still had the basic human urge to argue, and I liked to win. So I didn't get into quarrels that involved opinions, only facts, and I never lost these. It was a matter of common sense; I chose my scraps wisely and didn't dabble where it wasn't my place, but the success normally drew two responses. The first, 'You always think you're right', was fair comment. But as I explained, I don't argue when I'm not right; there are easier roads to a good time than contradiction. The second response got my goat. Backing down, my opponents would mutter: 'Well, of course you know how to argue, they train you to argue.' A reference to law, the big cheese, my course. It had undergone a surge of popularity when I was applying to colleges, which is one of the reasons I took it. It was the *plat du jour*, it had kudos. Law. It tripped off the tongue with insouciance and brevity. You could utter the syllable at Freshers' Week and stand back to admire.

The things we do for appearances. It's also the most pointless course in the world if you don't intend to be a lawyer. Two years after graduating, twenty per cent of what you knew has been overruled or new statutes have hustled it into retirement. The rest you just forget, fortunately. It's not important now, of course, like my degree; the point I wanted to clear up is that they don't teach you how to argue. Why would they? And how could they? What – after talking for an hour about Land Covenants, is the lecturer supposed to show *Perry Mason* videos and make us all repeat after the fat bloke, 'Objection!'? Honestly. No, I won my own arguments, and I never understood law.

So from time to time I had to work. A horrible thing to admit to myself; I always saw the need to study as a reflection of inadequacy. In school situations I'd never felt obliged to open my books outside grey walls or office hours. Here, my inability to ignore the texts and still shine was a source of concern, topsy-turvying my self-satisfied world. It was important to me not to make an effort for Jim McFadyean's tutorials, because I didn't want him to think I was trying for him, which is a pretty stupid reason to fail your degree, but it had been a pretty stupid reason that led me to the degree in the first place. Elsewhere, though, I didn't enjoy the long line of D minuses my essays attracted, and occasionally, just occasionally, I craved acknowledgement. It wasn't my inability to follow the lectures that bothered me because I've never been a quick thinker, always been slow to catch on. This may surprise you – the admission, not the fact – but I do know my limits, and I don't think it's necessarily an indication of stupidity. I always understood eventually, and properly. I think my mind just used to wander, and information had to form a queue before I could process it. This sounds very much like the desperate self-deception of a weak mind, but come on, it's not as if I was thick. Still, I could see this law thing was taking a different turn, and I couldn't see it improving. I was the class dunce, and living with some of the world's most diligent students didn't help. Apart from Mabel, who was a complete fuck-up, obviously, but that didn't matter anyway because she'd found a way out, a pass to the world of marriage and domesticity and having a husband, where things like degrees aren't important. Living with people who spend half their time in the library and the other half at lectures and the other half writing dissertations can make you feel scared. And competitive. So I was writing my first essay of the year, although I wasn't concentrating because I felt a little lonely that day, and wrote on my knee in the living room with some of the others there. Heather and Finlay and Mandy had all gone out to see a film together. I was going to go with them, but I felt too mean to give them all lifts that day. I stayed in, like the dog in a manger I was, and listened to *Songs of Praise* and the other people in the house talking about whatever.

The doorbell rang and we looked at each other for a few seconds, the way you do when you don't want to get up. You size up each other's willpower. You think to yourself, Well, I know that no one *I* know would be coming round here on a Sunday and I'm fucked if I'm going to answer it. The most popular person will have to get it, although they don't want to, because they want to be told their friends are here for them, but they do anyway. Usually, this would be Heather, followed by Mandy, followed by Finlay, but with all three of them out of the house we had a hitherto unexplored hierarchy to work out and put into practice. I knew I wasn't at the top and enjoyed watching Richard finally do the decent thing.

'Oh, I'll get it, dammit!' he said, mock-angrily, and went into the hall. Then it all happened very quickly. We heard some men shouting in very deep voices and Richard shouted back in his deep voice and then he was being pushed into the living room by three men in balaclavas who were holding baseball bats. One of them hit Richard in the stomach with his bat, then on the legs, and the rest of us screamed. Richard fell over. The man who'd hit him stood over him and started yelling. I couldn't make out what he was saying for a moment because I was so shocked and terrified and he had a thick Manchester accent and a mouthful of acrylic.

'Shut the fuck up all of you. Nobody fucking move and you won't get fucking hurt.' He hit Richard again, this time across his head, and I screamed really loudly, afraid that he'd been killed. The man who hit him stepped over and started shouting at me, telling me to shut up or he'd hurt me, and I cowered and folded myself up and didn't make another sound. Richard was bleeding; his forehead was a red smeary mess, but he was conscious. Mabel, who was close to him, touched his face with her hand to see if he was okay, and the man shouted at her to sit down. We sat. Then two of them stayed with us, swinging their bats in the air, while the third stamped his way upstairs. The two shouted suggestions to their accomplice, as if he were in *The Crystal Maze*, and he shouted back from various locations in the house: 'It's all fucking shit, there's fuck all here.' He came back into the living room with a duvet cover from Mandy's room, put the (hired) video and television in it, then Richard's stereo stuff – his room was on the ground floor – and Mabel's ghetto-blaster and my portable television.

'Call yourselves fucking students?' shouted one of the men. 'You've got a load of fucking shite here. There's nothing worth fucking taking.' And then they ran out, hurling the front door open so it cracked back on its hinges and slammed shut, making us all squeak with genteel fright. The few seconds of silence before we spoke again seemed to last longer than the robbery.

Then the girls shrieked in unison and ran to Richard, while I rang the police, my hands shaking so much that I pressed all the other buttons too. The ice-cream voice at the other end made me want to be more hysterical but simultaneously made me feel I was overreacting on an epic scale. I panted details, which she took down. When that was over and she tried to terminate the call I didn't want to hang up. I wanted more, but she thanked me and cut me off.

'Oh, Christ, what if they come back?' Sara said.

'They're not going to come back. We've got nothing to fucking steal,' said Richard, and he almost impersonated them and we almost laughed. 'I can't fucking . . . Christ my fucking head . . .' He lolled forward disturbingly.

'Richard?' I shouted. 'Oh, my God, are you okay? We should get you to a hospital. You could be – I'll drive you – I'll call an ambulance.'

'Don't. I'm fine,' he said again. 'It just hurts a bit, that's all.'

'Of course it does, I'm sorry, I'm just so – so fucking scared. He hit you so hard I thought he was going to kill you.'

Heather, Mandy and Finlay wanted very much to talk about the film. Their entrance was timed to coincide with the cleverest part of a discussion on the symbolism of headwear in the cinematographer's vision. Even in my unstable condition I had time to think to myself: That's not the first time they've said all that today. We could hear them before they had even opened the door, and we waited for them with collective anger.

'What the fuck?' Mandy said, when she saw Richard's streaked face and the bloodstained tea towel Mabel was dabbing it with.

'What's happened, mate?' Finlay said. All together, we told them. 'God, they could have raped you,' Heather said.

'We really don't need to hear that,' Sara said. 'They didn't do anything. They didn't even take that much.'

Finlay suddenly ran upstairs to check his stuff. I called my parents, who panicked as much as you'd expect, but I managed to talk them out of hurtling across the Pennines that very second. None of the others called their parents. Heather made tea for us all and brought it in. I didn't drink tea, except for the occasional cup over at Adam's, and certainly never with milk, but there was something miraculous about this, soothing, although I found myself spilling a lot because my hands were still shaking so much. We told the story about a hundred times, and then the police came and we told it again. I couldn't remember a thing about any of the men. One of the policemen was young and attractive, and he smiled at me and told me it was very rare for this sort of thing to happen, and they certainly wouldn't come back. They took a look at Richard's head and said it was just a cut, and he'd been lucky that the men obviously hadn't wanted to hurt him, which must have pissed him off in a very big way. They hinted that, with our descriptions being so pathetic ('they had Manchester accents'), they'd do their best, but there wasn't much to go on.

'Did you have any parties recently, any local lads come round to a party at your house?' the good-looking policeman said, and I froze in horror. I wondered if anyone else was thinking what I was thinking. I wondered if the guilt showed up on my face. I started shaking again.

When the police had gone, I asked, 'Do you think it was the people who left the drugs coming back to get revenge?'

'Don't be stupid,' Finlay said. 'They don't know where they left them. It was just some Mancs.'

'Oh, Jesus, do you think it was?' Sara said. 'What if they know all about us, and they know we sold it?' We argued about this for ages, Mandy and the boys saying I was being immature and paranoid and silly and the rest of the girls agreeing and saying we had got ourselves caught up in the Moss Side drugs war, all for thirty quid and a bit of blow. By the end, I think I'd convinced them but, fortunately, they'd convinced me the other way, so that was all right. Finlay was in a perpetual state of excitement all night. He didn't stop talking, and those of us who'd been there were still shocked and subdued and he just sounded more and more irritating, like a little yappy dog. He seemed to be extracting some sort of benefit from our ordeal, especially as nothing of his had been taken. He was trying his best to be sympathetic and to act properly, but he was certainly more than usually animated, charged with secondary adrenaline. I was too tired to speak, and talking gibberish, but I was too scared to go to bed, to take a shower, in case someone burst in like Norman Bates and murdered me, my old shower-phobia never having been more rational. It was getting late, and the atmosphere, I realized, was not just strange because we'd been burgled, but because we had no television, no background noise. The silences punctuated our conversations with a menacing prominence.

I finally went to bed when everyone else did, and I took a shower because I can't sleep without one, but I didn't sleep. I felt small and vulnerable and I worried about Richard getting a brain haemorrhage years later like Stuart Sutcliffe in the Beatles, or did he die of something else? I spent the night trying to read, and not being able to, and thinking I heard noises downstairs, and looking out of the windows for intruders in the backyard.

We weren't the only people we knew to have been burgled, nor the only people who'd been in when it happened. Indeed, most people took it very well, turning the experience into an entertaining story. One house we knew had made toast and coffee for their thief, each person thinking he was one of their housemate's boyfriends or one-night stands. When he left, they realized he'd taken their CD players. And people had been mugged at checkouts, threatened with knives, gay-bashed, whatever. There was a lot of crime against students, it was a new, well-documented phenomenon. When I read about it, not feeling like a student, I couldn't have cared less, and always felt they deserved it for discussing Nietzsche loudly at cashpoint machines, and singing Simon and Garfunkel songs on the top decks of buses. Now I just felt sorry for myself. Most students don't know what's going on. We never stop believing this is like school with all the parents out at a party, and all the teachers not giving a shit. We're aware there's an absence of the parachute of adult intervention, but we don't quite believe it. We think it'll flap into shape just in time and save us when things get really hairy. We drink frantically, expecting our mothers to come in and snatch away the vodka; we ignore essay deadlines, believing that the tutors will let us know when we're cutting things really fine; we spend all our money because we know it only has to last the year, and we can always get some more when real life begins. We know we can always get a bank job before we have to resort to doing one. For the first time, real life had intersected,

Venn-like, with our happily trivial circle. I listened to the wind roughing up the trees outside, and my windows felt flimsy.

By the end of the week it was just another story. I found myself telling it to people who'd heard it before from other people, and those who'd heard it before from when I first told them. Time to give it a rest. Richard, I must say, did very well out of it. There's something markedly pleasing about a man with the scars of combat still visible on his face. The baseball bat had left a deepish cut, and it broke up the squarely handsome blandness that made Richard so cleanly out of bounds for some of us. Coupled with the heroic tale, he found himself inundated with offers the next time we all went out. It didn't matter that four of us had been trounced by three, because most of us were girls, they had been armed, and they had had the advantage of surprise. Of course, it could have been that these new Richard groupies had always fancied him from a distance, and now they had the ideal topic with which to break the ice. They could admire his bravery, shudder with fear at the scary parts of the tale, and then cosset him with sexy, maternal concern.

This party was at Daniel's house. He was the boyfriend Heather had been so excited about only a few months ago, but now she seldom talked about him, and phoned him less. She planned to end things at this party. I asked her what had changed about him, why the passion had died so quickly when everything had been going so well. She said that things hadn't been that great, what was I talking about, and that he was a really nice guy and everything, but he voted Tory. I spotted them, deep in conversation in a deep sofa. He looked miserable as hell and she looked stunning. It's always good to call things off when you're looking great. It helps make them miss you. I was looking around the party in the mercenary, teeny-slut way I did back then, seeing if there was anyone interested in possibly necking with me at any time in the evening, but it all seemed so pointless, for once. I decided I'd rather just have a laugh with Mabel, who had come out with us all, for a change. She had completely forgiven Jonathan, although we had forced her not to tell him. So the wedding was officially still off, but it was only a matter of time before it was really all on again. A slim, floppy-looking blond boy with bee-stung lips came and knelt in front of us. There was something foppish and delicious about him. Mabel, for her part, was playing with her ankle bracelet, looking coy. What the hell was happening?

'What's up, Toby?' Mabel said.

'You look amazing tonight,' he almost whispered, letting his salaciously puffy lips remain parted for a few seconds. I wanted to chew them. But he was looking at Mabel.

'Grace, Toby. He's in my tutorials. Toby, this is Grace. We live together.'

'Hi, Toby.'

'Listen, this is really rude of me, but I have to show you this book I found yesterday in the second-hand book sale. It's upstairs,' Toby said to Mabel. Oh, right, then if he has any time he'll go on to his etchings, I thought. His pretty face was draped decoratively with lust.

'You live here? This is your house?' Mabel said.

'Yeah, I thought you knew that,' Toby said, blinking.

'So you know Daniel, then?' I said.

'Well, we have met a few times in the hallway.' Toby smirked. And he took Mabel upstairs with him to see his incredible book. I was a little lost for a moment. The decision had been made for me: I'd have to circulate and see who I could pick up. With exemplary efficiency, I homed in on a moody-looking youth wearing hip checked trousers, and asked him if he could help me get the cork out of my bottle. It was sticking, I explained. Naturally, I could have extracted it with any part of my anatomy and very little fuss, but you have to give these boys a chance to feel tough. Unfortunately he wasn't very tough at all.

'I'll get a knife,' he said, and we went into the kitchen. Finlay was there, alone, smoking. He looked quite good. My new friend exerted himself for a few minutes, growing redder and redder and making panting sounds. He had started hacking at the cork with a knife, and dusty pieces were flying about. Finlay and I watched each other coolly. Finally I grew impatient.

'Let me have another go,' I said sweetly. I eased out the cork. There was a long silence, heavy with anticipation, and an understated plunk. Mr Hip Trousers got a couple of paper cups, and I filled them for both of us. Finlay still wasn't saying anything. I pretended not to know him.

'Who do you know, here?' my bloke said. It's the standard question at parties. You establish which people you have in common. There are always a few.

'I know Daniel. He goes out with a girl I live with,' I said, sounding very boring. It's impossible to chat someone up when you're being watched, particularly by someone who's keeping score. The boy sat down at the kitchen table. I stayed standing, wanting to go somewhere else. 'Well, thanks for your help,' I said cheerfully. 'I'm going to go and, er, find someone now.'

'No, don't go,' the boy said. 'I don't even know your name yet.' I looked at Finlay, who was sneering.

'It's Grace,' I said, and turned to go.

'Grace, come back.' Finlay said this, probably to demonstrate to my new companion that he had more influence over me.

I swivelled on a heel. 'Mmmm?'

'I haven't talked to you in ages. Sit down.' He was far drunker than I'd ever seen him, which was saying something. What I'd taken to be a bemused, detached silence had been a hazy state of semi-consciousness. 'Who's he, anyway?'

'This is . . .' Fuck knew.

'I'm Graham,' the boy said.

'Graham,' slurred Finlay, over a long, bendy syllable. 'Hello, Graham. I'm Finlay.'

'How much have you drunk tonight?' I asked him.

'I don't fucking know. I couldn't give a fucking shit.' There was the old implied danger in his intoxication, and his words, still slurred, were sharpening at the ends, like the crack of a whip. I still hadn't sat down.

'I'm sharing this bottle with Mabel,' I said. 'I'm going to find her now.' I started to go. Graham stayed where he was. I wondered what they were going to find to talk about.

Mabel was nowhere to be seen. Was she with Toby? Heather was still deep in conversation with Daniel. I smiled at them both, but it looked pretty heavy and I didn't interrupt. Richard was talking to an almost beautiful girl with dirty blonde plaits. I couldn't find Mandy or Sara, and I wondered if they'd left. I thought I might just get a mini-cab and go home early. I wasn't in the mood for a party. If I went now I could still catch the repeat of *The Word*. I called our favourite company, Jetson Taxis. They were a nice firm, and once or twice, when I didn't go a long way, the driver didn't even charge me, as long as I talked to him all the way and sat in the front. They had one horrible driver, whom I'd had twice, but never alone. He drove me and Alice into town once, when she stayed, and asked us if we were lesbians, and whether we preferred it in the front seat or the back seat, if we knew what he meant. We knew. I didn't find it very frightening, but Alice was jumpy about that sort of thing, and I'd been trying to convince her what a safe place Manchester was and the cabbie from hell hadn't helped any. But I still trusted the firm, who were generally sleaze-free, and I booked a car and waited for it outside. I wanted to feel the air, and to hear the click of my heels echo in a quiet street. The party throbbed behind me, and I tried out a couple of tap-dancing steps I'd learned when I was about five.

'Are you going?'

I turned round to see Finlay, who was standing at the door leaning against the threshold. I didn't know how long he'd been there. 'Yep.'

'Can I share your cab?'

'I suppose so.'

'Well, don't do me any favours. I wouldn't like to *impose* on you.'

'I just wanted to be . . . Sure, okay.' I said it ungraciously.

We stood in silence. I started tapping again a little, finding the sound comforting. He looked as if he was ready to fall over. The cab came and he eased himself into the back, rolling into the seat like a wino. I took the front.

'Your friend is very drunk,' said the taxi driver.

'Isn't he?'

'Do you think he'll be all right?'

I realized he didn't want Finlay to vomit in his cab. 'I think so. I think he's just tired,' I said, and I changed the subject to make the driver happier. We talked about the jazzy radio station he was tuned in to, and about how he drove at night because he was at the poly all day, he was a student, from Cameroon. And when he dropped us at the door, I gave him a big tip and a wide smile.

Part of me was glad Finlay was here, now. I couldn't be sure Mandy and Sara had come home, and I was always terribly apprehensive about going into the house alone, after our break-in. I got home in the evenings later and later, so I'd be sure there'd be someone else there, and I spent all day out of the house. I unlocked the door, but I let him go in first.

'Are you scared?' he said.

'Scared of what?'

'Of finding someone in the house.'

'Oh. Sometimes. A little. No, I'm fine now.'

I followed him in. He turned on our new rented television. The rental people had been very nice and understanding and quick to send a replacement but the new television was an ancient seventies teak-effect affair, with a big knob to tune in, rather than separate buttons. It probably had valves in the back. *The Word* was still on. Yippee. But I didn't much want to talk to Finlay when he was this pissed.

'Don't go to bed yet,' he said. 'I want to talk to you.'

'I'm tired.'

'Who was that loser you were with?'

'I don't know him. Graham, he said his name was.'

'I can't believe you'd rather snog someone like that . . .' he said, peevishly, then tailed off. I went to the kitchen to get myself a Coke.

'Do you want a Coke?' I said. He said he did, and I brought it, conscious of the fact that I was serving him. We post-feminists love playing at Doris Day because we don't think there's the slightest chance we'll ever have to do it for real. I wonder if we're right. 'Are Mandy and Sara back, do you think?'

'I can't see their coats or anything. I think we're alone.' The wind blew, and the house shivered. I was very sober now, the way I always got at the end of parties. I seemed to reach a soberer state just after alcohol wore off than I had been in before I'd drunk it. My voice grew low and husky and I sounded very grown-up.

'Richard seemed to be doing very well.' I smiled.

'You really fancy him, don't you?'

'I fancy Richard? Are you mad? Of course I don't.'

'You sounded jealous then.'

I couldn't rule this out. I always wondered why Richard never seemed attracted to me. He'd had flings with Sara and Mandy, and flirted with Mabel, and teased Heather a lot, sexually, in a rumbustious, playful fashion, but he never once made a pass at me, even before we lived together. We had our Wednesday lunch dates, but they were very much platonic. No games were played.

'I don't fancy Richard.' And yet, after we'd been robbed together, I found myself as seduced by the cut on his face as the little blonde-plaited chick had evidently been tonight. I had felt a stirring of envy as Mabel had cradled his head when she ever so gently cleaned his cut. But I didn't fancy him. Not much. Not enough. 'He's a sexy bloke, though.'

'Well, I wouldn't bother if I were you. You're not his type.' He could be cruel, as well as pathetic.

'Goodnight, then.'

'Wait a minute.'

'What?' Impatient.

'Sit down.' A tentative request.

I thought about it, nearly sat, thought better of it. 'No. I'm tired.' I picked up my keys, purse, coat, and started climbing the stairs. A huge crash outside the back door made me scream and freeze.

'What was that?' Finlay said, coming into the hall.

'I don't know,' I said. 'Oh, my God.' Finlay went into the kitchen and turned the light on. 'Don't go in there, for Christ's sake.'

Emboldened by the dazzling strobe of the fluorescent bar, he started looking out of the kitchen window. 'It's the bin,' he said. 'I think the wind just knocked it over. There's no one there.' He opened the back door. 'It's just the bin,' he said. I couldn't tell whether he was very brave or very pissed. I didn't know what to do for a moment. The excitement had ruined my exit. I stood there, still hiding behind the kitchen door a little.

'Well, that was scary,' I said, trying to sound tough and sarcastic, and failing.

He locked the back door again and looked at me. 'Why do you do this?' he said.

'What?'

'Sometimes I manage to convince myself that you're this complete bitch and then you go all . . .'

'What?'

'This vulnerable thing you do. It's very . . . attractive.'

'Well, that's the effect I'm going for. I'm ever so glad it works. Lip-gloss and being fucking afraid. I think I read about it in Germaine Greer's *How to Pull Men*.'

'It must have been pretty horrible for you, when those Mancs broke in.'

'Well, it was.'

'I wish I'd been there.'

'No, you don't. Why? So you could have been beaten up like Richard?'

'I wouldn't have let them –'

'Finlay, they had baseball bats. They were scary big men. There was nothing Richard could do. We weren't going to help him fight them.'

'I wouldn't have let them hurt you.'

'How macho. They didn't hurt me, they hurt Richard. Are you missing a page?'

'Don't fucking laugh at me,' he slurred. He rubbed his face, pulling it into strange rubbery shapes, the way you can when you're pissed because you can't feel. 'What I'm saying . . . What I'm trying to say is . . .'

'Just don't,' I said. I didn't want to hear some pissed romantic bravado, some importunate manly bluster. I'd never been interested in his strength, but enjoyed his weakness, the ease with which I could manipulate him, affect him. I didn't want him to spoil it by saying something I would have wanted to hear from someone I really wanted. He leaned forward, as if to tell me a secret. The expression on his face was ghoulish and painful-looking.

'It was when Greg was coming round a lot, then that night you went home, that was when I first really noticed it.' He stopped. I waited. 'You were really . . . I just found it really sexy. I was completely turned on by it,' he said.

For a moment I was stunned. 'I'm thrilled that my anxiety has this side effect – you know, that my ultimate motive is always to titillate you,' I said, as if I was extremely offended. I should have been offended, and nearly was, but I just couldn't manage it. In fact, I was amused, curiously flattered, and I almost liked him again.

'No, don't be angry,' he said. 'It's just, normally you're so nasty all the time, and you have this way . . . this habit of going tiny and vulnerable. It's just, very, you know, very sexy.'

'I don't believe you,' I said. 'You're the –' A can rolled on the concrete yard outside. I jumped about a foot. Then I composed myself, exhaled, exasperated by my own cowardice, and turned towards the stairs again.

'Wait,' he whispered. I turned, and he stepped forward and kissed me. And still shaking, still afraid, and now suddenly needing more than anything to be held, I wanted him to. He cupped my face with one hand, then his fingers were in my hair and I felt my knees weaken and he steadied me. We staggered back a couple of steps on to the couch, still kissing. Oh, fuck, I'm going to have sex with Finlay, I thought. This can't happen. This can't be happening. He was unbuttoning my shirt with one hand, and I felt him gasp slightly when he touched my breasts. We were breathing very heavily, he was pushing my legs apart with his knee. 'Come upstairs,' he whispered into my throat. Oh fuck oh fuck oh fuck, I was thinking. I can't do this. I can't. I'm not even pissed any more. I'm not pissed enough. I have to stop.

That was when Mandy and Sara came in.

They had a pizza and a large bag of garlic bread.

'Ay ay, what's going on here?' Mandy asked, and then realized that something was. 'Oops.'

'We'll just go in the kitchen,' Sara said. They were both grinning all over the place.

'It's all right, girls, come back, there's nothing to see. It's all over,' I said. 'You don't have to go into the kitchen.'

'Come out here,' Finlay whispered, as he helped me up. I went into the hall with him, but the mood was broken, although he clearly didn't know that yet.

'Finlay, forget it. I don't know what came over me. I'm sorry. I'm not about to sleep with you. I just . . . Let's just forget it, shall we?'

'You can't do that to me,' he said. 'You want this too.' I was buttoning my shirt up, using all the wrong holes, and he reached out and stopped me, taking my fingers in his.

'I'm really sorry. That was bad of me. But if we . . . We live together. Can you imagine how terrible it would be?'

He laughed quietly. 'I can *imagine* how good it would be.'

'Well, it wouldn't. I'd be a big disappointment. And it's not going to fucking happen, anyway.'

'Grace . . .' he said, softly, reaching out to twist the long piece of hair that always fell in front of my face.

'Don't.'

'You were so nice a moment ago. Those fucking bitches.'

'Thank God they came in when they did, eh?' We both smirked at this. He didn't seem mad at all. If anything, he looked quite happy. I think he thought it was progress. I thought it was the end.

'All right, I'm going to bed,' he said. 'You could still . . .'

'I'm going to have some pizza,' I said. 'Don't wait up.'

I had to go back in to see the girls to quell any gossip that might have been beginning.

'Were you about to have sex with Finlay then?' Mandy asked me.

'I'm afraid I was,' I admitted. 'I'm ever so glad you came in and brought me to my senses.'

'So you're sort of back together, then?' Sara said.

'What's this "back together"? When were we ever together?'

'But I thought you . . .'

'There's never been anything between me and Finlay, except a wall, and there never will be.'

'Poor Finlay,' said Sara. 'You mean you just led him on again?'

'I made a mistake. It's his fault. He started it. It's very hard to live with someone who makes passes at you all the time.'

'God, yeah,' agreed Mandy. 'Last year, when we lived with Geordie Matt he was always following me into the kitchen and begging me to go out with him, and getting stroppy when I wouldn't. Then he used to cry. Or we'd stay up late watching old films together and he'd try it on so many times. I know how hard it is. It's really hard. It's hell. But you have to draw a line some time and say no. I thought you'd done that.'

'I had. I was pissed, that's all.'

'You don't seem very pissed,' said Sara.

So I went to bed. Finlay was in the hallway waiting for me. He tried to scoop me towards him as I walked past.

'It's not going to happen,' I said, twisting away from him.

'So that's it, then?'

'Yes. I just want to go to bed now.'

'You can't do that to me.' Same old same old – only this time it wasn't the same. A line had been crossed; I couldn't kid myself that he hadn't noticed the switch in my intent, he knew me too well. So he waited. But it was too late, I'd recovered, the logical armour was back in place. As the realization hit home that I wasn't going to carry on where we'd left off, his temper soured. The good humour brought on by our unusually ardent snog had vanished with the heat. My sense of guilt matured into defensive resentment.

'Look, I changed my fucking mind. Live with it.'

He stepped forward and pressed his chest against me. His arm was on the wall behind me. 'I thought you . . .' he said, and sighed. He had no plans to finish that sentence, no hope of presuming whatever had been on my mind. He left it hanging there, willing me to fill in the blanks. I didn't move away, because I wanted to show him he didn't intimidate me, but also because I knew he was enjoying standing there like that, feeling powerful, and I enjoyed it too, on an aesthetic level. It was very Gene Kelly.

'Go to bed, Finlay. You'll have forgotten this by the morning.'

'I won't.'

'I don't really care, then. I'll have forgotten it by the morning.'

'You can be a real bitch sometimes.' And now we were back.

'Ho hum,' I said. He slowly pulled himself off me. 'Goodnight,' I said. I didn't look back again, heard my door click shut and dropped forward on to my bed. I lay there for maybe another hour before my thoughts let up on me.

Wednesday

The morning after we had sex he made me fresh raisin toast for breakfast; warm, sweet and buttery.

'You look beautiful. I really have to go to work,' he said, kissing me while I ate greedily.

'That's fine. This is *sensational.* Who taught you to make this?'

'My father. He thought I should be able to make at least one thing well. But I *am* a great cook. Take your time getting up. Don't let the cleaner scare you. Are you free for lunch?'

'Well, I'd better not, today,' I said. 'I have some stuff to do.' Actually, I was thinking that I'd never get home, wash and set my hair, think of something to wear and make it anywhere in time for lunch.

'How about dinner tomorrow?'

'Dinner tomorrow's good,' I said.

'Oh, wait, I'm meeting my agent tomorrow evening.' He found his diary and flicked through it. 'Jesus, I'm so embarrassed – this is quite a busy week. How about Friday?'

'That's fine too,' I said.

'Would you like to meet for lunch before then?' he said.

'No,' I said. I wanted it to look like I had a bit of a life. 'I can wait.' And he went to work.

He called later that morning, when I'd just got in.

'So what are you doing with your day?'

'Well, since I didn't get that fabulous research job I'd set my heart on . . .'

'Don't be unfair. You'd be very bored, anyway. It's not as glamorous as it looks.'

'It *doesn't* look –'

'I know. Can you even *begin* to imagine how dull it must be?'

'So what have you been researching?'

'It's really not exciting. It's about a man with an obsessive-compulsive disorder. When he thinks he isn't in control of his life he bashes his head against walls until it bleeds.'

'He sounds extremely self-indulgent. I hate people like that.'

'He's depressed. He's destroying himself, and he can't help it. Or control it.'

'Can't he just take Prozac like normal people?'

'He tried. It didn't work. That's the thing about depression. You can't just make yourself get over it like a bad mood. Do you mean to tell me you don't feel sorry for him?' Cod horror, an invitation to unroll the full ugliness of my opinions. I loved that I could be mean with him and he made it seem attractive. It was as if all the time at college I'd been careful and guarded and *nice*, and a lot of people still thought I was as selfish and thoughtless as I worried they'd think I was. Now, the honesty was like a release. I used to think I had to pretend to be better to attract someone good enough, and now I could see I'd missed the point: that someone good enough thinks you're better anyway. I could be as bad as I liked and still feel a mensch. I had no doubts; I wasn't afraid of who he was, and I wasn't afraid he'd work out who I was. That was the thrill of it – he already seemed to know.

'No. It makes me so mad. If he thought about someone else for a change he might realize he doesn't have any real problems. So why doesn't he just kill himself if he's so unhappy? What's with this big obsession with living anyway, if his life is so terrible?' I rolled the callousness around with pleasure; I could hear him smiling.

'I had no idea you were so . . .'

'So what? So unsympathetic? Do you think I'm horrible?'

'I'm in love with you. So I find it excessively charming that you can't sympathize with a man who's drowning in self-hatred and despair.'

'Okay, well, I know you're being sarcastic, but I'm not sure how far. Are you trying to tell me you do feel sorry for him?'

'Of course I feel sorry for him. Anyway, fuck him. When am I seeing you again? Meet me for a drink tonight.'

'I'd love to. But I'm supposed to be a little more hard to get than this. I know I should be pretending I have some fulfilling circle of activity somewhere else. You know, I just don't think I can cope with a proper relationship.'

'So we'll have an improper one. Jones's. Eight o'clock.'

So I did all the stupid stuff, the movie set pieces. I spent every day singing in the street and smiling in public and just being stupidly, always happy. I'd dance ineptly and gleefully in front of my mirror, pirouetting without co-ordination until I lost my balance. I bought three new dresses and a pair of kitten-heeled sling-backs. I called my mother and Alice and told them about the presents he'd bought me, and that we were going to Rome in a week, and how I was going to get married and thoroughly pregnant. I loved that it was all such a cliché, that all this intensity and emotion had been done before. I was unfashionably late and it was grand. I finally felt normal.

'Alice,' I said, 'you know I love you and you're my best friend in the world and I . . .'

'What is it? Say it. I won't be offended.'

'It's not that it's offensive. It's just. You know? Wow. He's just . . . the best . . . *person* . . . I ever met.'

'Good,' Alice said. 'It's about time.'

Early on Friday morning, two weeks after we first had lunch, the phone rang, getting me out of bed. It was my father.

'Grace, something terrible's happened. I don't know how to . . . He's dead,' he told me quietly. 'He . . . suffered a brain haemorrhage last night.' When my father said his name, he got it slightly wrong, which made me think he was mistaken, and I started crying, but I kept telling him it wasn't him and the name was wrong. He said it was him.

'How do you know?' I said.

'It's in this morning's paper,' he said. I ran out of my flat wearing jeans over my pyjamas and bought about five newspapers. His picture was in all of them. I stood in the street, unfolding newspapers and dropping their pages all around me and crying. I wanted to scream, but I waited until I'd got home, where I scrunched the newspapers into balls and buried my face in their folds and wept and wept.

1992

9

Mabel's infidelity had kicked off something of a celebration. The girls decided that this was the only way to teach the evil Jonathan a lesson, not to mention a sign that she was well on the way to getting over him. I wasn't so sure. Of course, even my opinion of Jonathan had changed since the herpes affair. The images of venereal disease somehow illustrated the fact of his cheating, bringing it into colour and making it more serious for me. I couldn't think of his polished, handsome face without mentally picturing his spicy penis, and the thought repelled me. I could no longer daydream about the wedding in white, romantic terms, and it spoiled my fun. I didn't really want Mabel to have anything to do with it, or him, any more. So this time I had been firmly behind the rest of the house when they tried to wean her away from him, but while they were hailing it as a panacea, I didn't see Mabel's most recent penetration as being any kind of breakthrough.

She didn't want to see the beautiful Toby again, which baffled everyone. He was heartbreakingly ornamental, like a Pierre *et* Gilles picture of an angel. Mabel said he was too pretty, too blond. The issue now was whether she told Jonathan or not. Of course, everyone wanted her to. Not so she could start talking to him again, nor to get everything out in the open. They wanted him to suffer. They suspected him of having those double standards you always see on soap operas, where philandering husbands choke on the idea of their wives taking a lover. Mabel acknowledged that she was in a stronger position, but said that if she wanted to hurt Jonathan she might as well just walk away from him for ever and have nothing more to do with him, but if she loved him she shouldn't want to make him unhappy. But then, if she loved him and wanted to marry him, perhaps she should be honest. I told her that honesty was a much overrated thing, and that the fact that he told her everything had never helped their relationship much. That went down very badly with everyone, who said there was no such thing as commitment with secrets. And so we tossed the debate about for a few days, during which, I must say, Mabel looked rosier and healthier than she had in months. Perhaps there was something to this sex they were all so obsessed with.

Our landlord, Gareth, came round and fitted a large iron portcullis to our front door. We'd told him about the robbery and he was quite distressed. He was a nice young man, and he cared about his tenants, really, coming round every so often to fix things. He had several houses, but he knew us all by name and was pretty laid-back if one of us failed to pay rent on time, which happened a lot. 'That should stop any more robberies,' he said, and he winked at us.

When he'd gone, and we were playing with our new stronghold, Finlay said, 'What Gareth's forgotten is that you lot let them in. So it's not really going to help, is it?'

'We didn't let them in, they forced their way in,' Sara said. 'And of course it will. We speak to people at the front door through the gate. That's how it works, you idiot.' Finlay didn't seem to have considered this, because he went very quiet.

'It's like living in a cage,' Heather said. She disapproved of technology.

'Perhaps if you'd been here when it happened you wouldn't give a shit about living in a cage,' Sara said. Everyone in the house was pissing Sara off at the moment. She had told me this one day, politely excluding me from the list of irritants, but I suspected I was just as much a part of it. She said she couldn't stand being in the same room as Finlay and she just wanted to kill him whenever he opened his mouth. She hated everyone who didn't get robbed because they'd all made jokes about it but talked about it outside as if it had happened to them. She said she had nightmares all the time, and she had booked into the student health centre for some counselling.

'Counselling?' I'd said. 'Is it really that bad?'

'I'm depressed about a lot of things,' she said. 'The break-in just sent me over the edge. I can't cope with things any more. I'd do anything to move.'

'What, you want to leave college?'

'No,' Sara seemed surprised at the thought. 'No, I love my course. It's just living here. I just want to move out of the house. If I could find someone to pay my share of the rent I would.'

'We're all just a bit tired of each other,' I said. 'We've never lived like this before. So many of us in one tiny space. We're just getting on each other's nerves. I think everyone feels it.'

'It's more than that,' Sara said.

Depression is contagious. Within a week of this conversation the house had reached the point of optimum unfriendliness. When one person left a room, the rest talked about them. We were falling out over everything and nothing. One Sunday, Heather told me to clear up the papers a bit, and I launched into a mad rant about how the purpose of Sundays was to be surrounded by papers, and her voice cracked, and she said, 'I don't know what I've done to upset you, Grace, but it seems I can't say anything to you these days.'

It was the first time I'd noticed she and I weren't getting on, and I knew it had to be my fault because she was so easy to get on with. I wasn't talking to Finlay because, although I used to boast that I'd grown out of embarrassment, I couldn't think of anything to say to him any more. Thankfully, he seldom stopped working now. He was older than the rest of us and his finals were this year, which meant he could remind us that our exams didn't count and had a licence to behave as badly as he liked and blame it on the pressure. Mabel and Sara also spent most days together at the library, even though Mabel was supposed to be telling her tutors that she wanted to quit the course soon but it seemed likely now that she would be staying to the end of the year, whatever happened. She went about like a caged animal, sighing and pacing and waiting for something to change. Mandy had boyfriend problems that she didn't want to talk about but she was more than happy to complain about in an abstract fashion, only nobody wanted to listen. The party was over. The things we used to do as a pseudo-family, like putting on videos and talking all the way through them, hardly ever happened now. When we tried to drag out the old catchphrases and clichés they sounded forced and artificially bright. I went home for a few days, and when I came back, the house seemed dirtier, nastier and less like it had when we first moved in. The weather was improving, and I couldn't stay inside in the blue gloom any more. It was as if the house was collecting all our bad vibes, storing them up until the venom was soupy thick. I started taking books outside and perching on a wall to soak up the sunshine, to feel the scorch of yellow light on my black clothes.

Adam came out, holding the cat. He bobbed a little so I could scratch her head.

'I heard about your break-in,' he said. 'Pretty scary. Are you all okay?'

'Richard was hurt, but he's fine now, I think,' I said.

'Yeah, he's the one I was talking to about it. I've always felt pretty safe here. It's a quiet street. But you never know.'

'They knew we were students, that's the thing,' I said. 'Students are a good bet, that's what the police said. They know you're a bunch of fairly rich kids with, like, a telly and a stereo each. That's why they were disappointed to find out we just had a load of crap.'

'Still, it's a horrible thing to happen. How've you been, anyway?'

'Me? God, I'm always fine. What about you?'

'Yeah,' he said, nodding.

'And . . .'

'And that's all over and done with but I'm okay about it. It was probably what I wanted anyway.'

'I don't think anything's ever the end of anything, unless you want it to be. If that helps. It's not like you have to say, conclusively, 'Well, it's finished and over and I can never go back.' So if you feel like that, maybe it *is* what you wanted, and then maybe you'll change your mind and do it all again. Only better.'

'Sometimes, though, you've got to let it go.'

'I hate getting rid of anything. I'm a hoarder.'

'I used to be. Then I started running out of space.'

'Aren't we deep?' I said. 'I love talking to you. It's such a change from everyone I live with. I mean, you can come out and toss around metaphors about the most important things in the world, and in there it's pistols at dawn over the washing-up rota. We all hate each other now. Everyone's taking everything very seriously. I hate it when that happens.'

'You're not just here to have fun, you know.'

'Sure we are.'

Adam chuckled and stretched out on his bit of wall. We were very close, but we were still in our own backyards. I watched his chest tauten and caught a flash of the hair on his lean stomach as his T-shirt popped from under his waistband. He was so much fitter-looking than any of the other men I knew. Perhaps it was a gay thing. Men are sticklers for youth and beauty, regardless of their sexuality. Maybe gay men have to make more of an effort. Or it could have been a single person thing. Growing up I'd never met older single men. You don't. You meet your parents' friends, and they're all married, and your friends' parents, and they're all married too, or have been, so they stop trying. I imagined touching Adam's hard stomach with my fingertips.

'It's hot today, isn't it?' he said. 'I hope it lasts.'

I went to a Jim McFadyean tutorial. I was conscious of its solemnity, and missed the friskiness that had once charged these gatherings, but I just sat there looking surly. I realized, with some pleasure, that I was the reason the tutorials had been so enjoyably unorthodox. They were dependent on my playing along. He kept looking at me and frowning noticeably, as if I were a sum he was trying to solve. Sometimes he tried to involve me in whatever he was talking about, but I just pretended not to know. I didn't digress or act cute. Life was suddenly full of men I couldn't have or didn't want. They seemed to be able to hop from one group to the other in the space of a witty sentence or a stupid remark, never being in both places at the same time. I felt as if I'd exhausted all the possibilities here. There were the same faces at the same clubs, the same stories about the same people, only they appeared in them in different combinations. Nothing was going to happen to me until I moved away somewhere. The thought of another year at this place was hurting my head. If I'd had a dentist I'd have forgiven everything and gone off to have his children. Just for a change. The tutorial was over before I'd even noticed it, although it had lasted an eternity, so long that I assumed it would never end, and I'd eventually die there, sitting with a group of dreary people in a claustrophobic semi-circle. I heard the other students start to pick up their papers and things and it reminded me of where I was.

'Is anything wrong, Grace?' Jim McFadyean said. 'Are you finding the work difficult?' Finding it difficult? Ha! I thought. I'm not finding it at all. I'm above all that, beyond it. Nothing matters any more, don't you get it? I'm just keeping my head down, doing my time. I felt existential and reckless and wanted to flare my nostrils with haughty gypsy defiance like Gina Lollobrigida. I said, 'I'll be fine. I just need to get organized.'

'Have you seen *Nikita*?' he said.

Give it a bloody rest, I thought. Is that all you ever talk about? I said, 'No, I haven't. It's good, is it?'

'It's a great movie. You should go. Take one of your boyfriends.'

And now he sounded like my dad. What a way to let me down. I couldn't leave it. 'My boyfriends?' I said, drenching the word with scorn. 'Oh, yeah, I'll do that.' I felt my lip curl. Had he ever wanted me? I searched his dark eyes for something. He held my gaze, the way he always had. Some people do this, and they shouldn't. It makes you think they're in love with you. And to leave those gaping silences, the way he did. Also not on. When I left silences like that I expected to be kissed at the end of them. We'd both seen enough movies to know the form. I turned to go.

'Your essays are good, you know,' he said, stopping me. 'But they're too short, and too scarce.'

'That's what makes them good,' I said. 'If I wrote pages and pages you'd see the flaws. If I wrote a lot of them you'd soon be blasé about them.'

'Keep 'em keen by restricting the supply, is that what you mean?'

I meant to smile slightly, with irony, but a surge of genuine pleasure took over; the smile twitched, then widened. 'Well, anyway,' I said. I wanted to go before he dismissed me, to end the chat myself rather than linger until he'd had enough. To restrict the supply. I couldn't tell if he found me attractive, and it didn't even matter because I could see now that he was never going to do anything about it. So I left. I never wrote him another essay.

And then the mice came. I thought they were just things that sounded like mice at first, the uncurling of a crisp packet, the creaking of old timber, something else that might sound like a host of small animals living with us but was really reassuringly non-organic and non-alive. Then one night we were watching John Carpenter's *The Fog*, together, unusually. We watched it seriously, as we used to, in the dark with the curtains drawn so it was more like the pictures. I was not afraid of horror movies as long as there were other people there. Alone in the house, adverts for childhood vaccination scared me, *Crimewatch* scared me; anything that mentioned the devil or ghosts, or featured women being stalked and assaulted and I'd have to turn off the television and think of my favourite Julie Andrews musicals. But we were all there, and I wasn't afraid. Which was more than could be said for the others. And it was a truly preposterous film, featuring a zombie pirate with a hook who limped around very slowly, killing people. The others were really into it, shouting out, 'Oh, my God, what's he going to . . .?' and passing each other cushions and making squealy noises. I sat there looking cool and tutting, and spreading out my limbs to show I couldn't be more relaxed under an anaesthetic, and calling them wimps. I went into the kitchen to find a snack, to show I could even eat through the gory bits, and then a mouse ran over my foot.

I ran into the living room, screaming, and screamed several more times. Then I stopped. Everyone had been distracted from the film by this, and they gathered round me, asking what was wrong, none of them, incidentally, going into the kitchen to have a look. I screamed a couple more times. I was actually hysterical.

'It was a mouse,' I said. And then I stamped my feet and screamed quietly into my hands for good measure.

'Fucking hell!' Richard said, as if this was the biggest anticlimax he'd ever experienced, an operatic disappointment.

'Is that all?' Mandy said, in the same tone.

'I thought you must have seen a face at the window,' Finlay said. They looked thoroughly disgusted, and then they went into the kitchen to look for the mouse. It had scurried somewhere and there was no sign of it.

'Christ, I thought it was something serious,' Mandy said. 'I can't believe you could scream about a mouse.' For the next hour, she said the same thing several times, each time managing to sound more superior. She went on to talk about how there were rats the size of Yorkshire terriers where she lived, and they used to squabble over who got to kill them with a mallet.

'I'm scared of mice,' I said, pissed off. 'Surprisingly, I'm not scared of actors wearing ugly make-up, but I am scared of disease-carrying rodents that crawl around in your cornflakes at night, especially when they run over my foot. I know how wussy that makes me, but there it is.' Mandy had succeeded in making me feel kind of stupid.

'I knew we had mice,' Sara said. She hadn't joined in the communal contempt session that my behaviour had prompted. 'I keep thinking I can hear something at night before I sleep. Jesus, that's it, then. I don't know if I can stay here now. I'm really, really scared of things like that.' I warmed to her. She looked a lot more serious about this than I'd been, even mid-scream. Of course, she was depressed, still, and looking for an excuse to leave. Maybe she was pretending, setting things up for her departure.

The next day we called Gareth, and he came over with a bagful of traps.

'Wait, does this mean we're going to be finding half-dead mice everywhere?' I said.

'Not *half* dead,' he said, with a hearty smile.

But the mice didn't take the bait, which was bacon fat – apparently the best thing for the job, cheese being a myth propagated by the cartoon industry, who are probably in cahoots with the cheese industry. Over a couple of days the bacon fat curled up and dried but the traps remained empty. Gareth considered this a victory. 'No, there are no mice here. It'll have been pigeons you heard,' he said.

'But one of them ran over my foot,' I said. 'I saw it. I felt it.'

'It was probably just a fieldmouse, going through the house,' he said. 'If you had mice actually living here, there'd be one in one of them traps. But there's nothing. See?'

'I can hear them all the time,' Sara said. 'All night. I'm afraid to sleep now.'

'It sounds like mice,' Gareth said patiently, 'but it's more likely to be pigeons, nesting in the eaves. They make the same noise.' He collected his traps, carefully putting them into a carrier-bag with delicate fingers. But there were mice here. Sara and I knew it. The appearance of the mouse had shuffled all the mutual hostility in a positive way. It injected our day-to-day lives with a surge of virtual caffeine. With so many things to be afraid of – failure, rejection, burglars, rodents – none of us could afford to relax; the complacency which familiarity had been breeding was dwindling and we were jauntier, punchier and more inclined to laugh about things. The authenticity of my mouse sighting was increasingly questioned, and Sara's aural evidence of mouse activity was generally secretly agreed to be the paranoid ravings of an unstable person, but beneath the bravado and the mocking, we still acted as if we were sharing the house with a mouse colony. We became fastidious about leaving food out, we started seeing things in our peripheral vision and discussing whether or not it was hallucinatory, and we had something to talk about, a fresh source of jokes. Sara didn't find them very funny. Her bedroom was newly barricaded against mouse invasion; all the gaps along the skirting board were stuffed with paper, and closed over with masking tape. There was something slightly excessive about it, but I filled in similar holes in my bedroom.

Finally, there was another sighting. A yell from Heather's room, a scramble upstairs and a confirmation that, on the second floor, this was no fieldmouse. After that, the mice got cocky. We got used to them hurtling from one hole to another, although they never stopped scaring us. Gareth was called in again, and this time he brought poison. He deposited the blue powder everywhere, which can't have been hygienic, but he wanted to hear the end of it. The first mouse casualty appeared three days later. Finlay ran into the living room and told us we had to see something. In the kitchen, a tiny grey mouse limped in approximate circles around the table, and finally fell over, exhausted and panting. I watched it from behind the door, feeling terrible. We were killing things. We argued about how we should dispose of it, and who, until Finlay picked the creature up by its tail and threw it out of the kitchen door.

'What if Adam's cat finds it and eats it?' I said. He looked at me and tutted silently, but he went outside, found it and put it in one of our bin bags. As always, we had a dozen bulging sacks in the backyard. We could never remember to fill the wheelie-bin. Surprisingly, no more mice died in front of us, which led Sara to surmise that there were probably dozens of decomposing corpses in every hidden part of the house. This was a gruesome thought, and it kept me awake many nights. I still heard mice, too. As did the others. Richard said that, eventually, some mice became genetically immune to poison.

We were still meeting on Wednesdays, Richard and I, talking about how grim the atmosphere in the house was. The mice had been useful, serving as a common enemy post-mad-Greg, but the tension would not go away. I liked the fact that the two of us could commentate on it, as if above it all.

'Are you doing anything in the Easter break?' I asked him. The holidays coming up was just what we needed. We could escape the house and each other, and perhaps we'd even start missing the place.

'I'm probably going to France for a couple of days with some mates. We were thinking of taking my friend's van down.'

'That sounds good,' I said. 'Is Finlay going with you?'

'No, it's some friends from home,' he said. 'It's going to be a sort of shagathon, if we're lucky.'

'Lovely,' I said, pulling one eyebrow higher to show how little I understood the world of young men and their indiscriminate sexual pursuits. 'That'll be nice for you all.'

'What are you planning?'

'Nothing. I'll just hang out with my friends at home,' I lied. As if there were plenty. There were two girls I went to the pub with, and maybe to the town's only nightclub, Karizma, which was as good as it sounds. One of the girls didn't really like me, even. I wouldn't be doing much hanging at all.

'Finlay says he's going to stay,' Richard said, concentrating on cutting his potato precisely. 'He says he needs the library and he's going to work.'

'God, yes. His finals. He won't be living with us next year. That's so odd, isn't it? What's the house going to be like without him?' Richard looked like he was going to say something important, and considered it, fork in mid-air. Then he changed his mind. Then he changed his mind again. He cleared his throat.

'What is it?' I said.

'Have you thought about where you're going to live next year?' he said.

'I don't know. I suppose I assumed we'd stay together,' I said.

'Well, the thing is, some friends on my course have asked me to live with them, and I thought I would.' He looked at me for my reaction.

'Oh. Do you hate us all that much?'

'I wish to see you all dead,' he tried. Then he looked more serious. 'I just don't think I can live with a house full of girls,' he said. 'I'm blokier than that. I'd feel a bit overwhelmed living with no other men.'

'You managed okay this year,' I said, and he gave me a disapproving look. I lowered my head in mock-contrition. 'Of course you would.' I acted like I understood and didn't care, but I was hurt, and it probably showed.

'And we're not exactly getting on, are we? I mean, you and I are. And, you know, other people, but it's pretty intense sometimes, isn't it? I just feel like I need to be surrounded by a little more testosterone in my final year.'

'Have you told the others about this?'

'I've told Finlay.'

'Who also won't be here. Jesus. I wonder what it'll be like with just the girls. And probably without Mabel.' The next year suddenly looked like it was going to be a horrible place to live in.

'Well, look, don't mention it to everyone else yet. I mean, I haven't decided. There's a long time to go.' But there wasn't a long time. The weeks were being sucked up at an alarming pace. I felt a little insecure and lonely, the way you feel when you're waiting somewhere in the cold. 'Can I get you another cake?'

'I'll have some rice pudding,' I said. 'And make sure it's hot.'

*

The news got out, news always does. But there was worse to come. It seemed that Richard was not alone in already making plans to live elsewhere next year. In fact, I was alone in not doing so. Sara had been holding talks with an already established house of four. They would turn it into a five next year. Heather was moving in with a girlfriend. They wanted to try a more mature sort of flat-share; just two of them, like working girls. And Mandy was planning on going back into halls, like Michelle. She said the stress of finding food would be too much for the third year, and she wanted to be cooked for. She didn't want any extra bother when she was working for her finals, and what with the burglary and the mice and all the other shit that had happened recently, she'd made her mind up. These decisions had all been taken secretly, unilaterally, and I was shocked and momentarily worried. I would be alone. I had to find someone to live with and somewhere to live in my final year. It wasn't going to be easy. I wasn't happy with anyone in the house, couldn't even talk to them for a few days. So it was official – we really weren't friends. I felt rejected, naïve and unpopular. But free.

I was extraordinarily relieved that the Easter holidays had arrived because I couldn't keep up my end of the hostility for very long. I didn't want to look needy, and I didn't want to go too far and alienate these people for ever, in case I had use for them at a later date – always planning ahead – but I felt I ought to register my disapproval too. There had been underhand tactics in play, and I couldn't be seen to support these, and didn't want to relinquish immediately my right to make the rest of them feel a little guilty. When you have a trump card you don't throw it away on a weak round. I packed up my car the day before we were all set to go, and drove off without telling anyone. Really, I was too pissed off at them to offer them the usual five different lifts to the station. And I wanted my journey to be completely mine, to start as I meant it to continue, with me, a stash of tapes and a big, long, throat-ripping sing-song all the way over the Pennines, zipping past lorries and hat-wearing old men on the Snake Pass. Now that was living. I got through all of *Evita*, singing every role, before I started choking on the high notes. I made the crossing in record time, despite being trapped for several miles behind one of those lorries that carries hay. And then I was home, where the surfaces were hygienic to the touch, the carpet clean enough to lie on, and the only four-legged animal was domesticated and friendly. I unpacked the zillion books that I hawked back and forth whenever I moved from one house to the other, even though I didn't touch them in either place. I let my mother make me a sandwich.

The next day Alice called. We went to the local pub and got drunk and kissed some boys we didn't look at in school, and on Saturday, complete with raw, cloying hangovers that felt like Prairie Oysters taste, we had an Activity Day, a contrived tradition of ours, where she pretended she'd had a deprived, fun-free childhood and I pretended I'd had a *Blue Peter* one. The idea was that we spent time bonding over something creative, like potato-printing or finger-painting or tie-dyeing, and the differences in our lives that changing circumstance and maturity imposed would be forgotten, as nothing. It worked very well. For while we no longer had mutual friends or visited the same places, and the fashion-conscious reputation of my university was at odds with the aspirational profile of hers, the language of plate-painting was universal, and we could resume our old roles effortlessly. It was even better now that we could drive. We bought plates and bowls, paints and brushes, and set to work. Fun for the whole family, too, because my father and brother would pass by occasionally and sneer derisively, and my mother, who was talented but never got a chance to prove it, would show us how it was done; so everyone was happy. On Sunday we took the finished products to a car-boot sale at the racecourse, where hundreds of people stopped to admire, and a woman bought a jug, the one thing my mother had painted. We managed to get a pound out of the woman, which would have been daylight robbery for something so exquisite – the blank jug had cost us at least two pounds – except we hadn't used proper plate-painting materials, and the chances were she'd be left with a plain piece of pottery if she ever tried to wash it.

We spent the rest of the day driving around the countryside, stopping at pubs to see if they had electronic quiz machines. Our friendship was a perfectly evolved compatibility. We had shaped each other, we matched. We had a whole back catalogue of memories: like how we used to shop in Sheffield together and were taunted on the way home by cooler girls because we'd bought stupid things and taken them out to look at them on the train. How we'd kissed the same boys and been to the same parties and first got drunk together. She'd taught me to like coffee: we spent hundreds of evenings sitting at her kitchen table with steaming mugs and Kit-Kats, imagining what our lives would be like, who would lose her virginity first, whether we'd have kids.

But she had nothing to do with my other life, the one in Manchester, where I was forced to act like someone I wasn't. The trouble was, the Manchester situation was the direction I was choosing to take my life in. The future lay there, in the world where I smiled a lot and pretended to know about politics. I could never fuse the two successfully, so I'd never have another friendship in which the other person knew me so well, and liked me despite everything. Because of everything. So, although we sank easily back into the life we'd always had, it was coloured with a sense of urgency. It was like running alongside a train that is leaving the station, waving to one of the passengers as they gradually, inevitably, get further away. We spent the few weeks at home flipping over the possibilities of our futures like in the old days, with humorous detachment, as if it wasn't really real, but just a conceit, a consequence that wouldn't happen, even though it got closer every time. We hugged each other when I dropped her off at her house. Hmm, she's put on weight, I thought, pleased.

Wednesday

A few days after his death, the obituaries started appearing. I got to learn about the man I was in love with from the press, the way I'd learned about his death. And it was horrible, not knowing anything about his life when I felt so completely linked to him. Nothing the obituaries said was surprising, because I knew him and understood him; they were just dates, names, facts; just his life before he'd met me. Then there was the bad one, in the tabloid that thinks it's so respectable, which told me he was an alcoholic and a womanizer, and sometimes that made me feel worse, because I would have liked the idea that he lived like that; it would have suited his casual, confident swagger and added to his charm and I just wanted him more. Then sometimes I found it comforting, because it allowed me to believe that he'd been lying when he convinced me he was in love with me, that I was just one of many and we wouldn't have had any kind of future. I *wanted* to hear that he was a bad person, I wanted reasons not to be in love with him. But the things written about him were never bad in a way that mattered. I read everything, over and over, still checking the name and the pictures in case there was some mistake, and I called his number to hear his voice on the machine, but someone had disconnected it. I listened to the dead line for a long time before hanging up.

I spent the next week getting out of bed only to go back there, hugging myself in a foetal position for hours while I moaned softly or screamed into the sheets. I couldn't believe I could feel so much, that I could suffer physical pain from something so emotional. But it was real and it hurt, as if someone had ripped out part of my stomach. I cried constantly: sobbing, hiccuping, until my cheeks and neck ached from the strain and I felt strangled, and my eyes disappeared under puffy folds. Death isn't the end enough.

I still hadn't fully come down from the intense excitement I had felt when I was seeing him, and the expectation of the date we never had, which lined my depression with false hope. The feeling that there was something unfinished, something fabulous coming that would make everything better just wouldn't go away. Every day I had to tell myself that it wasn't coming, it wouldn't happen, there was no future, and every day it felt worse, not better, when I had to face that. I'd sit and go through everything that had happened and the thinking didn't stop with the memory. I added new dialogue and imagined new situations, and I'd be at home, alone, finding myself saying, 'Let's go and see a play tonight and have dinner,' aloud, and then realizing how stupid I sounded. Then I'd laugh at myself, horribly, and force myself to say, 'No, you can't do that, he's dead, remember? Dead.' Aloud.

I quickly became desperate about the future, my mind working with crazy, impossible logic. As I dressed, carefully, slowly for the funeral, in the black shift I'd bought for our next date, I was thinking, Maybe I can meet one of his friends today and he'll be the same person, and I can go out with him instead. I thought that someone who knew him would be like him, like enough for it not to make much difference. The emptiness tore at me; I wanted a replacement. I hadn't known him long enough to miss him. I couldn't grieve for him, only for myself, I could only be mad at him. And at the funeral a dozen people stood and told stories of how much they loved him, and I sat at the back, crumpled with fear and depression and raw, angry jealousy.

People called and expected me to be happier. There was a time when I thought I was good at cheering people up, because I'd noticed that sad people, if you change the subject and make them laugh, don't act sad any more, and I thought I'd helped. Cured them. It was only now that I knew that, sometimes, you just have to be sad, and even if you can forget for a moment and be happier, it's not enough. I'd assumed before that everyone wanted to be happy, always; I thought that was obvious. Now, sadness was the only thing that satisfied, and feeling happier, or even acting happier for other people, made me sick. So I didn't, but they were insulted when they couldn't help, when I wouldn't pretend they were easing the pain. If I softened, smiled, I felt as if I was letting them off the hook, when I wanted them to suffer too. I was mad at everyone and resented them and couldn't talk to them any more because they didn't understand what I was going through. I wanted to be dead more than anything, but I would never have killed myself. I just wanted it to happen; I'd shut my eyes and wish I wasn't there. *Wuthering* fucking *Heights* started making perfect sense, even though I'd mocked it at A level. I thought about heaven and ghosts, and sometimes even believed in them, but that wasn't why I wanted to be dead. I just wanted the pain to stop. It hasn't.

1992

10

We hadn't called each other at all in the Easter break. I never made much of an effort anyway, but in the first summer holidays there had been phone calls, the odd meeting, substantial contact of all sorts going on between us. Of course, in the first summer holidays we were smitten with each other, the best of friends. Still, we pretended we'd missed each other when we met again now and compiled verbal essays on what we'd done in the Easter break. Lizzy, a shrewd beauty I'd lost touch with since the end of the first year, remarked once on the inverse correlation between the warmth of a friendship and the warmth of a greeting after separation. 'When you hate someone, you're, like, "Hi! How are you?! God, it's soooo great to see you!" And with your best mate you just grunt,' she'd said.

There was only a grunt from Finlay. I couldn't help thinking sometimes that we had missed out on a potentially wonderful friendship because we were both so preoccupied with sex. But, then, I suppose it's the same with everyone.

When six of us had been back for a few days we started wondering if Mabel was ever going to join us. So, as a house, but principally through Heather, we called her. Her mother, who sounded tired, said she had gone back already, and she'd be there in the evening. But she wasn't. We didn't know whether to call her mum again and worry her, but we were worried ourselves. Had something happened on the way?

'Let's leave it a day,' Mandy said. 'If she wanted her mother to know she'd have told her.'

'But what if she's been killed travelling up?' Sara said. We left it a day, all the same.

'We could call Jonathan and ask him if he knows where she is,' Finlay said.

'But we don't know what's going on between them,' I said.

'Does it matter?' said Finlay.

'Yes. That's a good idea,' Heather said. 'Does anyone have his number?' As if.

So we waited another day, and by now we were worrying quite seriously. Not that we really thought she'd met with some sort of accident, but that, if she had, we'd all be held responsible for not alerting anyone to the fact that she was missing. But then she called.

'I'm in Oxford with Jon,' Richard said she said, when he got off the phone with her. 'We're just going to do it. I mean, what the fuck, eh?'

'Well, do you want us there?' Heather said, when she called Mabel back. 'What about all your stuff? What about your mum? Mabel, you can't just do it now without telling people.'

'No, I'm coming back to Manchester. I'm staying to the end of term because Jon's doing his finals and he says I'd be a serious distraction around then.' According to Heather, Mabel giggled at this, as if he was next to her while she spoke, feeding his tongue into her ear. 'But I'm spending the week here living with him. It's like a trial period.'

'A trial period of a week?' Heather said. 'That should give you a good idea of married life.'

'Don't make it hard for me, Heather,' Mabel said. 'I'm frightened enough as it is.'

'Well, doesn't that tell you anything?' Heather said.

'Please, Heather. I know what I'm doing. Anyway, this is good. It means I get to do the end-of-year stuff with all of you and I don't have to keep paying rent to the house for nothing or force you lot to find someone to live with you for one term. It's all perfect. And then we can have a wedding party and you can all come.'

'It hasn't been the best-organized wedding, has it?' Heather said. We were listening to Heather's half of the conversation in the living room, and we all gasped loudly at this criticism and pulled faces at each other. According to Heather, who didn't usually skip bits, Mabel said, 'Well, we can't all be obsessively organized, can we, Heather?' Heather sniffed and waited for Mabel to break the silence. 'This is it, Heather, I'm not just thinking about it. It's not up for discussion any more. I've chosen. Be pleased for me.'

'How can I be pleased that you're ruining your life?'

'You can be pleased because I'm happy. That's all.' Heather hung up and came back to us and repeated the conversation, her voice hushed with concern.

'The thing is, she has made her mind up,' I said.

'The thing is, she can still change it,' Heather said.

If I had been Mabel, I wouldn't have come back. Living with all of us at our lowest, the threat of mice still lurking (even though Finlay said Gareth had pretty much fumigated the place when we were away) and no point to her days, no lectures to go to, or exams to study for, seemed like the most depressing existence I could imagine. But she did come back, and I'd never seen her so happy. Responsibility hadn't suited Mabel: she wore it like a heavy grey overcoat. Jon was taking the pressure away from her. She had returned to her old role as soother, peacemaker, laughing at our problems, repelling our cruelty with a warm smile. She was understanding and noble, the way you can be when you stop letting things bother you. If she hadn't come back, I'm not sure we wouldn't have started fist-fights among ourselves before the year was over. We existed in a state of what felt like permanent intoxication, caused by late nights and poor diet and fear that what we were doing for the next few weeks would affect the rest of our lives.

One day the doorbell rang, and I was standing in the hall

when Richard answered it. Through the bars of our portcullis I could recognize Greg, although it took me more than a moment. He had put on at least fifty pounds.

'Wow. Security gate,' Greg said, greyly. Richard was enthusiastic and I was wary as we let Greg into our house again. As we asked him questions about what he'd been doing for the last few months, I was reminded of some work experience I'd done at a geriatric hospital for my school, and the overwhelming sensation of being kind. He was very quiet, but seemed grateful for being spoken to. His face looked paralysed until he spoke, which was infrequently by normal standards; as this was Greg, who had dribbled through breathless, unlikely tales as he hurtled into his mania, the silences were more than awkward, they were sad.

'So what's going to happen, mate? Are you still taking the exams?' Richard said.

'No. I'm going to do the year again.'

'Right. Can you do that? Is that all okay?'

'Yeah. I came up to talk to my tutor. I just thought I'd drop in and see you all.'

'So, is everything okay now? Wha – were you – was it stress?' I said, wondering how intrusive I was being.

'No, I was mad, man. I was just mad,' Greg said. His eyes widened when he said it, and we glimpsed a souvenir of his more frantic alter ego. I was somewhat relieved he was calling me 'man', although from anyone else it would have been really annoying. There was a longish pause. Greg made no attempt to fill it, and finally Richard and I clashed dutifully, feigning politeness to avoid revealing whatever trite conversation we'd come up with. We 'no, you say'-ed for as long as we could, and then, thankfully, Greg said he had to be getting back or he'd miss his train.

'Poor Greg,' I said, when we came back in to sit down. We were still quiet, but this time we were being respectful.

'Yeah, the poor guy,' said Richard. 'He was so . . . spaced. And so . . .'

'Fat,' I said. I held my straight face as long as I could, and then we both pissed ourselves.

Sara was the first to leave. She went home to London when her lectures finished. She said the libraries there were just as good, if not better, and she could concentrate on revising when she didn't have to live in the house. She said she was always afraid there, and it was doing her no good, and that she'd come back to sit the exams. I saw her leave very early in the morning, without telling us. I could have gone down and said nice things, offered a lift, been generous and female and the friend I was supposed to be, but I didn't want to. And she didn't want me to. She was walking purposefully with a heavy rucksack, and two cardigans knotted around her waist. It was almost summer, but the mornings were still brittle. I squinted through the column of gold dust that floated at the window, and let her go. Later, I faked surprise when Heather reported her absence. We stopped discussing Mabel and Jonathan for a few days. We had a new target to raise our eyebrows at and call strange. Mabel alone defended her when we came up with unkind, pseudo-psychoanalytical reasons for Sara's premature departure. She knew what it was like to come under the collective disapproval of the rest of us, and she decently answered for Sara whenever her name came up. With six of us in a house that had been used to seven, there was a feeling of being able to breathe a little more easily. Sara would have enjoyed the place more with herself away.

'Daniel has a new girlfriend,' Heather said, hurling a hot tray on to the kitchen table. 'Ow! Burned my hand. And she's a complete moose!'

'You've met her?'

'I haven't met her, but I've seen her. She's a moose.'

I wasn't sure what 'moose' meant. The world of hip, I believe, can be divided into fashion and trends. Fashion is the god I worship. It's big and solid and predictable and rational. It moves steadily forward and crushes everything in its path. Fashion makes the world turn. Trends are fickle and irrational. They can be attractive, but they can never be important. They're the means by which people who don't understand fashion fool themselves into thinking they do. Buzz-words, or in-words, if you haven't guessed where I'm going with this, are trends. I've never been any better at pre-empting trends than even very ordinary people, and it's with in-words that I exhibit myopia most often. I speak the same way from year to year, more or less, occasionally adopting Americanisms because I like the feel of them, with their casual rubberiness and disdain for convention. But all societies have hip words and phrases that they flirt with for a season or two and then dump cruelly, treating them with derision when their moment has passed. I never notice such words until they are commonplace and on their way out, by which time I know it would be folly to attempt to use them. Students, who dabble in the illegal and are anxious to prove themselves all over, are particularly susceptible to the lure of these verbal trends so I was always at sea, language-wise. I supposed 'moose' was a straightforward physical insult, conveying a condition of obesity or ugliness, or both. But for all I knew, it could have been a specific and compact by-word for a whole behavioural discipline. It could even have been 'mousse'.

I bluffed my way on. 'So how do you feel about this? Are you wishing you were still with him?'

'God, no. I just think it's funny, that's all. I think it's really funny that he's gone from me to a complete moose.' And she laughed, and threw a wooden spoon into the bubble-filled kitchen sink.

Other people were still having parties, the rascals, and we were still going to them. Not to go would have been like admitting you were a swot who had to work for exams. The shared obsession with underachieving is peculiar to British scholars. Visiting Americans and Irish students never quite get the hang of it, which seems strange to us because it is so obviously the coolest stance. To confess that you tried, that you did your best when the possibility of failure still exists is hara-kiri for your intellectual reputation. Doing well is only respected in Britain when it is preceded by minimal effort, because anyone can work hard but only a few are born clever. Just as French teenagers manifest a studied indifference to personal safety in the way they ride mopeds without helmets, smoking, we take pains to conceal any mental slog. So, even though we were fed up or, as I was, feeling fat and plain, we had to do the rounds on the social circuit. We still tended to set out together, like a family who meets for the usual occasions; reluctantly but without question.

That evening I was relatively excited about seeing the moose girlfriend of Daniel's, and perhaps having the word's mystery implications illustrated to me in succinct physical example. When Heather cocked a subtle knuckle in the girl's direction, I found myself staring until she pulled me away. The girl was gorgeous. She was tall, sturdy to the point of plump, but ravishingly sexy. Her natural, raven ringlets, as glossy as wet paint, bobbed and danced as she turned her head and laughed. And she laughed a lot, without affectation or self-consciousness. If I had been gay I would have loved her shyly, from a distance, and thought myself unworthy. And I was fairly attracted to her as my sexuality stood.

'But, Heather, she seems so nice. She's lovely,' I said.

'She's a moose,' Heather said angrily.

'She's not, though, is she? She's just lovely.' And I turned to look at her some more, and Heather disappeared into the crush of people.

Mabel told me later that I had upset Heather profoundly, and she was letting the whole house know about my cruelty. I was astonished. The moose's shimmering aura had made me neglectful of Heather's feelings, but I hadn't for an instant considered the possibility of her being hurt by my opinion. Heather had dumped Daniel. She had slept with other people since then. I assumed she just wanted to laugh at his pitiful post-Heather decline for fun, and it seemed unfair and unbelievable that she'd want to use such a nice-looking girl to do so. That was all. But according to Mabel, Heather had called my comments 'unsupportive', which, in Heather's language, was the lowest form of treachery. The sisterhood she expected of me included an embargo on extending the same solidarity to certain other sisters. I found myself fighting my case to a complete stranger as I sat on the stairs, steeped in remorse.

'Do you know that girl?' I said, to a little thin girl sitting on a higher step. I find it easy to talk to small women. Being small myself, I believe there is a level of adversity faced by all small women that makes them automatic friends, a rebuttable, but fairly reliable assumption.

'No, I don't,' she said.

'She looks really nice, though, doesn't she?'

'She looks really lovely.'

'That's what I thought. But I've gone and got myself into trouble by telling her boyfriend's ex-girlfriend that. She doesn't fancy him any more, the ex, but she wanted me to say the new girl was horrible and I couldn't and now she hates me.'

'Ex-girlfriends are always bitchy,' said the small girl. 'It comes with the territory. Even nice girls turn nasty when it comes to their exes. You should have just nodded.'

'Well, I know that now,' I said. 'So have you got an ex here? I can point at his new girlfriend for you and call her names. Get some practice in.'

The girl laughed. 'It's not his new girlfriend, it's his old one,' she said. 'She's a total bitch, and she's not even very pretty, apparently, but he couldn't get over her.'

'Then you should treat him badly as well. Obviously that's how he likes it.'

'Well, I finished with him, but he didn't seem too bothered. That's as nasty as I get. I think she must have some incredible sex technique that I can't do.'

'Christ. I couldn't even begin to compete with something like that. Sounds far too much like hard work. Is he worth it?'

'He's not worth it. I'm far too good for him. I suppose I just want what I can't have.'

'Don't we all? Just ignore him. He'll soon come round. Men want what they can't have too.'

'I'll try it. But I really hate playing those sort of power games.'

'Yeah? I love it. Maybe that's where you're going wrong. You're actually a nice person.'

'I think you're right, because she – the other girlfriend – was always screwing him up. God, so men want bitches. That's so pathetic.'

'No, we all want bitches. But not really. It's a fear-of-commitment thing, this is my theory. We go for the wrong people to put ourselves off the whole idea. It passes the time while you're waiting to fall in love. That's why you still want him.'

'It's true. Well, maybe I'll start being really horrible. If it doesn't make him fancy me, at least it'll make me feel better.'

'That's the spirit.'

'I really am too good for him, though.'

'I really don't doubt it for a second. But I don't think you've convinced yourself yet. As soon as you do you won't be able to get rid of him. Anyway, I suppose I'd better get back to my friend and try to make it up to her. Maybe I can think of something bad to say about that girl.'

'Good luck. She looks pretty perfect.'

'Well, the word on the street is that she's a moose.'

'Mmm. Yes, you could say that. If you were Satan. Tell your friend you've thought it over, and you can see how false the girl is. That covers everything.'

'False. That could work. Okay, wow, thanks. I'm Grace.' The thin girl scooped some strawberry blonde hair out of her eyes and extended an exquisitely dainty hand to me.

'Donna,' she said.

Finlay still made a few perfunctory attempts to rekindle the waspish jealousy that had once diverted the pair of us so efficiently, but his heart wasn't in it. One night three of us came in together – me, Mabel and Finlay – and I made a batch of dry, chewy popcorn because I had nothing else. Finlay and I had almost come to blows earlier when he made a clumsy sort of advance and my refusal was even clumsier, and although it had lacked enthusiasm and conviction on both sides the crossness still bristled between us. We were going through the motions, but the emotions weren't fully dormant. We had come so close to proper sex and I thought – hoped – he realized that that was as close as we'd ever get. Sometimes I felt exposed and vulnerable when we were alone together, as if we had had sex. Now, we sat round the kitchen table, while he glared at me and I played with the popped corn. For some bizarre reason, which I forget, Mabel and I kept breaking into a chorus of 'Yes, sir, that's my baby' and then cracking up into hysterical giggles. Finlay became irascible and started throwing popcorn around and swearing in a dark, slurring voice laced with gin and malevolence, and for a moment it brought back old memories, when everything was more fun, and life had an edge. Mabel's presence neutralized any threat he might otherwise have presented. I sat with my chin on my hands and smiled at him, drunk and sweet and sleepy.

'Why are you always so cross, Finlay?' Mabel asked him. Finlay picked up a handful of popcorn and scrunched it mercilessly in his fist. He let the few crumbs drop from his palm, and the rest of it, too chewy to disintegrate, reinflated to its original shape on the table.

'Oh, leave me alone,' he snarled. We started singing again, then broke it off to do the silent laugh that hurts your chest. Finlay began throwing popcorn across the table, like he was skimming stones across a pond. He looked very narky indeed.

'Why are you always so cross, Finlay?' I said. I was newly, recklessly happy, in the way that made me want to squeak. It suddenly seemed important that he should feel better too. But he wasn't used to niceness and he looked wary, suspecting sarcasm or a veiled remark. By now he had made quite a horrible mess with the popcorn. 'I hope you're not expecting me to clean that up,' I said, trying for a pretend-scolding tone, aiming for a joke.

He took it badly. 'Do you think I give a shit about this fucking house?' he said. 'I don't give a fucking shit, okay?' He was behaving as he always did, the usual phrases, the usual bad temper. Mabel and I, still a little booze-happy, found it funny this time, and he knew it but couldn't prevent it. The more surly he became, the more we smiled. The more popcorn he snatched and mutilated, the more we had to restrain our laughter, which only made it harder. 'Look, I can see I'm, er, amusing you both no end but –' He broke off, too drunk to formulate a suitable reprimand. And then he smiled, one corner of his mouth twisting into something that was part grin, part grimace.

'Lighten up,' I said. 'It's nearly the end of the year.'

'Exactly my point,' he said.

The next day a letter arrived from Sara, except it wasn't a letter, it was a cheque for the gas bill with a small piece of paper folded around it that said, 'This is for the gas bill.'

'God, what did we do to upset her so much?' said Richard. You slept with her, I wanted to say. That can't have helped. I took pains to avoid people I'd snogged; I couldn't imagine what it was like ducking people who'd seen you naked when you actually lived with them.

'It's the mice,' I said. 'She has a real phobia about them.'

'Whereas you handle them like a man,' Richard said. 'Just remind me – how many times did you scream when you saw the first one?'

'I was surprised,' I said. We smiled privately at each other as the conversation rolled on.

'It's everything,' said Mabel. 'She's been under a lot of pressure.'

'She could have written us more of a letter, let us know how she's getting on,' Heather said. She sided with Richard all the time.

'It's funny,' Mabel said, 'but when you're away from this place, you don't feel like you owe it anything. When you're here you do. I miss you more when I'm here, alone all day, than when I'm at home or at Jon's. It's like they're different worlds and when you're out of this one you almost don't remember living in it at all.'

'God, we're going to lose touch, aren't we?' I said. 'We'll stop phoning then writing, then we'll forget all about each other.'

'That's not going to happen,' Mabel said. She didn't even try to look like she meant it.

After my unscheduled encounter with Finlay's maddeningly charming ex, Donna, another coincidence that occurred when I made an appointment to see the careers adviser gave me a feeling that there was a circularity to life, and maybe, even, a meaning. I was going through an identity crisis, or a future crisis or something like that. An intense tunnel of self-doubt and fear. And everyone else was going for advice there, and I wanted to be told something great, like I should be a movie star or a newsreader. I filled in the forms and sat and waited, chewing bits of skin from my fingers. The adviser was a little Irishman, who pretended to be kind and nice and with it but I could tell I made him impatient and he didn't really like me. He kept giving me really dull and obvious lectures and then said, 'This isn't how these interviews normally go.'

'Oh, really?' I said. 'What usually happens?'

'Usually I say a lot less,' he said, rolling his thumbs around each other. I sincerely doubted it. There was a long silence, which I now felt entitled to leave to him. 'You just don't seem to have any idea what you want to do.'

'Well, precisely,' I said. 'That's what I'm here for. For advice.'

'I can't tell you what you should do,' he said, with the kind of hackneyed wisdom you acquire with practice. It grated. 'I can only advise you on your choices. Look, I'll tell you what, you should speak to Mr Collins about this. He's our resident man for your particular faculty, and he should be able to help you more than me. He's more specific, you see?' It's a sign of age, saying 'you see'. Nobody under fifty does it. Everyone over fifty joins every part of every sentence together with it, as if it's some sort of verbal glue, like taking a breath or saying 'um'. But I said I'd see this Mr Collins and thanked him for his time.

I destroyed more of my thumb as I waited and tried to listen through the door to what other people were saying to the Irishman. He seemed to be dominating the conversation exactly as hoggishly as he had with me, just as I'd suspected. The door opposite opened and Mr Collins called my name. I recognized him, but for a few moments I couldn't place his face. I remembered with a freezing shudder. He was the man who stole my parking space, the one whose car I'd left notes on, the one who didn't like swearing. I had stood up partially at the sound of my name but not acknowledged myself. He was looking at me, but I didn't know if he recognized me.

'Are you Grace Benjamin?' he said. I opened my mouth and then I saw him squint and remember. I could see the scene playing out in his head. His jaw tightened and throbbed. We stood looking at each other, the way we had the first day I met him. Then he said, 'Oh, I know you, don't I?' in his quiet, television-paedophile voice. I made a small squeaky sound and ran away. At the door, I heard him call my name again. I turned and caught his eye, but I didn't stop.

'So how did your careers talk go?' Mabel asked me, and laughed when I told her. 'Well, now you'll never know what you should be doing,' she said. 'It serves you right for picking fights with strangers.'

'He's a total get and he needed to be shouted at. But you're right. I don't know what I should be doing and I don't know who to ask and I can't be bothered doing it myself. This is so much of a hassle I want to die. I wish I were you. I wish I wasn't doing any of this. Swap?'

Mabel pretended to mull it over. 'You'd have to shag Jonathan,' she said.

'I could do that.'

'You'd have to go down on him, too. He likes that.'

'How hard can it be?'

'That's part of the problem. But I won't corrupt you any further. Abstinence suits you.'

'I don't think it does any more,' I said. 'I need to get laid. I think I'm ready.'

'Well, I'm sure Jonathan would oblige,' she said, but there was too much bile in her tone and I changed the subject.

I found some people to live with, purely by a chance conversation in a late-night bar that pretended to be a club so it didn't fall foul of the licensing laws. They were people from my course whom I'd hardly spoken to in two years of studying with them. I had seen a little more of them recently, what with everyone turning up at the faculty building for last-minute exam-related lectures. I strolled over to sit with them for a moment.

'I can't believe we're all coming back next year to do this again,' I said. 'This isn't my idea of fun.'

'This year doesn't count anyway,' said one of these people, a tall, wholesome blond called Jason. 'They take your top five exams. We do four this year and five the next. So I'm only revising two topics this year and three next.'

'Is that true?' I said. 'Why do I never know these things? I should talk to more people on my course. Everyone I live with does something different, and we're not interested in each other's work at all.'

'Why don't you live with us next year?' said Jason's friend Tony. Tony was fat. 'We need another girl.'

'Do you all live together?' I asked. There was a third, a little blonde girl whose name I actually didn't know but was pretending I did.

'Yeah,' said the girl. 'But we want a bigger house next year. Three's a bit small.' She seemed a friendly sort. Not too fashionable, not too scary. I thought it over.

'Are you serious about this?' I said, 'because I'm looking for someone to live with next year. Everyone in my house has fallen out.'

'Why?' said Tony.

'Because we're all impossible to live with,' I said. 'No, it's a joke, we're lovely. It's . . . it's complicated. Someone's leaving, someone's getting married, the rest of us hate each other . . . Look, are you really serious?'

'Come on, live with us,' said Jason. 'It'll be fun.'

The warning signs were there, but we swapped telephone numbers all the same.

When the exams finally started I couldn't have been happier. I love everything about exams. The silence alone is always something of a turn-on, but there's so much more: the discussion beforehand where you try to get across to everyone exactly how much work you haven't done, the big wads of fresh, clean, lined paper, the suspense, the race-against-time urgency, the cod-seriousness of the teachers as they walk up and down to deter cheats, the way I took in forbidden food and practised the excuse I would give if I was challenged about it (I get hypoglycaemic and faint if I don't eat something sugary every half-hour), the fag that stopped me being able to feel my lips and feet that I used to sponge from Michelle after every exam, and the fact that it felt just like those big fun end-of-term quizzes we'd had at school since the infants', which I used to love because I was clever, and never stopped getting excited about even though I didn't know the answers any more.

It is, of course, desperately easy to cheat in these things. You can simply write any useful information on loo paper and stick it in the front of your knickers, take a loo break and enjoy the interesting reading you've taken with you, then flush away the evidence like a hardened criminal. Or put it back in your knickers – they don't do strip-searches. This was my plan, but I was too self-conscious to be seen to be the kind of person who might require a lavatory, and I started having crazy, paranoid ideas that they had hidden cameras in the bathrooms, and it wouldn't have helped me because I revised the wrong things, all the wrong things, and nothing but the wrong things, although no one will ever believe you when you tell them this. If you happen to be luckier, or revise in a more bet-hedging manner than me, there's no reason that this devious plot shouldn't work marvellously, depending, of course, on your course. You have my permission to give it a go, but don't blame me if it goes wrong.

On the bad side, Sara was back, although she was trying her best to be cheerful. It seemed like she'd hardly been away, although it had been weeks. She seemed, bizarrely, to have developed a quietly affectionate friendship with Richard, of all people, after scarcely speaking to him for the best part of the term. Perhaps they had got round to talking about their brief, long-forgotten affair, perhaps the statute of limitations on feeling dreadful about a bad-mistake shag was up, or perhaps they'd started having sex again to relieve exam tension. Who could say? But they talked a lot now, and exchanged sensitive glances and even touched each other. It is always annoying when one of your friends decides to start liking someone you've both been bitching about for ages. He made me feel like some sort of rodent when I tried to joke about her faults, and as a result, our Wednesday lunch dates cooled, then chilled, then iced into extinction. My own fault, I suppose, for breaking my own rule: never choose sides when sex is involved.

'How are they going?' I said to Finlay, in the spirit of pretending to care when he came in one evening.

'Pretty good,' he said. 'Yours?'

'Oh, I've failed everything, I expect. It hardly matters now.'

'Ah, I forgot. You still have to keep up that "I'm so cool I don't give a shit about exams" image.'

Amused, and a little aroused by his roughly perceptive, but amiable insult, I couldn't help stretching and smiling and implicitly inviting him to stay and chat. 'You forgot. I really am that cool. It's not an image.'

'Everything you do you do for effect. You only have two emotions, you've never met half of your tutors, you blow-dry your hair before you take a shower,' he said. 'It's all an image – do you think I don't know that by now?'

'I'm flattered,' I said, 'that you think the tumbling chaos of my life is presentable enough to be considered in any way deliberate. I certainly don't do things for effect. I should have thought the fact that I tend to fuck everything up might have poked holes in your theory.'

'You don't really think you fuck things up. I've never met anyone quite so pleased with themselves. You've grown pretty arrogant since I first knew you.' When he added the last, nastier part of his evaluation I was a little lost for words but not shaken.

'As I'm so shallow and fond of myself I'm finding it hard to understand why you've persistently been so taken with me this year,' I said. I was beyond modesty now.

'I suppose I believed your advertising,' he said. 'Since you were so self-absorbed I assumed there was something worth pursuing.'

'Oh, really? And you've discovered that the truth is disappointing?'

'Let's say I've been a victim of creative, rather than false advertising,' he said, with some enjoyment.

'Been working on this, have you?' I said. 'Well, carry on. I wouldn't like to think you'd prepared an insult and missed your chance to say it.'

'Some of us are spontaneous, occasionally,' he said.

'You know, I'm going to have to think up something witty to say back to you. I'll keep you posted.' I shook out a newspaper loudly and crossed my legs.

Of course I'd found the exchange fairly enjoyable. It was almost comforting having someone being openly rude to me, after months of subtlety and paranoia and doubt. And even though there was a causticity to it, it wasn't a million miles from the way we had behaved when we liked each other. And there was a smooth levelness to his posture now that I preferred. I enjoy the predictable, and extremes of emotion make me uneasy. He seemed calmer and I was happy with that. I couldn't resist smiling as I thought about what he'd said and pretended to read the news. I was slightly taken aback at his impudence, but the confidence it gave me, the warm feeling that comes with a sense of recognition, outweighed the negative. In the end, all we want is to be understood, because that way we believe people will want the real us, not the illusion. He had made a good stab at working me out, and I was flattered. My normal sense of isolation had been slightly thawed. In fact, I hadn't felt so able to deal with the end of term in a long time. There were four official days to go. Quite unexpectedly, I found myself thinking I might stay on longer.

Wednesday.

I think

I still want to talk about it to people I meet because it explains me, it excuses my life. Everything I have become I became when he died. Things that counted before and things that didn't count seemed to swap places. Although I was angry at losing the future I thought I'd have, the future I have now seems much more predictable; thoroughly pointlessly certain. It's useless trying to explain to people that I won't fall in love again, because it irritates both of us. Me saying it, them telling me I'm wrong. And I'm not allowed to keep thinking about it in front of other people because they say I didn't know him long enough, and they tell me how in the first few days of anything they always feel like that too, and that's just the way it is. They're wrong. That was never the way it was for me. But then, once, when I told someone I'd never love anyone again, she said, 'Really? Do you think so?' completely credulously, which felt even worse, so I suppose they can't win.

The legs thing would have happened anyway, it was happening then, although I hardly noticed. Sometimes I think it's better that it ended before I put him off by getting worse. But I know that's not how it would have been. I know I would have taken risks that I won't take now, lived for the moment. More than that, I know it didn't make any difference. Which means maybe it shouldn't now, but what else do I have to think about? I know it would have been fine, I know it isn't now. I'm allowed to know anything I want, of course, because it's all conjecture. I still know.

I don't want to talk about it to the Orwell Street people when we meet again, these people I haven't seen in six years. It would be like I was turning my memories and anxieties into conversation, and I don't want to use him, despite what he did to me. Part of me is afraid I won't be able to talk to them at all, because nothing will have changed them, and I'll resent them for it. I'd be the same, too. If. It's only a couple of days away and then it'll be over. I shouldn't worry about it. Never worry about anything that won't matter in three months.

I took a bus into town today because the bus stop's on my side of the road, and I didn't think I'd be able to get across the road to the paper shop. I needed to sit down. Old women glare at me when they get on the bus and I'm in one of the seats near the door. There's no way to explain, so I tend to stand up for them after a while. The pain makes sweat weep hot tears down my back and my hair cling to the sides of my face in sticky claws. I should start carrying a crutch or wearing a badge. It wouldn't help, but it would show people there was something wrong with me. They should do T-shirts.

Most days, when I get in I strip at the door and run a deep bath. Lying there, cradled by the water, I don't have a body any more. I'm just head, the part above the foam. Then, cold and restored, I put on a record, eat, lie.

'What do you do with yourself all day?' my mother asked me, when she was last down here. She was ironing. I don't iron, myself. I don't know if it's a symptom of Letting Myself Go, if this is the first step to Bag Lady, but I can't see the evil of creases, the way other people seem to.

'I don't know,' I said. This is virtually the truth. I know what I do, of course, but I don't know where all the hours go or why it seems to be enough.

'Are you lonely?'

'Of course I'm not. I'm *alone* . . .' What a difference. How boldly deliberate one is, how desperately passive the other. ' . . . but I don't *want* to live with anyone. You know how I hated living with people.'

'I know you did. I just wonder what you do with yourself all day.'

I mope, I think, but I don't say this aloud. I regret. And I can, because I don't have to think about anyone else. Living alone is the ultimate selfishness, which is why it's such a luxury.

I bought the studio flat, part of it, with money my grandmother left me when she died. My dad pays the mortgage, which isn't all that much. Less than the rent used to be in Manchester. It was meant to be temporary, that arrangement, until I got a job, found my feet. Time passed, and we realized my feet were right at the ends of my legs. But I probably will work again, one day. The jobs I'm applying for are getting less exciting; as time goes by I'm learning to settle. Eventually I'll hit the landable level. Won't that be fun?

We meet on Friday. I have prepared my lines. I mean to lie extravagantly as Alice advised. I shall be the life and soul of the evening. I can arrive early and leave last, and that way they won't all get to stand in a line and watch me hobble towards them. I'll smile all the time, and tell stories of the brief period when I was happy, and make it sound as if it's still happening. Of course, if I'm too conspicuously unsuicidal, I won't have any excuse to make to Sara if she calls in the future about going somewhere. I'll simply have to screen my calls from now on, and keep screening until she stops.

I'm two pounds lighter, which is still heavy, but for some reason, when your weight is downwardly mobile, whatever it is, you feel slim, and when it's rising, no matter how thin you are at the time, you feel fat. So at the moment I'm fairly confident, and I think I'll be able to cope. If you dread something enough, you can take away its sting.

1992

The Wedding

Three weeks after the end of term I drove down to Oxford alone, and met the others in a pub in the middle of the city. They were all there, together, drunk and loutish by the time I turned up, rumpled and exhausted but still feeling cleaner than I ever did when I'd lived with them. I was quite pleased to see the gang again, caught up in the general enthusiasm and rowdiness. Their smiles were wide and eager, but their eyes were slightly downturned and anxious-looking. This reception had more of a ten-year reunion feel to it, than a we-just-saw-each-other-a-fortnight-ago familiarity. I sensed I should watch my behaviour. I got a round of Guinnesses, which for some reason they were all drinking, and a Campari for myself, and sat down.

'Your last day as a single woman,' I said to Mabel. 'I didn't think you'd do it.'

'I haven't yet. There's still time to run away,' she said. Sara and Heather exchanged glances.

'Fa!' I said. 'You don't even nearly mean that.'

'No, I don't. I just keep thinking, Jesus, the rest of my life. Jesus.'

'You're not having second thoughts, are you?' said Heather.

'No, she's not having second thoughts,' I said. 'She's having her first thoughts again. And they haven't put her off yet. Where are you staying tonight?'

'At Jon's.'

'No, you can't. What if he sees you in the morning and then you meet a pig on the way to the wedding?' I said.

'A pig?' Finlay said. He rolled his eyes up to meet mine, and I countered his gaze until he looked away. 'Why would they meet a pig?'

'It could happen,' I said. 'It's really unlucky to meet a pig on your way to the ceremony. Or lucky, I can't remember which. Anyway, the one about the bride and groom not seeing each other on the wedding day is definitely true.'

'Which is why he's spending the night with a friend,' Mabel said. 'I believe all that as well. I didn't know about the pig thing. But there aren't many pigs in Oxford. In the centre.'

'Perhaps it doesn't have to be an actual pig,' I said. 'Perhaps if a lorry drove by with a pig's face on it . . .'

'Maybe if you eat a bacon sandwich the register office will explode,' Richard said. They all had a pig gag to add, which was the point of the original pig story anyway. I'm so good at introducing fun topics into conversations.

'Where are you staying?' Sara asked me. 'You can come and stay at my friend Petra's.'

'Actually, I'm booked into a tiny hotel here tonight and tomorrow. I like the idea of it. I've never stayed alone in a hotel before and I'm quite scared and excited. I can't wait. And the ceiling has beams, and if you count the beams the first time you sleep in a new room you can make a wish.'

'How do you know all this bollocks?' Richard said.

'I'm a witch,' I said. Finlay smiled.

'It's such a waste of money,' Sara said.

'Yes, but there are three of you staying with this Petra girl, and I don't know her, and I don't want to squash even more people into her house. Thanks, though.'

Three hours later I was at the pissed stage where you tell people you love them and miss them and make promises you'll regret. And I meant it all, having fallen under the romantic spell of a summer evening in a strange city, feeling free from university for further than I could plan ahead. We made about a hundred toasts: to Mabel, to Jonathan, to the clap in Jonathan's pants, to each other and Manchester and friendship and Orwell Street, and Gareth the landlord and mad Greg and the extermination of mice everywhere and to the future. Every so often my mind wandered, and I fell into disturbing trances, seeing scary images of my own future which I couldn't quite clarify, and then I'd catch a word of the conversation which would bring me back into things. My mind was flooded with emotional déjà vu, a rebirth of the conviction that these people were my friends, my real friends, the people I could call in a crisis and tell secrets to. I wanted them to swear we'd never lose touch. I wanted to make plans, and set dates and to know them as well as this for ever. We relived the year in anecdotes, the good and the bad, except the good was better, and the bad better still as we remembered it. There were tears and group hugs and hand-holding.

In the morning these powerful feelings lingered with the smell of gin and Babycham and the grey haze of old fag smoke trapped in the curls of my hair. It was exactly the right mood to see a wedding in: sentimental and oversensitive. I looked like shit, obviously, but I felt like I was dreaming. It was the sunniest day in days, made all the more blinding by the pale stones of Oxford's buildings, which threw back the light, and I opened the window and leaned out in my vest. The headache felt good, as if the beauty of the world that morning was making my brain throb with its intensity. I showered and went back to sleep with the window open and the sun burning my face.

Mabel and Sara were standing outside the register office when I arrived.

'You look really . . . You look perfect,' I said. She was wearing the white Givenchy, the cut-price white shoes and she was holding a little posy of white roses.

'Jon had them delivered this morning,' she said, and her eyes filled with tears.

'Don't start that again,' Sara said. 'Your mascara'll run.'

'Are the others here yet?' I said.

'There's Finlay and Richard, over there. Can they see us?' Sara said. She started waving widely with her whole arm. They ran over.

'Well, Mabel,' said Richard. 'You look stunning.'

'Yeah, um, very, er, sexy,' Finlay said.

'I'm not supposed to look sexy,' Mabel said, 'I'm supposed to look pure and beautiful.'

'Yeah, that too,' he said, and kissed her lightly on the cheek. 'I'm actually very, er, jealous of Jon.'

'Thank you,' Mabel whispered.

'Where are Mandy and Heather?' Richard said.

'They'll be here soon,' said Sara. 'I spoke to them earlier this morning.' Some moments of standing wondering where they were passed, and then we saw them coming round the corner, arms linked.

'Your dress is old, your shoes are new . . .' Mandy said, breathlessly.

'. . . so we brought you something borrowed and something blue,' Heather said. 'Here. Wear this through the wedding, then you have to give it me back.' It was a little crystal bracelet.

'And tie this around your ankle,' Mandy said, holding out a piece of blue satin ribbon. All the girls started making high squeaking noises and pretending to cry, while the boys stood straighter and looked amused and baffled. Mandy kissed Mabel on the cheek. 'Now you're all ready.'

'And I brought a pig . . .' Richard said. 'Oh, no, oops, that's *bad*, isn't it? Have I got time to take it back?' And we took turns to hug her tightly and took a few photos of each other and Mabel took a deep, symbolic breath and we went on in.

'Mrs Ong,' Mabel was saying. She was more than drunk, she was internally saturated with booze. 'Mrs Fucking Ong. Eh? Mrs Bloody Ong. Mrs Ong. Mrs –'

'Mrs Ong, yes, we get the fucking point,' Finlay snapped, but he was being funny, not impatient.

'I think it sounds fucking good,' said Jonathan Ong, who was leaning back in his chair, almost as pissed as Mabel. He looked untidily crumpled and his face was somehow more asymmetrical. He was better this way, a little flawed, a little human.

'So, what are we going to toast this time?' Richard said.

'The happy couple,' said one of Jon's dentist friends.

'No, we've done that thirty times,' said Jon. 'What about a toast to our children? The little Ongs.'

'The little Ongs!' we all shouted.

'You can forget about the little Ongs for some time, darling,' Mabel said. And she leaned backwards and snogged Jonathan. 'I'm the little Ong, all right?'

'You know, I probably won't see you again after today,' Finlay said to me, quietly, when we were standing beside each other at the bar. He was there to help me carry over a round of drinks.

'You might,' I said. 'I mean, I'll stay in touch with everyone else, and you probably will too.'

'I don't know. I don't think that'll happen,' he said.

'He's right, it'll never happen,' said a bloke standing next to us. We both looked at him, a little surprised.

'Do you mind? This is a private touching farewell,' I said, with some sauce.

'Sorry,' he said, holding out the palms of his hands to us. I smiled, and bit my bottom lip provocatively.

'So anyway,' Finlay said. 'I just wanted to say that.'

'You just wanted to say that what?'

'I just wanted to say that. That we probably won't see each other again.'

'Right,' I said. 'Well, you never know. We easily could.'

'You won't,' said the strange man again. 'You think you will, but you won't. I never kept in touch with anyone I said I was going to keep in touch with. New people arrive, old people fade away. That's life, you know. It's constantly changing. That's what makes it so interesting.'

I turned round to fix the man with an evil glare. 'Thank you for your thoughts. We'll bear them in mind. Right now, this poor boy is trying to come up with something suitably final and weighty to conclude our torturous, long-standing relationship.'

'You can tell it was torturous,' the strange man said, 'by your eyebrows.'

'What's wrong with my eyebrows?' I said. 'I plucked them yesterday. I happen to think they're pretty great.'

'They are,' he said. I turned completely to him, away from Finlay.

'Who are you?' I said.

'Brendan,' he said. 'Brendan Mazzarelli.'

'Like the ice-cream.'

'If you say so.' Behind me, Finlay was pissed off, and trying to speak to me again. I still ignored him, but he kept saying things, and I kept talking over them to this Brendan fellow, until we were talking loudly at the same time, but neither of us was paying much attention to what we were actually saying. We were too busy listening to each other, and pretending not to, to care about what was coming out of our own mouths.

'Jesus Christ,' Finlay said, 'I must be stupid, but I actually thought that the last time we spoke you'd be able to pay attention to me for five fucking seconds instead of trying to cop off with some complete stranger you've only just met. I mean, obviously I am stupid, but I just thought, I just assumed, you'd be able to spare one minute of your time before we never speak again.'

'Oh, Finlay, let's not spoil things today. We've been pretty good recently, you and I, haven't we? I thought we'd reached some kind of understanding.'

'Is that what you thought? You've got some bloody weird ideas about what constitutes getting on well with someone.'

'So what now? What are you shouting at me for?'

'I'm not fucking shouting at you. I just wanted to talk to you one last time.'

'Look, we've been talking and saying nothing for more than a year now. What makes you think this is going to be worth saying? What good is it going to do now? You said it already.

We're not going to see each other again. So fine. So goodbye, have a nice time doing whatever you're going to do.'

'Fuck.'

'Fuck indeed.'

'Let me have a word with him,' Brendan said, leaning forward conspiratorially.

'You want to talk to him? Why?' I said, turning to syrup again, like a tart.

'Let me have a word with him.'

So I took some drinks over to Mabel and Jon's table. I looked over to the bar, trying to imagine what they could be saying to each other. Finlay was nodding, and Brendan was gesturing, butchly, with his hands. And then they were both smiling.

'Who's that?' Mandy said. 'The guy talking to Finlay.'

'That's Brendan,' said one of Jonathan's friends. 'He's a great bloke. Junior doctor.' I hot-footed it back there, and as I approached, Finlay was on his way to the wedding table, looking pretty normal. We danced a little to avoid touching each other as we passed between some tables, and exchanged severe expressions.

'What did you say to him?' I said to Brendan.

'It doesn't matter,' he said. 'Do you fancy getting out of here?'

'Well, it is a wedding reception, and I'm kind of like one of the bride's friends.'

'They won't miss you,' he said.

'I'd like to think they bloody will,' I said.

'Of course you would. Come on.'

His car, parked outside, was a curvy black E-type Jag. He opened the door for me, and I got in. As we drove away into the azure summer evening, I shuddered with chilly pleasure at the terrifying realization that I was finally going to let myself get laid.

Friday
The Reunion

I'm early. It's a horrible pub, not one I'd have picked, but I don't get to pick. Full of students and people with beards. I can't see any of them, but it's a big place. I walk round a few times, feeling the usual self-consciousness, but also a confidence that comes from being able to walk around pubs alone without worrying. It's like pretend confidence, but it builds on itself, dividing and multiplying like amoeba. I buy a drink: Jack Daniel's and ginger. This isn't the sort of place that could make a whisky sour. It's the sort of place that gives you a glass of vermouth when you ask for a martini. I stand on one leg, leaning against the bar, letting the cold brass rail numb patches of my forearms. I'm probably unrecognizable from behind: my hair is shorn where it used to be long and young. Do I look older? It's only a few years, but I feel more haggard. Orwell said you get the face you deserve, and my face has earned its droop by putting in hours of despair. I just don't think I deserved the despair. I get another whisky.

I see Sara. She looks pissed off, a familiar expression. She doesn't see me. Her eyes are narrowed, her legs are fabulous. I wave and she comes over. We don't hug, because neither of us is the sort to initiate anything touchy unless we're drunk. And anyway, it's not all that long since I saw her last – a year isn't for ever, although it's a little hard to explain away when you live less than two miles apart. I can't think of anything to say so I ask her about her work, which is hard but fulfilling. Naturally, she says she's earning nothing at all, and we brag a little about how virtually destitute we both are. I'm not really listening to her, but wondering how long we'll have to stand here alone together, while thinking of the next question. But she has her own questions: she wants to know what I'm doing. I flit about, saying nothing. Which is enough, because she's not interested either.

Heather comes next. Her clothes are gorgeous, an extension of the innate style she flaunted at university, but supported by grown-up money. Her hair is short, too. We take each other in, and compliment each other at the same time. It's like nothing has changed, and there we are, ready for a night out, being mutually supportive, like we're supposed to be. Her career is just a whirlwind. It's incredibly engaging and important and, oh, she's rushed off her feet but she's loving every minute.

The rest of them have met outside and come in together. Mandy looks exactly the same, which means worse in real terms. Her smile is unmistakably, inexplicably false. Already. The boys have better hair, but look no different. And Mabel . . . Mabel looks like a woman. I'm scared of her. She's smiling and tiny and looks just as sweet as she always did, but there's something about her that I daren't even begin to approach. I raise my eyes timidly to hers.

'Let's get a table,' Richard says, with the efficiency of someone who was head boy at his public school. There's clattering as we take seats from other people around us.

'I haven't heard anything about you guys in so long,' Heather says, making it clear that we are only one little spot in her continent of acquaintances, a place she can visit to recall her roots and measure her growth. 'But I've been abroad the past couple of years, with work. I've been living in Hong Kong, and now I'm back, things are, like, in slow motion. It's incredible. I feel like I'm walking backwards. I can't get used to it.' I want to defend my city, but I realize how silly it would sound.

For a while, as we catch up, I find I can't think of anything to say, so I just smile, as if I'm listening to all of this, and for some reason I'm not. I don't care any more. I want to go home now. Okay, they're all alive. See you again in another five.

'And how is married life treating you?' Heather asks Mabel.

'We're divorced,' says Mabel, with the understatement of one who has been saving the killer blow. There's silence. We're too young to know how to react to a friend with a failed marriage. Then she laughs, and I think she must have been kidding. But her eyes are clear and sad, and she says, 'Oh, come on, people. Not one of you expected it to last. You're not pretending to be surprised now, are you?'

'Why didn't you tell me on the phone last week?' says Sara, the organizer of the reunion, who rounded everyone up after Heather called her. Mabel shrugs. 'You can't be divorced already. How long were you married?'

'Two years. One month. Four days,' says Mabel. I look at the floor. I wonder if anyone's still blaming me.

'Oh, my God,' Mandy says. 'So what happens now? What are you doing?'

'I work in publishing,' Mabel says. 'I lied to get the job, and they found out about a year later, and they didn't care, really. It's a good job. So I'm quite happy now.'

'And what about Jon?' Richard says. 'What happened? I mean, why?'

Mabel pulls a face, not a nasty one, just brings her lips up to her nose then twists it all around a bit. 'Who knows?' she says, as if we're collectively wondering whether there's life on other planets. 'It was just one of those things. One of those things with blonde hair and a breathy voice. Then another, and another, and I left him to them. I didn't feel like competing any more.'

'*You* left *him*?' Sara says, with a glint of humour. I mentally double-take.

'Go, Mabel,' says Heather, smiling. 'What was it with him and his dick anyway? I'm amazed he managed to pass his dental exams. When he told his patients to open wide, half the time he probably meant their legs.' We laugh raucously, then fade away into guilt. I worry about how this is going, but Mabel looks perfectly happy now, sitting swirling the ice in her gin and tonic. It seems rude to change the subject and I still can't think of anything to say.

'Do you still see each other?' is my best attempt.

'Not really. The other day at a party. We still have a lot of the same friends, but they're very . . . tactful. They do their best to keep us apart, as if we'll start wrestling when we're put in the same room.'

'God, I can't believe it. I know we all said bad things when you first told us you were getting married, but the day you did it, I really thought you'd be able to make it happen. You looked pretty good together. And he looked like he knew how lucky he was,' Sara says. I glance at Mandy, who looks, there's no mistaking it, triumphant. She wants to say, 'I told you so,' but she's biting it back, twitching with frustrated self-righteousness. We fall silent, as a mark of respect.

'What about the rest of you?' says Richard. 'What are you up to, Grace?'

I have a second to decide whether I'm going to lie or not. There's no going back. 'Oh, you know, stuff,' I say. 'This and that. Temping, mostly.' And we move on. Later, as the conversations divide and multiply, I find myself talking to Mandy.

'So where are you temping now?'

'I'm not, really, at the moment.'

'But you live alone, don't you? How do you afford it?'

I give a brief account of my finances. Somewhere in the middle of the dull statistics I slip this in: 'And I get disability benefit . . . That helps.'

'Nice one!' Mandy says, as if I've pulled off a confidence trick and I'm criminally cool. 'How d'you get that?' Suddenly, because it's her, I'm livid. Hypocrite's fury. I want people to not see – Mandy doesn't see, and I can hardly speak, I'm so upset.

'By being disabled,' I say. The voice is weak, but the tone is hideous, and mean.

'Oh, right,' she says, and blushes, and I know how unfair

I've been and feel bad and let her break into someone else's conversation.

There's nothing here I'm envious of, actually. Nobody's job is more tempting than Richard and Judy and *Fifteen to One*. Mandy's at Glaxo, Richard's in the City, Finlay's up to something that's too complicated for him to explain but it sounds like selling computer systems to businesses. It's all so *expected*. So I relax. Lower my guard, and my shoulders. The alcohol is diluting my inadequacy. I start saying some funny things, some cool things. Some of my lazy superciliousness is putting the starch back into my eyebrows. I talk about television – always my forte – and use some well-rehearsed lines that go down well. I knock back the bourbon in a lush, American manner, imitating the early-eighties alcoholic soap queens I still worship most weekdays. There's an opulent decay about my presentation that I'm enjoying. And for a time, if I don't scrutinize or check myself, we're the way we were, particularly me, and it's as if I'm the house know-all again and I've no idea what it feels like to hurt.

'So, Finlay,' I say. Until now he has pointedly ignored me. I can't work out whether it's embarrassment or hostility. I can't remember if we're friends or not. The last time I saw him I was leaving Mabel's wedding reception in Brendan Mazzarelli's black E-type. Brendan. Now he was a nice bloke. I almost wish I hadn't been so scared of everything then. I thought the more he saw of me the more he'd find to dislike, so I removed the problem by removing myself. But it wasn't true love and I don't think either of us minded. I wonder what he's up to. He was the ideal first shag: left-wing, sensitive, *Cosmopolitan* reader. Unfortunately a film fan. I took one look at the movie posters on his walls and realized I was still trying to sleep with Jim McFadyean. I had such conventionally bad taste back then that it was pretty lucky I chose as well as I did. Thank God I didn't let Finlay do the job. 'So, Finlay.' He looks at me, a little shyly. 'How are things?'

The others are talking among themselves. We've split into

smaller groups. There's no one listening and he can say whatever he likes. But he doesn't want to talk to me. I can tell. He's keeping an ear on Mabel and Richard on his right, looking for a way in. I feel a bit ridiculous. My body language is all wrong: leaning forward, breasts pushed together, a voluptuous smile that recalls the assured flippancy of our erstwhile cat-and-mouse, and he's the opposite. Reluctant, wary, leaning the other way. And I remember myself and crumble a little.

'Things are going really well, I'm very happy,' he says, with a tone I'd imagine he tends to reserve for friends of his mother. 'How about you?' I just nod my head from side to side, as if to say, 'so-so.' The normalcy of the conversation is stark. I'm trying to recapture something of the al dente substance we used to be able to create together but I can't. Just the facts, then.

'Where are you living?' I ask, and he looks upwards at his hairline, as if he's thinking of a lie. 'I'm not going to invite myself round,' I joke, a tad desperately, widening my eyes with disbelief. 'I'm just making conversation. You can make it up if you want to. I shan't check up on you later.'

'No, it's not that. I've just moved into a new flat, and I'm not used to saying the address,' he says. A likely story. For the first time, though, he's smiling. I can't save the situation now and I don't even attempt to. I ride the next silence. He doesn't. It's a sad reflection of the state of things. Our silences were indomitable, once, and proud. 'Are you seeing anyone?' he says, making it clear it's just conversation. His eyes wander, as if to underline the lack of interest.

'I was,' I say, and order myself not to say anything about it. 'He died,' I say then, because I can't stop myself. Richard overhears and I tell it to the rest of them, exactly as I'd intended not to. There's another polite lull, but it's buried efficiently by some healthily upbeat anecdote about Heather's life in Hong Kong, just related enough to be respectful, but really a complete non sequitur. I'm relieved, though.

Later, outside, as the others head off to the tube, Finlay

beckons a cab over. For me. For a moment, I forget that the situation has changed, make some rude, clumsy joke about his improved behaviour and he winces. His face is closed with wounded gallantry and something worse – something that looks like pity. I can't meet his eyes any more. I've behaved as if I affect him, the way I used to, and exposed the conceit unambiguously. It lies open, like a wound, and I can't cover it. He could flatten me with casual scorn, and I brace myself. But he just opens the cab door. The kindness is worse. I touch his arm, softly, to apologize for things, mostly for myself, but we don't smile, or say goodbye. It happens quickly. Nobody's there to see. I won't go back again.

Saturday

My answer-machine kicks in, the pre-recorded man's voice that came with the phone.

'Pick up, pick up.' It's Alice. 'I know you're there. You *are* there, aren't you? You didn't pull last nigh–' I pick up the phone.

'God, it was just awful. I hated it. It was really completely dull, but hard work at the same time. They haven't changed a bit. I didn't need to see any of them again.'

'What are they all doing now?'

'Oh, God, I don't know. Stuff. Who cares?'

'So nothing happened?'

'Nothing. Well, for a while it was okay. I was quite, you know, quite funny. For a while.'

'Well, I'm going to go, then. I'm still at work. I just wanted to know if anything exciting happened. I told you you had nothing to worry about.'

'Mmm. I'll call you this evening. But there's nothing to tell.'

Ten minutes later my machine man starts up again. I sit down on my sofa and watch it.

'Um. I don't know if this is the right number. Anyway, this is a message for Grace, if you live there. It's Finlay. We, er, we didn't really get a chance to talk last night and I was wondering if you, er . . . I wondered if you wanted to go for a drink. Or something. Soon, if you like. I'm on 0171 94–'

I pick up. 'I'm here,' I say.